Between the Seams

AUBREY GROSS

TABLE OF CONTENTS

Title Page
Table of Contents
Dedication
Chapter One
Chapter Two
Chapter Three
Chapter Four
Chapter Five
Chapter Six
Chapter Seven
Chapter Eight
Chapter Nine
Chapter Ten
Chapter Eleven
Chapter Twelve
Chapter Thirteen
Chapter Fourteen
Chapter Fifteen
Chapter Sixteen
Chapter Seventeen
Chapter Eighteen
Chapter Nineteen
Chapter Twenty
Chapter Twenty-One
Acknowledgements
Between the Seams Playlist
Preview: Baseball and Other Lessons
About the Author
Copyright

*To my Cowboy, who's my biggest supporter,
my best friend, and the love of my life.
I'm so glad I get to keep you.*

CHAPTER ONE

"Yo, Chase, did you hear a word of what I just said?"

Chase Roberts snapped out of his reverie and glanced over at Owen Daniels, his best friend, business partner and occasional pain in the ass. "Sure."

Owen snorted. "No, you didn't."

A pretty blonde entered the building across the street, and Chase fought the overwhelming urge to follow her. "Did you see the blonde across the street just now?" He asked instead.

Owen opened the driver's side door of his car. "I thought you'd sworn off women? Called them all second-hand groupies or something like that."

Chase looked at the building—Mitchell's Drug Store—one more time before climbing into the passenger seat of the low-slung Mustang. "I didn't say they were all second-hand groupies. There just happen to be more than I would like."

"Must be tough, being chased by hot, scantily-clad women all the time."

Owen pulled away from the curb and Chase fought the urge to turn and watch to see if the blonde came out of the drug store.

"It is when the only reason they're chasing after me

is because of my brother." Chase's brother, Matt, was Mr.
Baseball. The long-time ace for the Texas Wranglers, Matt
was well-loved in their hometown of Del Rio, Texas. So
well-loved the high school baseball fields now bore his
name. Without a sponsorship. So well-loved that he had
his own menu item at Francine's Diner. So well-loved that
there was a freaking Matt Roberts Day, complete with a
downtown parade. In November. After the World Series and
before Winter Ball started. Hell, his brother had been given
keys to the damned city.

As much as Chase loved his brother, he got tired of
the groupies who decided that if they couldn't have Matt
they would just settle for Chase. After one too many
stories posted about him on internet message boards and
questionable websites, Chase had decided about a year ago
that maybe a female hiatus was in order.

Besides, he had a business to run, and even with
his last name he still wanted to project the image of
responsible, trustworthy businessman—not wannabe
playboy.

"Boo-freaking-hoo."

Chase ignored Owen's sarcasm. "Anyway. Did you
happen to see her?"

"Who? The curvy blonde going into Mitchell's?"

"Yes. That one. Apparently you did."

Owen shrugged. "She looked like she had a nice ass."

"She looked familiar."

Owen turned into the parking lot of Roberts Ventures,
LLC, and swung into the space next to Chase's pickup.
"Previous one-night stand?"

Chase snorted. "No. Definitely not one of those."
Hell, Chase could count on one hand the number of one-
night stands he'd had over his entire lifetime. His brother's
groupies just made it sound like he was, well, a player.

They got out of Owen's Mustang and entered the

building. Chase's executive assistant and all-around office goddess looked up and smiled at Chase. As soon as Kimberly's gaze landed on Owen, her smile quickly turned to a frown.

Chase didn't know why Kim didn't like Owen, and no amount of gentle prying had managed to get the information out of her. "Good morning, Kim."

"Mornin', Chase. We got the Sutton contract in, and Frank Wimbly called earlier, said he found a spot out by the lake that he would like to take a look at."

Chase nodded. "Thanks. I'll take a look at the Sutton contract and give Frank a call back."

He made his way to his office, shaking his head as the sound of Kim scolding Owen could be heard from down the hall.

Never a dull moment he thought as he got back to work.

~~*~~

Jolene Westwood was usually pretty hard to embarrass. As a high school guidance counselor, she'd heard—and discussed—some of the most embarrassing things human beings experienced. From high school crushes to missed periods to kids grappling with their sexuality, she thought she'd heard—and seen—it all.

But embarrassment was much easier to deal with when it wasn't your own, and unfortunately she was currently knee-deep in it on this lovely evening.

She'd just been standing there, in front of the pads, tampons and Monistat cream that lined the back wall of the Del Rio Walmart, debating small pack versus value pack, when she accidentally backed up into someone.

A solid someone who radiated warmth and *man*.

Slowly, she turned around, her hands still paused mid-air, holding the bright yellow and blue boxes up like some sort of offering.

Or maybe as a big fat red light.

No pun intended.

Her gaze wandered up from the box of Crest toothpaste in one hand to the center of what was definitely a polo-clad male chest and up to a jaw shadowed with dark stubble. Firm lips. Slightly crooked nose. Brown eyes that made her think of warm, cinnamony Mexican chocolate. Dark eyebrows. Dark brown, almost black hair that curled out from under a blue YETI coolers ball cap.

Jo swallowed a gasp—or, more realistically, a longing-filled sigh—and took a quick step back.

Chase Roberts.

Childhood best friend.

Teenage crush.

The boy she'd long ago said goodbye to.

Her stomach flip-flopped as she slowly lowered her hands and her gaze. Mentally drank him in.

Six-one.

Two hundred pounds.

1.87 ERA.

At least, those had been his college stats. If anything, he looked like he might have gained a couple of inches, and whatever he weighed, it sure looked like it was pure muscle.

Realizing she was staring like an idiot, she mentally shook herself and somehow found her voice. "I am so sorry, Chase. I didn't see you behind me."

Stupid, Jolene. Of course you couldn't see him behind you, it isn't like you have eyes in the back of your head.

His melted chocolate gaze traveled up and down her body before settling on her face. "I'm sorry, you seem to have me at a disadvantage—you know my name, but I don't know yours."

Jo smiled, even though she was cringing on the inside, and she fought back the sense of disappointment his words evoked. They'd been friends for years and he didn't remember her? Hell, her mother had tried to end his parents' marriage, until the truth finally came out years later that Chandra Sommers had never slept with Bo Roberts. Ends up Sarah Roberts had known that for far longer than Jo had—Chandra was more than happy to let her daughter believe the worst. And he didn't remember her?

Serves you right, for ending things the way you did.

Her voice tinged with the disappointment she apparently couldn't hide, Jo responded. "Sorry. I've changed some since the last time we saw each other. Jolene Westwood."

Chase's brows drew together over those hot chocolate eyes. "I feel awful, but I don't remember a Jolene Westwo—wait a second. Jo? Jo Sommers?"

Jo could feel her cheeks warming and knew she was probably beet red by now. Could this be any more awkward? "Sorry. I changed my name a few years back, after my parents died."

"Westwood is your grandma's name, right?"

Jolene nodded and swallowed. "Yeah."

Lame, Jolene, lame.

Chase stood before her, a brown-eyed god with a 92 mile per hour fastball and a nasty curveball, looking for all the world like a pitcher who couldn't understand a single one of the signals the catcher was sending him.

~~*~~

Jo. Jo Sommers. His childhood friend and teenage crush. The captain of the cheerleading squad and smartest girl in the room (and hell, their class).

He'd known it was her as soon as she'd turned around and allowed that sea glass gaze to travel up his body oh so slowly. He'd never be able to forget those eyes—they'd haunted him for so long they were a permanent part of his psyche at this point.

She may have changed a little bit—her blonde hair was softer, longer and wavier than he remembered, and she'd gained some curves since he'd last seen her when they were in college, but he sure as hell would never be able to forget her.

So why was he playing stupid now?

She'd fueled more than one of his teenage fantasies, even after she'd suddenly stopped talking to him their freshman year of high school. As a teen he wondered if it had to do with the health issues—and eventual scarring—he'd had as a kid and young teen. Had she been embarrassed to be around him?

As an adult, he realized there could have been other reasons, but even a cocky teenage athlete can be felled by one simple brush off from the prettiest girl in school.

"So, uh, what brings you back to town?"

Smooth, Roberts, real smooth.

Worry briefly turned those sea glass eyes stormy, but the expression was gone so fast he wondered if he'd imagined it.

"Gran had a hip replaced. She refused to go to a rehab facility, and pretty much ordered me to come take care of her." A small grin played at the corners of Jo's generous mouth, and for a brief second Chase was reminded of the girl she used to be. The one who'd been his playmate and confidante.

"How's she doing?"

Jo waved her hand, and then blushed as she looked at the box she still held.

"I'm really not trying to accost you with tampons, I swear."

Chase barely managed to choke back the laughter that threatened to escape. "Well, at least they're not used."

Jesus, Roberts, that was awful.

Her blush deepened, and the chuckle that had been

threatening to escape somehow managed to rumble out. Jo shook her head, smiled, and tossed the box into her cart. "I'm glad to see you still have a sophomoric sense of humor, Chase."

"At times, yes." Unfortunately.

Their gazes met, held, and then a slow smile bloomed over Jo's face before she, too, was laughing. "How about we try this again?" She held out her hand. "Hey, Chase! Nice to see you again."

Chase wrapped his hand around hers, and he swore he felt tingles shoot up his arm. "Jo, it's good to see you, too."

Unsettled, he dropped her hand and stepped back. A look of confusion flitted across her pretty face before she once again replaced it with an odd, too-placid-to-be-real smile.

Had she felt it, too?

"Well, uh, I better get going." She gestured to her cart, which held a small amount of groceries and toiletries. "Gran's waiting for me to get back so I can cook supper. Can't let her starve."

Chase took another step back, feeling the need to put some amount of distance between them. He flexed his hand, still feeling slight tingles in his fingertips. "No, can't let her starve."

Jo began to push her cart away, and before he could take the words back he blurted out, "We should do lunch some time. Or supper. Catch up. For old time's sake."

God, he sounded like an effing idiot. Catch up for old time's sake? Yeah, because *that* sounded like a brilliant idea.

An expression Chase couldn't identify clouded Jo's eyes before it, too, was gone almost as quickly as it came. "Um, sure." She nodded her head once, her wavy blonde hair falling over one shoulder. "We'll have to do that."

Chase nodded in ascent and shoved his hands into

his pockets. Jo shot him one last glance before turning from him. Chase allowed himself to enjoy the view as she walked away.

Couldn't not appreciate it, really, as it was a damned fine view. The same damned fine view he'd seen just this morning walking into Mitchell's Drug Store.

~~*~~

"Jolene, is that you?"

Jo set down her grocery bags and blew a strand of hair out of her eyes. "Yes, Gran, it's me."

"Good, that rehab woman just left and I'm starving."

Jo rolled her eyes. "I think that rehab woman has a name."

"Yes, the Devil's Harlot!" Gran shouted back from the living room.

Jo sighed and yelled back. "She's not a harlot, Gran." Who even used the word "harlot" anymore? "She works for Val Verde Regional Medical Center. Last I checked, Satan wasn't on their payroll."

Gran harrumphed from the living room. Jo finished putting up the groceries and walked into the living room. "Did she make you do something new today?"

Her grandmother sat in a big, somewhat comfortable chair. She waved a hand in the air dismissively. "Just a new exercise. Nothing too bad."

"Then why the name-calling, Gran?"

Gran gestured towards the flat screen TV mounted on the wall across from her. "She was lusting after that Roberts boy. Acting like a cat in heat."

"Roberts boy? Chase? Why was Chase on TV?" Jo's mind went back to the embarrassing scene in Walmart, and realized it was a good thing Gran couldn't read *her* thoughts. Chase Roberts all grown up was definitely worth lusting after.

Gran waved the remote. "No, not the sick one, bless

his heart. The older one."

Sick? Was Gran referring to Chase's childhood illness, or did he only look like the picture of health? Hot, hot health.

"And we're back at the top of the eighth inning, and Wranglers ace Matt Roberts is back out on the mound."

Jo looked at the television and saw Chase's older brother, Matt, readying the mound for another inning. The camera zoomed in on his face, and Jo had to admit that he was definitely attractive. Always had been. Problem was, he'd always known it, too.

While Chase had been popular and well-liked in his own right, Matt had always had that "it" factor that just drew people to him. Throw in obnoxiously good looks and talent that had scouts looking at him as a freshman, and you had a combination that was hard for any girl to resist.

"The PT was openly lusting after Matt in front of you?"

Gran pursed her lips. "The shameless hussy wouldn't shut up about him. Went on and on about how 'hot' he is. Cat in heat, I tell you!"

Jo loved her Gran, she truly did, and while Jo was by no means remotely promiscuous, her grandmother's old-fashioned views sometimes came across as a little, well, old-fashioned.

"Well, Gran, in all fairness he's not an unattractive man."

"Don't you start acting like a hussy too, Jolene!"

Jo sighed. "Gran, just because a woman thinks a man is attractive, that doesn't make her a hussy. Come on, you thought Pawpaw was handsome before you married him, didn't you?"

Gran's eyes misted over and a small smile tugged at her lips. "Oh, your Pawpaw was so handsome in his dress blues. He had the most beautiful eyes—that's where you get yours, you know—and the sweetest smile. Curly black hair. Such a fine figure the first time I saw him. I knew right then I was going to marry him."

Jo smiled. "You just proved my point, Gran."

The older woman shrugged and absently massaged her hip. "Always been too smart for you own damned good."

Jo leaned over and kissed her grandmother's wrinkled cheek. "And you know you wouldn't have it any other way, young woman."

Gran couldn't hide her smile. "Don't go getting a big head, young lady. Now what's for supper?"

~~*~~

Later that night, feeling restless and crampy and borderline maudlin, Jo climbed out of the full size bed in the room that had been her's as a teen and pulled a box from the top shelf of the closet. She set it on the floor, brushed the dust off and opened it.

Inside were high school mementos.

Her Homecoming mum from her senior year, the bells still shiny but missing a glittery letter from her name. A set of royal blue and white pom poms. The corsage Billy Walther gave her for senior prom, the roses dried and in a protective plastic case, the lilac elastic band's color still as vivid as the day he'd slid it on to her wrist. There were other pieces of flotsam and jetsam, memories of years gone by.

A newspaper article talking about how she'd made valedictorian. The notecards from her graduation speech. An old report card. Her acceptance letter to Baylor. Notes she and her best friend Jenn McDonnel had passed during algebra.

At the bottom of the box lay her senior memory book and four yearbooks. She withdrew all of them and returned to the bed, leaving the other items on the floor where she'd left them.

She wasn't sure what had her feeling nostalgic. Maybe it was being back here in Del Rio, sleeping in the same room she'd slept in as a teen far too often when things went downhill at home. Maybe it was seeing Chase tonight. Or maybe Aunt Flo was just a mean bitch who made her do crazy things.

She opened the memory book, smiling at the memories and the thoughts of an eighteen-year-old girl hell-bent on changing the world. Or at least her little corner of it.

10 Years From Now I...
1. *Will be Oprah's go-to psychologist on all of her shows*
2. *Will own my own practice*
3. *Will be married with two kids—boy and girl—to a gorgeous man who owns his own business, makes a lot of money and will never cheat on me*
4. *Will be a great mom who never cheats on her husband or abandons her kids*
5. *Will be living somewhere super cool, like New York City or Chicago or San Francisco*
6. *Will be making a six-figure salary with no debt, a nice house and driving a BMW*
7. *Will no longer feel the need to be perfect*
8. *Will know what love really is*
9. *Will be a member of the Junior League*
10. *Will be gearing up to run for office*

Funny how the only one of those things that had happened was number seven.

Jo brushed away a lone tear that rolled down her cheek, hating herself for feeling maudlin but realizing that if she was there was probably a good reason for it.

She hadn't gone on to become Oprah's therapist, and

instead of opening her own practice had decided to help out high school kids. God knew as a high school counselor she certainly wasn't making a six-figure salary, her student loan debt was mind-boggling and her dreams of owning a shiny new BMW had been replaced with the reality of driving a Ford Fusion. Mr. Right still hadn't come along, and at thirty-two she was beginning to wonder if he ever would. The only guy she'd loved as an adult had been shipped off to Afghanistan, and he'd ended things before leaving the States. And she certainly wasn't a member of the Junior League or planning on running for office any time soon. As for her current town…well, she sure hadn't pictured herself back in Del Rio taking care of her grandmother, but she supposed her adopted town of Austin was pretty cool. At least that's what people and dozens of weekly Top Ten lists always told her.

Jo continued to flip through the memory book, smiling at the photos and random pieces of high school life she'd glued to the pages. Towards the back, folded up and tucked underneath a photo of her, Jenn and Chase, was a lined piece of notebook paper, which she unfolded.

Dear Chase,
I'm sorry.
I'm sorry I haven't been talking to you much. I think I've hurt your feelings. I never meant to do that.
But I can't. I can't talk to you knowing that my mom has a thing for your dad. It's weird and gross and makes me embarrassed and ashamed.
My dad doesn't care who she sleeps with. I think the whole town knows that by now. He probably doesn't care if I sleep with someone, either.
But I'm not my mom. And I can't be around you because I'm too embarrassed and hurt and afraid you'll hate me.

You're my best friend. You, Jenn and me. We're the
Three Amigos. I don't want to hurt you.
I'm so sorry.
Love,
Jo

She folded the paper back up and placed it in the
book again, tucked neatly under the photo of her, Jenn
and Chase. They'd been going into the ninth grade, the
best of friends since elementary school. Until that awful
day when Jo had overheard her mom on the phone with
Chase's dad. The things her mom had said had made her
hot with embarrassment and shame, and even though she
didn't think Chase's dad would ever cheat on his wife, Jo
still felt awful and as if it was somehow her fault. If she and
Chase hadn't been such good friends, her mom might not
have ever met his dad. So she'd done what seemed best to
a fourteen-year-old girl—she'd distanced herself from her
best friend even though it had killed her.

She'd written the note to him to try to explain, but
in the end had chickened out. She couldn't. She was too
embarrassed and ashamed and didn't want Chase to think
she was like her mom.

Instead, she'd folded the note and tucked it into her
diary. That night, after eating supper with her parents
and being told not to eat so much—that "thinness is
perfection!"—by the woman everyone thought of as The
Easy Mom, was the first time Jo made herself throw up.

CHAPTER TWO

"I saw Chase the other day," Jo blurted out to Jenn, her best friend since the third grade, as they waited for their server to bring them their food.

Jenn raised an auburn eyebrow. "Reeeallly? And how was Mr. Straight and Narrow?"

"Mr. Straight and Narrow?"

Jenn sipped from her Diet Coke. "Yes, Mr. Straight and Narrow. It makes perfect sense."

"I guess. I wouldn't really know." Obviously.

Jenn shrugged a shoulder. "He's always been responsible, but he's…changed."

Curiosity was getting the better of her, but Jo was afraid to give that away—even to her best friend. Casually, she swirled the straw in her iced tea before taking a sip. Unfortunately, ever since bumping into him at Walmart she hadn't been able to get those melted chocolate eyes and that slow grin out of her head.

"How so?"

"He's…" Jenn paused to take a sip of her drink. "He's really serious now. I mean, he was always a little more on the serious side than Matt, but I guess as we've gotten older he's gotten more serious. He owns his own business—

commercial real estate—and is pretty damned successful. He also owns a big managed game ranch off the Devils River. He doesn't really talk about his finances, but from what he has said I've gathered that it's a decent money maker."

"Y'know, none of that really surprises me, though. Chase was always smart. I mean, come on, the three of us were separated by—what?—a hundredth of a grade point in high school? 'Mr. Straight and Narrow' just sounds so uptight."

Jenn stared at something behind Jo and said, "I think he feels like he has something to prove."

Jo twisted around to see what Jenn was looking at. Above the bar was a big flat screen TV, camera zoomed in on Matt Roberts' face as he watched the game from the Wranglers' dug out.

"Matt again?"

"Matt always, you mean."

Jo sighed. "I don't get it. Matt's obviously a great pitcher, but he's also always been a bit, well, cocky. I mean, they've always been a bit competitive, but I never thought Chase would feel like he had something to prove."

"When you get a chance, do a Google search on Chase's name. That'll probably tell you a lot."

Jo raised her eyebrows. "Okay, now I'm really curious."

Jenn squirmed, as if she were uncomfortable. "Let's just say Chase has been the target of some not so nice women."

Jo took another drink of her tea, suddenly wishing she'd ordered something stronger. Her best friend was obviously not telling her something, but Jo couldn't figure out what or why. They told each other everything. Well, apparently not everything if Jenn's current reaction was any indication.

"Okay, now you have to spill."

Jenn sighed. "I want to tell you, I really do. It's just that Chase kind of confided in me one day and was really embarrassed and asked me not to tell anyone. I told him I wouldn't, and you know how I am about giving my word."

"Fair enough." Jenn had always been the most loyal, trustworthy person Jo had ever known. If you needed to confide in someone you knew would keep your secrets, Jenn was the person to go to. "I guess I need to get to Googling."

Jenn breathed an almost imperceptible sigh of relief as their waitress arrived with their food. After thanking the waitress and taking quick bites of their lunch, Jenn asked, "Why are you so curious about Chase, anyway? You haven't spoken to him or about him since you left for college."

Jo knew that her friend's comment was a statement rather than an accusation, but Jo still felt guilty for basically abandoning the boy who'd been her other best friend for most of her childhood. "To be honest, I've kept up with him a little bit. We ran into each other a couple of times in college at football games. And he doesn't know it, but every time the Texas baseball team played Baylor in Waco I went to all of the games while he was on the team."

Jenn paused, fork in midair, before slowly setting it back down on her plate. "You never told me that. Any of that."

Jo shrugged. "I didn't want to make a big deal out of it. You know what happened and why I stopped talking to him. I've always felt bad about it, but I was embarrassed and hoped that if I stopped hanging out with him that my mom would stop hitting on his dad. That obviously didn't work, but by the time I figured that out the damage had been done."

Jenn reached across the table and squeezed Jo's hand

before picking up her fork again. "And yet you kept tabs on him while we were all at our separate universities?"

Jo smiled. "It was pretty easy, considering he was the closer for the Longhorns. That, and I might have stalked him a couple of times via MySpace back in the day."

"Ah, the times before Facebook and Twitter."

"We're getting old, Jenn."

"Nah. We're just now hitting our prime."

At thirty-two, Jo sometimes *felt* old, especially after spending her days counseling high school students. There was nothing like being around teenagers all day to make you feel old, even if you were only in your early thirties. "Be that as it may, I was just curious. It was really good to see him. I've missed us, the Three Amigos."

"Chase is a good guy. Sometimes I wish he wasn't like a brother to me—there isn't exactly a dearth of attractive, successful, single guys around here. At least not our age."

"I think that's the case everywhere."

They both dug into their lunches, Jenn eating her salad, Jo enjoying her grilled salmon. After long moments of companionable silence, Jenn took a drink of her Coke then asked, "So how'd it go?"

"How'd what go?"

"Running into Chase again. All you said was that you ran into him, didn't really say anything about how it went or what happened."

Jo sighed, still a little embarrassed by the whole thing. "I bumped into him. Literally. With a box of Tampax Super in one hand and a box of overnight pads in the other. Just walked backwards right into him and then almost hit him with the damned tampons."

Jenn's laugh was full and good-natured. Familiar. Welcome and missed. "Oh wow. I'm not sure which of you was probably more embarrassed."

"I think I was. At any rate, it was kind of awkward. He

didn't recognize me at first, and I kept almost hitting him with the box of tampons. I felt like one of the teenage girls who comes to my office at least once a week, crushing on the starting quarterback and miserable over it."

"Crushing, huh?" Jenn's green eyes twinkled.

"Maybe not crushing. But seriously, Jenn, you couldn't have warned me that Chase grew up and got seriously hot?" Just thinking about those eyes and that smile made her feel like she'd just run a marathon—all hot and breathless.

Jenn shrugged. "You're the one who's been stalking him."

Jo felt her cheeks warm. "True. It's just…good Lord…I mean, he was cute before. But he was so tall and skinny in high school."

"He wasn't in college," Jenn pointed out.

Jo finished off her tea as she thought back to the few times she'd seen him face to face in college and on TV during televised games. "No, he wasn't. I guess I just didn't really notice it at the time." *Liar, liar pants on fire.* "I was still grappling with the shame of my mother's actions and just too wrapped up in it and my own issues."

"Your mom was a slutty bitch who didn't deserve you as a daughter."

Years ago, Jo would have jumped to defend her mom. After several rounds of therapy, though, she knew that her mom hadn't done anything to deserve her defense. "Be that as it may, I hadn't quite admitted that at the time. You know that by college I knew that Chase's dad had put a quick end to her bullshit and had never once done anything to encourage her. Mom sure as hell took her sweet time telling me that, though, and by the time I knew the damage had already been done with Chase."

"Jo, it's been like eighteen years since all of that crap went down. We're all grownups now. Maybe you should think about, oh, I don't know, just talking to Chase about it rather than avoiding it and him all together."

"Wait, I thought I was supposed to be the therapist here."

"I teach seventh graders, so I might as well be a therapist."

"So true. I don't envy you teachers one bit."

Jenn clinked her empty glass against Jo's. "And I don't envy you guidance counselors one bit, so we're even."

~~*~~

"Heard Jo Sommers is back in town."

Chase stilled before pushing his sunglasses onto his nose and climbing into his black F-350. Frank Wimbly followed suit, giving Chase a blessed few seconds to get his thoughts in order. "Yeah, I heard that, too."

Frank shook his head. "Damned shame what her mama did to that poor girl. And her daddy…didn't care one damned bit about either of them."

Chase glanced over at his gray-haired companion before pulling out of the parking lot and onto Highway 90 to head back into town. As Lake Amistad grew smaller in his rearview mirror, Chase considered his next words. "Yeah, I think they did a number on her."

The older man stared out the window at the passing scenery. "You were probably too young to understand what was going on back then, and usually I wouldn't speak ill of the dead, but if it hadn't been for Nellie Anne, well, I don't know how that girl would have survived and made anything of herself."

Chase mentally tried to connect the dots and figure out what the old man was hinting at. Despite the fact that he and Jo and Jenn had been best friends as kids, he'd always known that Jo hid stuff from them. He'd met her parents a few times, and they'd seemed ok. As an adult, he'd heard other rumors here and there, but nothing substantial. After both her parents had died in a car accident a few years ago, the rumors had kicked up a bit, but nothing solid or that Chase had thought had any merit. Now he was beginning to wonder.

"That Chandra Sommers…" Frank shook his head, "now there was a woman who hit on anything with an XY chromosome. Like a cat in heat. All the damned time."

Chase had fuzzy memories of Jo's mom in skirts that were just a bit too short, and tops that were just a tad bit too low. Very large breasts. Teased blonde hair. If he remembered correctly, she'd been a huge Dolly Parton fan, thus Jo's given name of Jolene. He had a vague memory of Jo being embarrassed when a boy in their class had commented on Chandra's breasts and how they'd grown in size over Christmas break. A few sizes, really.

He slowed as they entered the outskirts of city proper and the speed limit dropped. They neared Walmart, and he was taken back to their meeting the other night. He hadn't mentioned to anyone yet that he'd run into Jo. His thoughts had been uncharacteristically tangled since that night, and his dreams unfortunately just as confused.

It seemed that maybe his high school crush hadn't gone away after all.

~*~

Frank had been gone fifteen minutes when Owen sauntered into Chase's office and plopped into one of the big leather chairs in front of Chase's desk.

Chase looked up at his friend. "Don't you ever work?"

Owen shrugged. "Sure, every now and then."

The fact was, Owen worked his ass off, and had a capable crew that could more than take care of the day to day goings-on of his construction business.

Owen propped his work boots up on the edge of Chase's desk, folded his hands behind his head and said, "I hear Jo Sommers is back in town."

Chase pinched the bridge of his nose. "You and

everyone else."

Owen raised an eyebrow. "Oh yeah?"

Chase nodded his head and went back to looking over the details of the offer Frank had wanted him to draft.

"You're suspiciously silent."

"What am I supposed to say? I heard the same thing. So did Frank Wimbly. And apparently you, too. I'm guessing the entire town knows by now."

"Probably."

Chase flipped to the next page of the contract.

"You gonna see her?"

"Why would I see her, Owen? We've barely spoken since high school."

Owen snorted. Chase glared at him. "Come on, Chase. You were madly in love with her until we were in our twenties. You don't want some answers?"

Sure he wanted answers. But he didn't want drama, and dredging up things long past did nothing but stir up drama.

"I saw her the other night." Why the hell had that come out?

"And?"

"And nothing, really. I acted like I didn't recognize her, even though I knew it was her the minute she turned around." He would recognize those eyes anywhere.

Owen rolled his eyes. "Sometimes you are such a girl."

Chase threw a pen at him. Owen deflected and continued. "Seriously, man. It sounds like she's gonna be in town all summer, helping take care of her grandma. Maybe now's the time to get some of those answers you've been looking for for years."

He sighed. "It's not important anymore, Owen. I'm over it. Her. Have been for years. I still don't know what happened and I don't care. I'm not a kid with an unrequited crush anymore."

"Says the man who's sworn off women."

"Yeah, because they're only using me to get to my brother."

Owen shook his head, his expression uncharacteristically hard to read. "Yeah, keep telling yourself that."

CHAPTER THREE

"Hey, Gran." Jo dropped a kiss on her grandmother's cheek. "How was PT today?"

Gran patted her hip before turning down the volume on the evening news. "Only needed two regular ibuprofen today."

Jo smiled. "That's great!"

Gran nodded, a satisfactory smile on her face. "That woman says I'm 'exceeding expectations.' Pfft. Of course I am."

"She obviously doesn't know you, Gran." No one could ever accuse her grandmother of being a quitter that was for sure.

"How was lunch with Jenn?"

"Good. I swear that's the slowest Chili's ever, though."

Gran clucked her tongue. "If I'd known you were going there, I would have warned you."

Jo chuckled. "It's okay, Gran. It gave us time to gossip and make some tentative plans."

"Jolene, you know you don't have to hover over me night and day. If you want to go have fun with your friends, go have fun."

Jo resisted the urge to fidget; how she could be a thirty-two-year-old woman and still feel like a teenager asking for permission was beyond her. "Well, Jenn did mention going up to the lake on Saturday for a few hours."

Gran waved the remote dismissively. "Go. Have fun. Lord knows you haven't had enough of that in your life."

Jo swallowed past the sudden lump of emotion in her throat. "I love you, Gran."

"I love you too, Jolene. Now what's for supper?"

~~*~~

"You didn't tell me Chase would be here," Jo grumbled into Jenn's ear.

Jenn shrugged as she pushed her ball cap down over the braid that was somewhat taming her wild auburn curls. "I knew if I did, you wouldn't come."

"You don't know that for sure. I might have anyway."

Jenn's response was lost in the wind as Chase's big, speedy boat flew over Lake Amistad. Under them, the water was as blue as she remembered. All around them the shoreline rose in white, craggy limestone formations that still took her breath away.

As a kid, the lake had been one of her favorite places. After she'd pulled herself away from Chase, she hadn't visited as much for fear of being around him and causing embarrassment.

And now here she was, sitting next to her best friend in the back of her former best friend's boat, speeding across the water to God knows where.

Nerves jangled in her gut.

Chase and his friend Owen were at the steering wheel, laughing and talking about something. While Owen had stripped down to nothing more than a pair of flip flops and board shorts, baring an impressive tattooed and freckled chest that complemented his red hair, Chase wore a faded—and very fitted—Longhorns baseball t-shirt and gray swimming trunks.

Was he still self-conscious about the scars? Curiosity

burned in her gut, but she didn't know how to ask Jenn.

Chase's childhood illness, the surgeries and the subsequent scars were a topic that the three of them had rarely broached as they grew older. As children, Jo and Jenn had laughed and teased and joked with Chase in an effort to make him feel better. While he'd never told them as much, as they'd gotten older Jo had realized that the scars made him a bit self-conscious; he never took his shirt off at pool parties or during the numerous pick-up ball games of all sorts that would pop up among the neighborhood kids. As teens, when the other boys would proudly take off their shirts to show off for the girls, Chase kept his on, deflecting the gazes and questions with a joke and a smile.

She'd seen the scars once, after his very last surgery at the end of their eighth grade year. He had two long scars, slicing from hip to hip just below his belly button, each about an inch apart from the other. One was newer, still pink and tender-looking. There were smaller ones on his back, thin and faded from where the doctors had done all kinds of biopsies.

He'd been in his backyard, standing at the edge of the swimming pool with water dripping off his hair and his swimming trunks, and she'd come over because she needed to escape the madness that was her own house. Her dad's nose had once again been stuck in some dusty tome of research, and her mom had gone off with her hair teased and smelling of Opium perfume. She'd needed a sense of normalcy, so she'd gone to Chase's, where everything always seemed normal and perfect and right.

He hadn't seen her at first, as she'd come around the side and through the gate and his back was slightly to her, his attention drawn to something else. Despite the fact that they'd been friends since childhood, Jo had started noticing the changes in Chase—and all the boys in their class—in the sixth grade. As a fourteen-year-old almost ninth grader, her curiosity had grown, and she'd *really* started noticing the changes in Chase. Playing baseball and football almost year-round had caused him to develop muscles. His voice had deepened. Her best friend was suddenly a *boy*. A really cute boy.

A really cute boy who was causing her to feel really confusing things that she had no clue how to handle or interpret.

And standing there, staring at him that day and seeing the scars that marked his struggle and will to survive, Jolene Sommers had tumbled head first into puppy love with Chase Roberts.

He never knew—she was too shy and too embarrassed and too confused to even give him a glimpse of what she was feeling. So she'd plastered a smile on her face and continued towards him, the lump in her throat making speech impossible. She finally stopped a couple feet away from him and somehow managed to say—in a pretty normal tone of voice—"Hey, Chase."

He'd startled, whipped around towards her. She'd noticed the panic in his eyes, and intuitively knew that if she looked down it would only make him feel even more panicked. So instead, she'd kept her eyes on his face— despite the fact that she so desperately wanted to see what his chest and stomach looked like without a shirt on—and smiled again. "Sorry, I didn't mean to startle you. I snuck in through the gate when your mom told me you were back here."

Chase had swallowed, his Adam's apple bobbing almost frantically before he reached for the t-shirt lying in the chair next to him. He'd rapidly pulled it over his head, and Jo had taken the small window of opportunity to satisfy her curiosity. Chase without a shirt on made her breath hitch and butterflies dance in her stomach. He was more muscular than a lot of the boys in their class, and she could see a small trail of hair poking up above the top edge of his shorts, just below those hip to hip scars. She'd been through sex ed, she knew where it led. And suddenly she was really, really curious about Chase in a way she'd never been curious before.

Too soon, the shirt was on and covering his torso. Jo had to suppress her sigh of disappointment. When Chase nervously cleared his throat, she realized she was still staring at the place where shorts met skin, just below his belly button. Embarrassed, she'd whipped her gaze back up to his face. And seen embarrassment there, too.

Awkward silence had stretched between them for long moments until Chase had said, "They're pretty bad, huh?"

Confused, Jo had asked, "Bad? What's pretty bad?" She hadn't seen anything that looked bad at all. No, it all looked way too good to her fourteen-year-old, raging hormone mind.

Chase's neck and face had flushed pink for brief seconds. "The scars, Jo. They're pretty bad. Sorry you had to see them."

Jo shook her head. "No, they're not bad." She swallowed. "I, uh, barely noticed them."

Chase had snorted. "Yeah, right. They're pretty hard to miss."

"I wasn't looking at the scars, Chase. I was looking at you."

The statement had been impulsive and real and honest. She'd never been more embarrassed in her life. Awkward silence that had never been between them before was there at that moment, and neither of them had known what to do about it. As they'd stood there, staring at each other, she'd noticed how Chase's breath had kind of hitched, and his eyes had gotten a little darker brown. Nerves and butterflies had tingled in her belly, and despite the fact that she'd never been kissed before she just *knew* that Chase was about to do just that.

Until Matt had stepped outside and opened his big mouth.

It wasn't long after that moment that Jo caught her mom hitting on Chase's dad, and Jo had done the hardest thing she'd ever done in her life—she'd let her best friend and first love go.

Jenn's elbow in her rib cage shook Jo out of her reverie. She felt like she was coming out of a fog as her eyes focused and brought Chase and Owen into sharp relief at the front of the boat. Shaking the memories away, Jo opened her bottle of water and took a long, long pull.

"Earth to Jo. Where'd you go just then?"

She tried to tear her gaze off of Chase—she really did—but for some reason her eyes didn't seem to want to cooperate with her brain. Jo sighed. "Just a quick little jaunt down memory lane, that's all."

"I think that was more like a marathon than a jaunt. I've been talking to you for five minutes."

Jo finally managed to look away from Chase and the muscles that bunched under his t-shirt and his quick smile and the sunglasses that hid those melted chocolate eyes, and at Jenn instead. "Sorry. Being back here, and especially with you guys, it's just stirring up memories. That's all."

Chase laughed at something Owen said, and the sound carried on the breeze back to where Jo and Jenn were sitting. Jo's gaze once again made its way to Chase. And just like that day when she was fourteen years old, Jo felt like she was on very, very dangerous ground.

~~*~~

Chase could feel Jo's gaze on him—he'd always been able to—and it took every bit of willpower he possessed to not look back at her. When she'd shown up with Jenn today, he'd been surprised. He should have realized, though, that Jenn would bring her along; he, Jenn and

Owen had a tradition of going out to the lake on the third weekend of the month, and this was the first of those weekends since Jo had come back to town.

She made him feel nervous and awkward, just like he'd felt as a teen with a mile-long crush. Funny how a pretty girl could tie a man's tongue in knots, no matter if he was fifteen or thirty-three.

He turned just slightly towards Owen, so that he could see Jo in his periphery. She was wearing one of those short summery dress cover-up things that hid and revealed just enough of a woman's body to make a man curious. Her hair was caught up in one of those messy ponytail bun things women wore all the time.

It made him want to see her hair messed up for other reasons entirely.

Jenn was talking more than Jo was; he could tell by the way she fidgeted with her bottle of water that she was distracted by something.

Funny how even when you hadn't seen someone in about ten years—and hadn't really talked to them in eighteen— you could still read them like a book.

As the boat neared their favorite inlet near the mouth of the Devils River, Chase slowed and then shut off the engine once they were in shallower waters. Quiet settled, waves lapping against the side of the boat, and the drone of far-off boat motors the only sound for a few, blissful seconds.

"Have you ever been to this part of the lake before?" Jenn asked Jo from the back of the boat.

"I don't think so. Most of my time as a kid was spent at Governor's Landing."

"Well, then, you're in for a treat. As you can see, there aren't anywhere near as many people out here as there are there," Jenn said before hopping up, whisking off her ball cap, tank top and shorts and diving into the water.

Chase shook his head and smiled. It was their routine. They would arrive at this little cove, and sit in silence for a few seconds. Jenn would then dive into the water like some kind of fire-haired mermaid, Owen would open a beer and Chase would pull out his fishing rod. Owen would eventually join Jenn in the water, and they would wind up arguing about something while Chase tried to catch supper from the other side of the boat—away from all of the splashing. Sometimes he would take a quick swim, sometimes he wouldn't. Afterwards they would head back to one of their places—they rotated turns—and fire up the grill, drink a few more beers, maybe a glass or two of wine, and simply enjoy the easy company of friends.

He wasn't sure how Jo's presence would change that routine. Behind him, he heard another splash as someone else dove into the water, and then Owen's low whistle.

"You're missing the show, my friend."

Chase shook his head and tossed his line into the water. "What show? I've seen those two in bathing suits since we were eight years old."

It was true, even if he knew that Jo now was nothing like Jo as an eight-year-old.

"I'm not sure if you're stupid, crazy, or gay and I never knew it."

Chase raised an eyebrow and turned to look at Owen over his shoulder. "You know that last one isn't true. The first two are probably debatable."

Owen laughed before setting his beer aside. "You should join in on the fun over here on this side."

Chase turned back to his fishing pole. "Gotta catch supper."

He heard Owen snort. "Because I don't have plenty of meat in my deep freezer."

Chase decided to ignore Owen, and tossed the lure again. Considering they owned a managed-game ranch that teemed with wild game, Chase knew just how well-stocked Owen's freezer was.

"Your choice. I, however, am going to go have fun getting wet with two beautiful ladies."

Chase heard Owen's splash seconds later, and then Jenn's shriek. He smiled. Owen and Jenn teased each other like kids, dunking each other, dragging each other under, giving each other wedgies. He half expected to find out one day that they'd run off to Vegas and eloped—except as far as he knew they weren't actually attracted to each other.

He pushed the laughter and voices to the back of his mind, found the quiet place in his head and focused on casting, reeling and trying to hook. He felt a slight tug, set the hook, and reeled in his first catch of the day. He caught the largemouth bass in one hand, removed the hook with the other, and tossed it into the live well. He turned back to the water and was just about to cast his line when Jo appeared beside him.

"Nice fish," she nodded her head towards the live well.

"Thanks." Chase turned towards her, and froze.

Jo stood in front of him, sunglasses shading those blue green eyes that had always made him feel like he was drowning. She was wearing one of those two piece bathing suits that looked like a one-piece—a tankini, he vaguely remembered Jenn calling it one day. The top was dark blue, tight around her breasts while flowing away from her abdomen. It skimmed her hips, which were clad in red and blue polka dotted bikini bottoms that had these little ties on either side. Those ties made his fingers twitch.

There was nothing immodest or particularly revealing—he'd certainly seen less fabric out here on the lake—and yet his mouth was dry and his body was definitely responding to the beautiful, wet woman in front of him. The only part of his body that seemed capable of movement—his eyes—skimmed over her again, drinking her in like a parched man in the desert.

He didn't remember her breasts being quite so…big… the last time he'd seen her in a bathing suit. Granted, that had been sometime in early high school at a party they'd both been invited to, but still. His gaze tripped down her body and stuck on her legs before flying back up and noticing her arms and shoulders.

"You lift?"

God, she was going to start thinking he'd taken one too many baseballs to the head if he kept up such scintillating conversation.

His gaze returned to her face, and he noticed that her cheeks had pinkened. She grinned shyly, winked, and then flexed her right arm. "Yup. I even have a baby bicep to prove it."

Chase laughed and felt a little of the tension drain from his body. "That's a little more than a baby bicep."

She flexed again before dropping her arm. "A little more. How'd you know I lifted?"

He swallowed. "Your legs. And then your arms and shoulders." If she hadn't known he'd been checking her out behind the lenses of his sunglasses, she did now.

Jo took a sip of water before returning his casual perusal, raking her gaze from his head to his toes and back up. "I'm not the only one who lifts."

"No, you're not."

She turned and looked out at the water before turning back to him. "I shouldn't have come today. I'm obviously making you uncomfortable."

You have no idea, Jolene Westwood. He sighed. "Not uncomfortable, really. We're just…" Chase searched for the words that could most accurately describe what she was making him feel, without giving away, well, how he was actually feeling. *Like a horny teenager.* "We haven't seen each other in years. We're different people, but kind of the same."

They stood there in silence, contemplating each other before Jo turned her head and looked out towards the water again. She wrapped her arms around herself, the motion pushing her breasts up higher. Chase swallowed, tamping down the lust that clawed at his gut.

Funny how while some things had changed, others certainly hadn't. She still made him feel like a fourteen-year-old boy, all needy and antsy and itchy, like a bottle rocket waiting to shoot off into the sky.

She worried her bottom lip, shifted her weight from one foot to the other. As he watched her—he couldn't seem to take his eyes off of her, and wasn't sure he even wanted to—goose bumps scattered over her baby biceps and her breath hitched ever so slightly.

The sight reminded him of a day long ago, next to a different body of water, when she'd had a similar look on her face. She hadn't been wearing a swimsuit that day, instead had on cut-off shorts and a cherry red tank top. But she'd looked at him, and since he knew her moods better than anyone had been able to see her nervousness. He'd thought it was because of the scars—she'd never seen them until that day. But when she'd blurted out that she hadn't been looking at the scars, but at him, his fourteen-year-old brain had dared to hope that maybe the prettiest girl in school and his best friend maybe wanted to be more than friends.

He'd been thinking about kissing her, wondering if it would scare her or gross her out if he did. He remembered being anxious, fear and nerves churning in his gut. Her cheeks had been pink, she'd had goose bumps on her arms despite the summer heat and she'd drawn this really shaky breath like the ones he'd seen in movies right before the guy kissed the girl, and courage had blossomed.

And then Matt had broken the moment.

Out of the corner of his eye, he could see Owen and Jenn, about two hundred yards away, occupied with their usual race to the sand bar that gently bumped out of the water in the middle of the cove. Matt wasn't here, their friends were engrossed in their own game, and Chase suddenly felt the need to at least get *some* answers from the woman standing in front of him.

He dropped his fishing pole, causing Jo to jump and jerk her head around to look at him. "Are you…"

He cut her question off with his mouth, finally doing what he'd wanted to that summer day almost twenty years ago, and so many days after that. He nipped lightly at her bottom lip before licking at it with his tongue. His hands settled on her hips—those damned tempting strings twined around his fingers—and he coaxed her mouth open.

He felt her body's response before he felt her mouth's response. Her arms fell and he felt her hands on his waist, riding the waistband of his shorts. Her touch burned through his t-shirt.

And then she was kissing him back. Slowly, almost shyly. Their tongues danced together and lips caressed each other.

Languorous. That really was the only way to describe it.

Languorous.

Their bodies rocked gently with the boat, but he didn't move closer. Just an answer, that's all he wanted.

Just one fucking answer.

He heard her inhale deeply through her nose, felt her fingers tighten on his waistband, and knew he had at least one answer.

This was going to be a really long summer.

~~*~~

Jo blinked as Chase pulled away from her, breaking the kiss and setting her thoughts spinning in her head.

Chase had just kissed her.

Chase.

She wanted him to do it again.

He was an expert kisser.

She wanted him to do it again.

And again.

And again.

And again.

Except with more hands. Those big hands had stayed on her hips, but Jo realized with a sharp, jarring thought that she wanted those hands *on* her. Everywhere.

But he was Chase and she was Jo and despite having a degree in psychology and being a high school counselor she suddenly *felt* like one of the teenage girls she so often listened to. She vaguely remembered this feeling—the confusion and anguish and *want* that clawed sharply, desperately at a person's insides. She hadn't felt it often.

Oh, she'd wanted men before. She'd had men before. Not a lot, but a few. And she'd wanted them, been attracted to them, trusted them and in one case even loved. But this intense, sudden churning she'd only felt with one person.

Chase.

It hadn't been there the other night at Walmart—not like this. She'd recognized the spark, the stirrings of want, but it hadn't been like this since high school, when she'd loved him desperately and had stuffed it down because she'd been trying to protect him.

Okay, she'd been trying to protect herself, too.

Vaguely, the sound of Jenn's laughter reached her ears, carried on the wind and the waves, and Jo blinked as she returned to the present.

Chase was still standing in front of her, their bodies close enough that she could feel heat pulsing off of him in waves. Knowing her sunglasses were dark enough to hide her eyes, she took a moment to look him over, to collect herself. His body was taut with tension, she could see that now. Could feel that, somehow, like she'd been able to once upon a time, when she'd been attuned to his moods, thoughts and emotions.

His breaths were slightly uneven, and despite the fact that it had been some time since she'd been around a man in an aroused state, she was pretty sure Chase was, indeed, in an aroused state.

He wanted her.

Somehow, that made everything simpler and more complicated at the same time.

Same, but different.

Words and thoughts and feelings pushed at her throat, tripping over each other as they danced over her tongue. Her thoughts were spinning like Jessie Spano on diet pills.

Then suddenly Jessie was no longer excited, and her thoughts were calm, and the only words that mattered— really mattered—spilled over her lips.

She pushed her sunglasses onto the top of her head, removing at least one of the barriers between them, and looked him in the eye. "I never meant to hurt you, Chase."

"Then why did you?"

She shook her head. "I was trying to protect you. Myself. My mom…"

He looked off to the side, and she followed his gaze. Owen and Jenn had just reached the sand bar, were walking onto shore with their backs towards the boat. Chase glanced back at her, grabbed her sunglasses and his, tossed them to the side and then pushed her over the edge.

Jo came up sputtering, spitting water as she scooped hair out of her eyes.

What the hell was wrong with him?

She looked up at the boat, trying to find him, and felt something brush against her leg. She shrieked and kicked, paddling towards the boat, away from whatever was lurking under the surface. She was scared to look down, for fear of what she'd see in the clear water.

Please don't let it be a snake. Or a gar.

Just as Jo reached the side of the boat and began to tread water, Chase's head popped up right where she'd been, and she realized with at least some relief that she'd probably felt him brushing against her leg under water.

At least, that's what she preferred to believe.

He stroked towards her, stopping about a foot away.

"What the hell was that for?"

He grinned as he tread water. "I wanted some privacy."

She pushed a hank of wet hair out of her eyes. "And we didn't have that already?"

"They always turn around once they reach the sand bar and wave at me. They would have seen us and then we wouldn't have heard the end of it."

"And disappearing over the side of the boat and out of their sight won't make them give us hell?"

He looked away for long moments, long enough that Jo wondered if he was going to answer her at all, and then he swung his gaze back to her and she felt her breath catch somewhere between her lungs and her throat before leaving her body on a long, hard *whoosh*. Did he even know what those eyes did to a woman?

"We're just swimming."

"You don't sound like that you believe that." She sounded much braver than she felt.

His laugh was slightly choked; with wonder, disbelief, or anger she didn't know. "You know me too well. Somehow, you still know me too well."

And she did. They might be same and yet different than they had been, but the fundamentals of who they used to be were still present.

"I made you uncomfortable. So you threw me into the water." She skimmed her hand along the surface, splashing him in the face. He wasn't the only one who was uncomfortable.

He laughed and splashed her back. "Slightly. Maybe."

Her lips twitched, holding back a laugh. He splashed her again, and she closed her eyes and splashed back, the laughter now bubbling over. She opened her eyes just in time to see him take a deep breath and dive under the water, and knew exactly what he was doing.

Jo moved quickly to the right and then used the side of the boat to push off with her legs. When he surfaced where she'd been, she was a good ten feet away from him.

Their gazes caught and she raised an eyebrow. "I bet I'm still the better swimmer."

Instead of answering he dove back under the water, and Jo moved again, swimming to her right.

Apparently she wasn't still the better swimmer, because seconds later she felt his hand grasp her ankle. Knowing what was coming next she took one last deep breath before he pulled her under.

It had been years since she'd gotten into a water fight with anyone, and even more since that person had been Chase. But some things were a lot like riding the proverbial bicycle—same, but different.

Instead of fighting to reach the surface and get away from him, she instead twisted in his grip, knowing his hand wasn't incredibly tight around her ankle. She opened her eyes, and could easily see him in the clear water. He was right in front of her, his eyes closed, and she took advantage, reaching out and lightly running her fingers along his belly where his shirt had floated up, exposing his skin there.

He jerked, and the movement propelled them upwards. Their heads broke the surface, both of them gasping for air.

"You tickled me!"

Jo snorted. "You're lucky that's all I did."

Chase narrowed his eyes in an attempt to look menacing. Jo giggled—actually giggled—which made him laugh.

They treaded water, laughing, for long moments before Chase smiled and said, "I've missed you, Jo."

Jo was suddenly glad for the water running from her hair down her face, because it helped hide—at least a little—the couple of tears that managed to escape.

"I've missed you too, Chase."

CHAPTER FOUR

"Stop feeling guilty."

Jo glanced towards Jenn and took another sip of her wine. "Guilty about what?"

"I can read you like a book, Jolene Westwood. You're feeling guilty about leaving Gran all alone tonight."

"She just had hip surgery, and I was gone all day already."

"And she told you she was perfectly fine and to not feel guilty and go have fun with your friends. So stop it."

"It's just…hard not to feel guilty." Jo sighed and sipped more wine. She did feel guilty, sitting here in Owen's backyard, drinking wine while her grandmother sat at home by herself with still somewhat limited mobility.

Jenn *harrumphed* beside her before reaching for the bottle of wine to pour herself some more. "This is really good. Where'd you get it?"

Jo knew better than the trust to change in subject as being permanent, but answered her friend's question anyway. "Spec's."

Jenn raised an eyebrow. "You purposely packed wine to bring with you?"

Well, theoretically she could have stopped in San Antonio on her way from Austin. "I wasn't sure if I could find my favorites here."

"You're such a wine snob," Jenn teased.

"Yes, such a wine snob that I packed a few bottles of my favorite ten dollar red moscato to bring with me."

Jenn looked at the bottle again. "This stuff's seriously only ten bucks?"

Jo smirked. "Yup."

"Hot damn. I hope they do sell this stuff in Del Rio. Somewhere. Even Uvalde. I'll drive to Uvalde for this."

Jo laughed, the tension starting to drain from her shoulders.

Jenn flashed her a knowing smirk. "I got you to stop feeling guilty."

Jo sighed.

"Guilty about what?" Chase sauntered over, a long neck of Shiner dangling from his fingers.

She had the oddest sudden desire to be a beer bottle.

"Jo's feeling guilty about leaving Gran by herself."

Jo rolled her eyes. "She just had her hip replaced!" She said for the second time that night.

Chase sat down beside her, casually rested his free arm along the back of the wooden glider they were both sitting on. Every nerve in Jo's body jumped to attention. She grabbed her glass of wine, tried to take a casual sip, but gulped instead.

Coming to Owen's had been a bad idea.

For one thing, Gran might need her. For another, her emotions were still too raw from her and Chase's almost confessions this afternoon. Not to mention the definitely happened kiss.

Who knew he could kiss like that?

"How's she doing?"

Jo mentally shook herself. "She's actually doing really well. She hates physical therapy—which I knew she would. Stubborn woman."

"Well, at least you come by it honestly," Chase quipped.

Jo elbowed him in the ribs.

Jenn raised her eyebrows and peered at the two of them over the rim of her wine glass. "So what *were* the two of you doing while we were at the sand bar?"

"Swimming."

"Horsing around."

They spoke at the same time, causing Jenn to lift her eyebrows even higher—which Jo hadn't thought was possible.

"Swimming. Horsing around. Hmm." Those eyebrows eased into a lascivious waggle.

Jo forced herself not to squirm under Jenn's gaze. Damn her and her seventh grade teacher perceptiveness.

Or whatever it was.

Grasping for something—anything—she picked up her iPhone, started up an iTunes playlist on shuffle, and said, "Oh, hey, I love this song!"

Owen stepped out of the house—the fish were apparently ready to go on the grill—and asked, "You know Kelly Willis and Bruce Robison?" His expression clearly said, *I don't believe it.*

"Any Texas girl worth her salt knows the first couple of Austin's country music scene."

Jenn chuckled. "Oh, I think the gauntlet might have just been thrown."

Jo looked quizzically at Jenn, who smiled and explained, "These two," she tipped her wine glass first towards Chase and then towards Owen, "are the two biggest music geeks in Del Rio."

"Little do these two," Jo pointed at Owen and then Chase, "know that I'm also a music geek, huh?"

Chase's fingers brushed against Jo's shoulder—almost as if by accident—as he asked, "But are you a Texas country music geek? See, Owen and I are very, very picky."

"Snobby, even," Jenn nodded enthusiastically.

"More of an overall music geek, with a soft spot that borders on obsession for all things Miranda Lambert."

Chase laughed. "I should have known."

"Should have known what?"

"I'm just not surprised, that's all. So, you up for a friendly competition?"

Jo narrowed her eyes. "What kind of competition?"

Jenn almost bounced in her seat. How many glasses of wine had she had? "I play DJ. It's kind of like Jeopardy or Family Feud or something. First person to slap the table gets first guess at the song. Each correct guess is one point. Each wrong, you get a point erased."

"Do we listen to a song or what?"

"Jenn pulls up iTunes, shuffles stuff, and then starts playing. Sometimes we'll listen to the full song, sometimes we just skip through," Chase answered.

"Sure, I'm in."

"You're brave, Jolene."

"Nobody's called me Jolene in years, and I swear between y'all and my gran I've been called that more times I can count since I've been back."

Chase shrugged. "Sometimes it just fits."

Jo raised an eyebrow before turning to Jenn and smiling. "Bring it on, boys."

~~*~~

Jo's hand slapped down on the table and she shouted out, "Nobody's girl by Reckless Kelly!"

Beside him, Chase could feel her hips twitching. Playing their stupid game with Jo had been fun—and an added challenge since with every sip of wine she took, the more her hips twitched on the seat next to his.

Owen set the now cooked fish on a platter in the middle of the table, and Jenn let the song play as they took an official time out for supper. As Jo speared a grilled filet with her fork, he could hear her humming softly along with the song. He chuckled, remembering how as kids she'd put on more than one "concert" in his backyard, most often to Madonna and Bon Jovi.

Chase surreptitiously glanced down at her, noticing how emotions seemed to fleetingly cross her face before they were gone, so different from how guarded she'd been that night in Walmart when they'd first bumped into each other. As the song neared the bridge Jo's body seemed to hum with barely suppressed movement. Something told him that had she been alone she would have been bouncing and pumping her fist in time with the music and the words that expressed the heartache of a woman growing up in a broken home and finding herself repeating the cycle.

Jo's home hadn't been broken in the traditional sense, but he knew enough to know that it hadn't exactly been whole, either.

How many nights had she spent on her own, he wondered, before telling himself that it really wasn't any of his business.

The only problem was that while everyone else assumed he'd long ago stopped caring about Jolene Sommers—no, Jolene Westwood, now—he hadn't. Not really. He'd just done a good job of stuffing the feelings down and ignoring them like she'd ignored him.

He sounded like an angry kid, even to himself. Chase supposed that somewhere inside he probably was still a little bit of an angry boy.

Conversation ebbed and flowed as they ate supper, with Chase lost primarily in his thoughts the entire time. When they'd finished, Jenn and Owen volunteered for kitchen duty, gathering up dirty dishes and carrying them inside.

Alone with nothing more than Jolene, iTunes and

alcohol, Chase wondered if his friends had planned this. He wouldn't put it past them.

The song switched from Pat Green's "Take Me Out to a Dancehall" to Eli Young Band's "Guinevere," and Jo once again softly hummed along.

"I really didn't take you as a Texas country fan."

She looked over at him. "No? Why?"

He chuckled. "Well, considering the last time we were around each other for any length of time your locker was decorated with pictures of matchbox twenty and Third Eye Blind…"

Jo laughed. "For what it's worth, matchbox twenty is still my all-time favorite band, and I've been known to crank up 'Semi-Charmed Life' a time or two. Besides, the last time you and I spent any sort of time near each other I'm pretty sure you had 'Smells like Teen Spirit' on repeat."

"Fair enough. People change."

"Exactly. But, as for how I got into Texas country," she paused, her brow furrowed, "I guess it was a kind of slow progression. I would listen to some stuff, the more popular stuff like Pat Green and Jack Ingram, but then I dated a guy who was in a band so any time we were together all we would listen to was Texas country. I got a little sick of it—I mean, you can only listen to 'Boys from Oklahoma' so many times before you feel like you might actually *need* a joint, even if it is rolled all wrong—and didn't listen for a while. But then KOKE FM came back on the air, and most of the stuff on mainstream was, well, not very good, and I started listening more and more and, well, that's that."

"Wait, back up. First—you once dated a guy in a band?" That seemed a bit incongruous with the Jo he'd known and the Jo he'd spent the past eight and a half hours with. Not that he was counting or anything.

Jo shrugged a shoulder. "It's the Austin thing to do."

"So was he in Ragweed or just a fan of Ragweed?"

"Fan of Ragweed. In both senses of the word."

Chase threw back his head and laughed. "You're surprising me, Jo."

"Honestly, it wasn't my proudest moment. I'd just moved to Austin right after finishing my master's degree. I was lonely, didn't know anyone, and he approached me at a bar one night. I was just drunk enough to dance with him, and then got drunker enough and accidentally gave him my real phone number. That relationship lasted a whopping three weeks."

"Is that even long enough to be considered a relationship?"

She snorted. "Who the hell knows? God knows to the teenagers I work with it is."

"How in the world do you do it?"

She looked up at him. "Do what?"

"Counsel teenagers?" He shuddered. "I can't think of a group of people that would be harder to deal with."

She shifted in her seat, fiddled with her now empty wine glass before angling her body towards him. "That's precisely why I do it—they're difficult and emotional and desperately need someone they can talk to who won't judge them. You remember what it was like to be a teen, right? I mean, we're not *that* old."

He thought about his teenage years. They'd been difficult, yes, but fun. He'd had a good family, a promising future in collegiate baseball, friends and plenty of girls who were willing to be his girlfriend, even if he hadn't really been interested in any of them. Yeah, he had his scars— literally—but other than his childhood illness, the hardest thing he'd had to deal with as a teen had been the sudden loss of Jo's friendship.

He'd actually cried over her one night, after sneaking home from a homecoming bonfire at which there may have been copious amounts of alcohol passed around among all of the underage participants.

It was the first and only time he drank until he was of a legal age.

Aside from that, though, he guessed he'd probably had it pretty easy. Some kids, he knew, weren't so lucky.

"Being a teenager kind of sucks," he finally said.

"Exactly. It's just…I weirdly relate to them. My life looked great on the outside, you know? But I was a mess on the inside. My home life was a clusterfuck, to put it bluntly. There was so much pressure to be perfect. From my mom. Myself. I always thought that maybe if I was smart enough, pretty enough Dad would pay more attention and actually be a dad. I know now that there's nothing I could have done to make him pay more attention—he was who he was, and that man was content to hide in his books and not deal with the real world, much less his cheating wife and his needy daughter. And Mom. God. There's a great example for a teenage girl to follow. I developed an eating disorder, had it until I was halfway through my junior year of college and ended up in the hospital and started working with a therapist who specializes in EDs. I gained a lot of weight in recovery—you wouldn't have recognized me— and lost a decent amount of it afterwards when I started treating myself right, lifting and actually feeding my body. Up until that point I'd planned on going into psychiatry and opening my own practice, but once I was out of the thick of it and could think about it without feeling crazy and out of control, I realized that I could have used a really good counselor in high school, someone to talk to who wasn't a friend but who still got it. So I changed majors slightly and decided to be a high school counselor. And I'm rambling and saying way more than I should have and I'm out of wine. I need more wine."

Behind Jo, Chase saw Jenn and Owen approaching the back door. He subtly shook his head and motioned for them to go back inside. He needed this conversation to continue, even if what Jo was telling him made him feel equal parts sick, angry and protective. Luckily, Jenn actually listened for once.

Chase set his beer on the table before taking the empty wine glass from Jo's hands and setting it on the table, too. Then he did the only thing he could do—wrapped his arms around her and kissed the top of her head, realizing that somewhere in that jumbled, rambly mess she'd accidentally poured out, was another answer.

~~*~~

Jo felt Chase's arms wrap around her as her head swam. Whether it was from wine, emotions or embarrassment she wasn't sure, but it was probably a combination of all three. Vaguely, she heard Imagine Dragons' "Demons" coming from her phone's speakers. Fitting.

She felt like she should warn Chase that she had demons hiding inside. Danger. Stay away. Don't get too close.

"Well, that's not Texas country."

She snorted into his shirt before taking a deep breath. He smelled like sun and skin and everything she'd ever wanted but couldn't have. She'd noticed it earlier on the boat, when he'd kissed her.

His scent made her mouth water.

"I told you, I listen to a little bit of everything, just mostly Texas country."

"Who is this?"

"Imagine Dragons." She shrugged. "I like their sound."

"It's interesting."

She pulled away from him. "You don't like it."

"I didn't say that."

His voice was slightly teasing, and she finally chanced a look up at him. Their gazes met, and Jo felt like she'd been punched in the gut.

"Don't feel sorry for me, Chase."

He twirled a lock of her hair around his index finger, his brow furrowed in thought, before he met her gaze again. "I don't feel sorry for you, Jo. I feel bad for the girl you were, and I wish you would have just told me that stuff was going on instead of pushing me away."

She drew a deep breath, and had apparently drunk just enough wine to loosen her tongue, because the next thing out of her mouth was an unplanned, "That wasn't what did it. Not really. I overheard my mom on the phone one day. She was hitting on someone—very explicitly telling whoever it was what she wanted to do to him. I'd suspected she cheated on my dad, and when I heard her…I was disgusted and embarrassed, and thought I might be sick because that was my *mom* saying those things, but I couldn't move. It was like I was frozen in the hallway. And then she said your dad's name, and I really did almost get sick then. She got kind of mad, and then sweet again, and hung up. I knew your dad loved your mom and wouldn't ever cheat on her, but at the time I felt like it was somehow my fault, that if you and I hadn't been friends maybe she never would have hit on him. I was embarrassed and sick and disgusted with my mom and very, very stupidly pushed you away in an attempt to protect you and your family from my mother."

She chanced a glance up at Chase's face, only to find his expression incredibly difficult to read. Wine. She needed more wine. There was none. She blindly groped for his beer.

"I'm not sure which one of us needs that more right now."

Jo almost choked in relief. He was speaking. Thank God, he was speaking.

"All this time, I thought it was me."

"You?" she asked stupidly.

"The scars. You saw the scars. Not long after that you stopped talking to me."

She reached up and cupped his cheek. "Oh, Chase. No. It was my stupid mom and me being a dumb, scared teenager. That day I saw the scars? I wanted you to kiss me so bad my teeth hurt. It was my stupid, stupid mother."

~~*~~

Jo's words, her hand on his cheek, the tears glistening in her eyes and answers—thank God finally, some more answers—gripped Chase and had his brain spinning.

He ached. Ached for the girl she'd been and the boy he'd been, caught up in and victims of stupid adult decisions and teenage angst. Ached for what they could have been and the time they'd lost. Ached for her.

He just…ached.

So he did the only thing he could think to do, the only thing that made any sense in the swirling morass in his head. He kissed her.

For the second time that day.

It was meant as comfort. For him. For her. He really wasn't sure.

Just…comfort.

He'd meant to gently brush her lips with his own, just once or twice.

For comfort.

But he ached.

And comfort quickly turned into something more than comfort as her tongue tangled with his and he could feel her shuddered breath beneath his palms. He'd purposely kept distance between them in the boat earlier, needing to know and yet not ready to fully know just how deep his attraction still ran. Now, though, there was no distance. Their bodies were pressed against each other on the small glider, and he could feel the skin of her calf brushing against his knee.

He ached.

She sighed. A breathy, ragged sound as her fingers dug into his shoulders. He could feel her breasts pressing against his chest. The softness of her hair between his fingers on one hand, and softness of the curve of her thigh under his other hand.

He *ached* dammit.

Chase vaguely heard the sound of voices inside the house. Jo apparently did too, as she slowly backed away. Not wanting to lose her just yet, he chased her mouth again with his, caught her lips in one more far too brief kiss.

Jenn and Owen's voices intruded again, closer now. Chase shifted in the seat, and he noticed that Jo did, too, and that her cheeks were slightly flushed. But she didn't look like she was going to cry anymore. Thank God for that.

Sensing they were on borrowed time, he dropped a quick kiss on Jo's forehead. She looked up at him, and he could see the relief, embarrassment and confusion mingling together on her face, knew she probably saw similar emotions on his.

And he ached.

CHAPTER FIVE

Jo woke the next morning with a pounding headache and a slightly queasy stomach. She shielded her eyes against the bright sunlight filtering in from her bedroom window and groaned.

How much wine had she had to drink last night?

She started to count, ended up at three glasses. God, she was a lightweight.

Then she remembered her conversation with Chase.

And almost threw up.

She breathed in through her nose. In. Out.

In.

Out.

Slow and steady like she advised her teens when they came to her panicky about test results. Of all kinds. Didn't seem to matter if it was a math test or a pregnancy test— that simple four-letter word seemed to invoke panic like no other.

Had she really drunkenly spilled her guts to Chase last night? Her stomach churned in a resounding yes.

Fuck.

Jo sat up slowly and reached for the bottle of water on her night stand, opened it and drank slowly. Thinking back, she realized that part of the problem was that she probably hadn't had enough water yesterday prior to drinking that favorite red moscato. Normally, three glasses spaced decently far apart would maybe make her tipsy, but not drunk.

Well, in all fairness she hadn't really been drunk. Rather, she'd been in that place between tipsy and drunk where she was fully aware of everything she was saying but her tongue was just a little too loose to stop. Her thoughts had jumbled and jostled and pushed to get out, and they had.

She'd been tired of holding all that in, and Chase deserved the truth. Hell, she deserved the telling of the truth.

Jo finished the water and crawled out of bed, padded to the bathroom and took a long, hot shower before getting dressed. She joined Gran in the kitchen.

"There's a plate warming for you in the oven."

Jo glanced at the time. Eight-thirty. Her grandmother hadn't been up and out of bed too long either, then. She bussed a kiss on the older woman's cheek.

"You didn't have to do that, Gran."

Gran shook out her newspaper. "Eggs, bacon and biscuits with gravy. I put a few bottles of Gatorade in the fridge for you, too. Might be cool by now."

Jo turned slowly, carefully placing her breakfast plate on the small eat-in breakfast table. "I'm not sure if I should be embarrassed or thankful." *No use beating around the bush.*

A hearty chuckle shook her grandmother's body. "Just be thankful, young lady. I was young once, too. There's nothing wrong with enjoying yourself every now and then."

Jo opened the Gatorade she'd snagged from the fridge, deciding to be thankful to her grandmother as the cool liquid wet her parched mouth. She sat, chewed thoughtfully on her eggs and swallowed. "You do know it's only every now and then, right, Gran?"

Gran didn't even bother looking up from her newspaper this time. "Of course I do, Jolene Dolly. You're a good girl, always have been. A couple drinks every now and then ain't gonna hurt nobody."

Jo groaned. "Please don't call me that, Gran."

"It's your name."

"It's awful is what it is. And it's not my name anymore."

Gran dropped the newspaper to the table. "It's not?"

"I thought I'd told you? When I changed my last name to yours, I changed my middle name to Sommers. I didn't really want their last name anymore, but, I don't know, I couldn't quite let go of it completely I guess."

Gran picked her paper back up. "Like I said, you're a good girl, Jolene. Now eat up and get hydrated. It'll help the headache."

"How do you know I have a headache, Gran?" Jo teased.

"Because you're my granddaughter, that's how."

Jo smiled and ate up.

~~*~~

Later that afternoon, while Gran was doing her PT homework in the living room, Jo changed into workout clothes, popped her earbuds in, and headed out to the garage for her own version of physical therapy.

She queued up her workout playlist and slipped her phone back into the tight pocket inside her workout shorts. She moved her kettle bells to the center of the garage before grabbing her dumb bells and setting them beside the kettle bells, wishing she'd been able to bring her entire rack with her but thankful she'd finally been able to get in a workout.

She'd been here…ugh, two weeks. Two weeks without exercising.

No wonder she was getting emotional—she needed some endorphins. Stat.

Jo warmed up, moving fluidly from stretch to stretch. She paused to drink some water before picking up her dumb bells and beginning her normal routine. Somewhere between upper body and lower body, her earbuds started slipping out and refused to stay in. Frustrated, she ripped them out of her phone, which she sat next to her water, volume turned up all the way.

She'd just finished Russian kettle bell swings and was in the process of moving into a set of goblet squats, Eminem's "The Monster" blaring from her phone, when she heard Chase's voice behind her.

"You really do listen a variety of stuff, don't you?"

She almost dropped fifty pounds of cast iron on her foot.

Almost.

Instead, she turned around, the kettle bell dangling in her hands, and asked, "Don't you know better than to startle someone in the middle of a workout?"

"Hey, I waited until you were done with the swings. I was pretty sure Gran wouldn't appreciate having a hole in her wall."

"The Monster" gave way to "Gunpowder and Lead," and Jo suddenly felt angry. "Why are you here, Chase?"

He shrugged, obviously uncomfortable. "I wanted to make sure you were okay."

Determined to finish her workout, Jo dropped into a deep squat. "And why--" Up. "Wouldn't I--" Down. "Be--" Up. "Okay?" Down.

He raked a hand through his hair and looked over her shoulder before turning his gaze back to her. She waited for him to respond.

Up.

Down.

Breathe.

Up.

Down.

Breathe.

"I got the impression you hadn't planned on all of that coming out last night. Not like it did. And not last night."

Up.

Down.

Breathe, Jolene.

Up.

Down.

Breathe.

"You would be correct."

Up.

Down.

Breathe.

Why did he have to be so fucking gorgeous?

Jo's heart was racing, and she wasn't sure if it was from the workout or him or both.

He was ruining her workout.

Maybe.

The eye candy was nice.

Being watched so intently, however, was unnerving.

She finished her squats in silence, concentrating on counting each rep. As Jo set the kettle bell down on the floor and grabbed her water, she almost laughed out loud as the lyrics of Sugarcult's "Pretty Girl" pummeled her ears.

Leave it to iTunes to have impeccable timing. She almost skipped the song, but then realized Chase probably wouldn't see the irony in an angry song about a girl falling in love playing at this precise moment, and instead drank her water.

"I haven't heard Sugarcult since I was in college."

She almost choked on her water. "You know this song?"

Chase shrugged, the fabric of his t-shirt stretching across his shoulders. Thank God this one was looser than the one he'd been wearing yesterday. That one had fit like a second skin. This one at least kept her from drooling quite as much.

"I did go to school at UT and play baseball. There's a really wide variety of stuff played in the locker room."

"Not to mention all those walkup songs."

He grinned. "Those, too. One time we paid the PA guy to switch out Shawn O'Malley's usual walkup song with Sir Mixalot."

Jo snorted. "What was his usual walkup song?"

"Garth Brooks' 'Ain't Going Down'."

"Seriously?"

"As a heart attack."

"That's classic." Her anger was apparently fading.

"Yeah, he was pretty mad about it. But then he jacked a grand slam out of the ballpark. He wasn't so mad anymore."

"Until he realized he was stuck with it."

"We baseball guys are a superstitious bunch."

Jo chuckled and set her water aside. She grabbed her phone and turned down the volume slightly.

"I'm sorry I interrupted your workout."

"It's okay. Squats are the next to last thing I do anyway."

He shuffled his feet. "Do you want me to leave?"

She considered him for a few seconds before dropping to the floor and picking up the kettle bell she'd previously abandoned. "You can stay if you want."

"Pretty Girl" drew to an end, and as she heard the opening strains of Alex Clare's "Too Close," Jo began her Turkish Get Ups and wondered why she had so many angry songs about love.

~~*~~

Chase tried not to watch Jo as she went through the motions of her final set, but it was incredibly difficult not to.

Incredibly.

She was wearing a pair of those short, tight workout shorts that seemed to be so popular among women these days—booty shorts, he privately called them—and a light blue sports bra that really did nothing to diminish her breasts.

They were kind of glorious.

He noticed the dumbbells sitting off to the side, and almost did a double take. Those weren't the dainty pink dumbbells he was used to seeing women use, but rather honest-to-God, serious dumbbells. He looked closer and saw the 75 etched into each one and almost swallowed his tongue.

She really did lift.

Curious, he looked at the kettle bells she'd set beside the dumbbells. Thirty-five pounds each. Looked at Jo and the bell clutched in her hands. Fifty pounds.

"You were just doing fifty-pound swings?"

She lifted an eyebrow, but didn't speak until the song switched over. Matchbox twenty's "Busted." This was one he definitely knew.

"This was my walk out song my freshman year of college."

She set the kettle bell aside, pushed up off the floor and grabbed a fresh bottle of water. "I know."

"You know? How?"

She drank, and he had the feeling she was buying time more than quenching her thirst. Finally, she spoke. "I may or may not have gone to a few games."

He cocked an eyebrow. "But you never said anything."

"Embarrassed teenager?"

"Right. So how many is a few?"

She took another gulp of water. This time he knew she was stalling.

"How many, Jo?"

"Does it matter?"

He shrugged. "Not really, I'm just curious." *Yes, it matters, dammit.*

"Every game Texas played at Baylor. And a few down in Austin when Baylor played there."

"Every one?"

She nodded. Slowly. Barely.

"Even the one that went to twelve innings and lasted 'til midnight?"

"You were amazing that game."

He had been amazing that night. The bullpen was drained when they put him in at the bottom of the inning, game tied at one run each. He pitched a shut-out ninth inning. And then a shut-out tenth, eleventh and twelfth, after Maldonado had jacked one out of left field in the top of the twelfth. He'd gone in at the bottom of the twelfth, finally in a place to close the game.

He threw six strikes in a row. The third batter came up, popped up to short on the first pitch he saw, and that had been the ballgame.

It was one of his favorite memories, and she'd been there.

"So who'd you cheer for?" Why he asked, he didn't know. He wasn't one of those men who needed to have his ego stroked by a beautiful woman. For some reason, though, he wanted to hear that she'd pulled for him despite everything that had happened.

How fucked up was that?

"I have to admit that there were times when I was a terrible Baylor fan. I always cheered for the Bears, unless we were playing Texas."

"So you cheered for the Longhorns while going to

Baylor?" That was an interesting little fact he wasn't quite sure what to do with.

"I think it's probably more appropriate to say I cheered for you—that way it didn't feel quite like cheating on my school."

He laughed. "No one ever questioned where your loyalties were?"

She shook her head. "I always went to those games by myself so that I wouldn't get that question."

"So you were secretly in love with me and went to all of my baseball games in Waco. What other secrets are you hiding?" he teased, which caused her to sputter.

"Not to bruise your ego, Roberts, but I wasn't secretly in love with you." Something flashed in her eyes, making him think that maybe she wasn't telling the complete truth, but he decided to let it go for now.

"Ouch."

She poked him in the chest. "It's not like you were secretly in love with me, either."

Chase felt his stomach tighten, and the words were out before he could snatch them back. "Are you so sure about that?"

So much for letting it go for now.

Jo froze, her eyes round, an almost panicky expression on her face. It would have been comical had his gut not been churning with his own anxiety.

"You...you never said anything."

His voice was surprisingly calm when he said, "I could say the same thing to you, Jo."

She drew in a sharp breath. Yup, she'd definitely been skirting the truth. "I guess I deserved that."

"Kind of. But I didn't mean for it to sound so harsh. Just, that, both of us were stupid teenagers."

"And this is why I tell my kids to actually talk to their problems," she muttered.

"Talk to their problems? Not about them?"

"Oh, about them, too. The thing with teenagers, though—and I know this from far too much personal experience, remember—is that their problems tend to be people more than anything else. Parents. Teachers. Boyfriends. Girlfriends. Friends. Crushes and unrequited love. Every now and then I get through to one or two of them, and they actually follow my advice and talk to the person. Sometimes it works out, sometimes it doesn't, but they always feel better for having at least tried."

"They're lucky to have you."

She smiled. "Thanks. Speaking of occupations…we've talked a lot about mine. What do you do these days?"

He shrugged, uncomfortable with the focus of the conversation swinging back to him. "Commercial real estate, wild game ranch management."

"Well, that's a bit divergent."

He laughed, and some of the tension eased between his shoulders. "I actually was wondering if you'd like to come up to the ranch with me. I've gotta take some feed and supplies up. That is, if you don't already have plans or need to help your grandma."

"Let me check with Gran and take a quick shower. Come on in, I'll grab you something to drink for while you wait."

As he entered Nellie Westwood's house, Chase wondered if he was crazy to ask Jo to spend that much time alone with him.

And then he looked down at her ass in those booty shorts and realized the real craziness was in asking her to change clothes.

CHAPTER SIX

"Oh, Chase, it's beautiful."

Several hours and errands later, Jo leaned forward as though to better see the vista spread out in front of her as an automatic gate swung open. Over the gate was an arch that proclaimed, "Devils Ranch." She chuckled at that.

"Creative, huh?"

Chase grinned as he pulled the truck and attached trailer through the gate. "Not really. We couldn't all agree on a name, though, so we flipped a coin and Owen won."

"So Owen named it?"

"Kind of. He, Matt, a buddy of Matt's and I tossed in a bunch of names and came up with that and another one. I can't even remember what it was now."

"So all four of you own it?"

He nodded and pulled up to a huge barn. As he put the truck in park, a young lanky cowboy strode out of the barn and met them at the front of Chase's F-350. The two men shook hands in greeting before Chase gestured towards Jo. "Daniel, Jolene Westwood. Jo, Daniel Hernandez."

"Nice to meet you Miss Westwood," Daniel smiled and tipped his cowboy hat.

"Oh, just call me Jo. Miss Westwood makes me feel like my grandmother." She smiled, and the younger man winked at her.

"Jo, then. Nice to meet you."

"Likewise."

Jo suddenly felt the gentle pressure of Chase's fingers on her lower back. Was he being possessive?

Well then.

"Daniel's our ranch manager. Kind of like a foreman, only even more important."

"Basically, I do all the work while Chase's lazy ass sits in air conditioning all day."

Jo couldn't help but laugh at the friendly banter. She gestured towards the outbuildings and main house and said, "Well, it certainly looks like you work your ass off."

"Good staff, Jo, good staff." He winked at her again, and the pressure on her lower back increased.

Chase *was* being possessive.

Interesting.

"I brought up the alfalfa you emailed me about Friday, and the other supplies you mentioned, too."

Daniel nodded. "Thanks. I'll get Jose and Lawrence to unload it. I've got something I wanted to show you anyway."

He called two teenage boys over, gave them instructions, and then they headed towards one of the out buildings, a small log building nestled in between the barn and the main house. Once they stepped inside Jo realized it was an office.

The desk was clean, a laptop and wide screen monitor the only things taking up space. A credenza behind the desk was polished to a high shine, a stuffed bobcat lounging on top of it.

At least, she was pretty sure it was stuffed. It looked pretty freaking real.

Daniel placed his cowboy hat on the credenza before taking the seat behind the desk and turning the monitor to face Jo and Chase. Chase took a seat and gestured for Jo to follow suit. Without the hat, Daniel looked like he was about twenty-five with dark blue eyes and sand-colored hair. Very attractive in a young, rugged sort of way.

"I pulled these off of Shorty's game camera earlier, hadn't had a chance to tell y'all about them yet."

Jo watched the screen as Daniel clicked through folders and photos of what looked like nothing but the night. And then Daniel stopped on one, enlarged the photo to full size, and sat back.

She looked at the dark image on the screen, then to Chase. "Is that what I think it is?"

Chase nodded. "That's the second black bear this month."

"I didn't think we had bears in this part of the state," Jo said.

"We do, they're just not incredibly common. With the drought the past few years they've been coming further east out of west Texas and the Big Bend area. They've also been coming up from Mexico. We have quite a bit of water on the ranch, what with the Devils River bordering it on one side, not to mention feeders everywhere." He turned to Daniel. "Have you let Miranda know?"

Daniel nodded. "Yup. She's out in Comstock today, said she probably wouldn't be able to get down here 'til tomorrow. She wants to take a look at Shorty first and the area around it, see if she can figure out where they're coming in from. She's debating between trapping them and taking them somewhere else, or tagging them to study them."

Jo watched Chase as he mulled that over. "I'll let Miranda form her own opinion first, but there's a lot to consider. It's their breeding season right now, which means we could have bear cubs come January."

"Which means a pregnant, hibernating mama bear

during busy season."

Chase nodded. "I don't want to drive them out of their natural habitat, but we have to take safety into consideration. And I really don't want Miranda and Texas Parks and Wildlife jumping on our asses if one of our guests sees one and gets trigger happy, thinking he's taking home a trophy."

"They're endangered, right?" Jo asked, trying to recall what little knowledge she had of black bears, which wasn't much.

"Yes, so they can't legally be hunted. If one of our guests was to kill one we could lose our license, permits and be shut down. There's also that whole threatened species thing, too. We manage our wildlife population, which means helping threatened species flourish, among other things."

Daniel tilted his head towards the screen. "There are a couple of others here I thought you might like to see, too."

Jo watched as the photos changed from night to early morning. Daniel stopped on one, and she gasped. "Is that a baby buffalo?"

Chase smiled. "Correct again. We've been waiting to see if we had any this year. This one's the first we've caught on the trail cams so far."

Daniel smiled. "It gets better."

He clicked through a few other photos until he stopped on a photo of three white tail does, four small fawns close by, their legs long and gangly and their fur dotted with ivory colored spots. Chase's smile widened, his eyes crinkled at the corners, and Jo fought to keep her heart at a steady pace in her chest.

Good Lord the man was sexy when he smiled.

"We're seeing signs of a good fawn crop this year. Early, too."

Daniel nodded and closed the photos. "That, we are.

Figured you'd want to see those. Good and not so good."

They all three stood and Chase turned to Jo. "Wanna see some of it? We don't have time to tour all of it, but I can show you around a little bit."

She smiled. "I would love to."

~~*~~

Chase turned and grabbed a set of keys off a hook on the wall. "We're gonna take Shirley. Radio me if you need anything."

He resisted the urge to grab Jo's hand as they left the office.

Bears and bison and white tails. Oh my. And here they'd all figured this summer was going to be quiet.

They entered the barn and Chase led them to Shirley, a two-seater utility vehicle that was used primarily by staff to get around the ranch for fun and minor projects. Before he climbed onto the seat he checked the gun boot across the back of the roll cage, made sure the rifle inside was on safe and loaded. Satisfied, he shoved it back into the boot and climbed onto the seat.

"Can you open the glove box and make sure there's a first aid kit and box of thirty ought six in there?"

Jo opened the small glove box. "I see a red kit with a first aid cross on it." She reached in and shook the box of bullets. "And it looks like we're good to go on thirty ought six."

She closed the glove box and he started the engine, released the brake and moved out of the barn. "Have you hunted before?"

She shook her head. "Nope. My dad's idea of hunting included rare texts and libraries. Mom's idea of hunting… well…she was a different type of maneater."

Chase turned the UTV onto a well-worn trail, away from the main buildings and towards one of his favorite places on the ranch.

"What's Shorty?" Jo asked as they bounced along the rutted, rocky trail, dust kicking up behind them.

"One of our feeders. It's the shortest one we have, thus, Shorty."

"You name the feeders?" Amusement laced her voice.

"It helps us keep them straight."

"Makes sense."

He grinned. "We thought so."

Jo gestured towards the wide expanse of scrub brush and cacti surrounding them and asked, "So how in the world did you get involved with this?"

"Well, you know Matt and I grew up hunting. As kids we would stay up late some nights, dreaming of owning a ranch where we could raise cattle and have horses and hunt when we wanted without having to pay for a deer lease. This place was foreclosed upon a few years ago. Being so big, and with the economy being what it's been, no one bit and it went to auction. Owen heard about it from a client, mentioned it to me. I mentioned it to Matt, who mentioned it to his agent, who's also a good friend of his. We decided to give it the old college try—why not? If we bid and lost, we were out nothing, but if we bid and won we could potentially get this place at a steal. Needless to say, we won. And with that, here we are."

He killed the engine and opened a toolbox on the inside of the dump bed of the UTV and pulled out two pairs of snake gaiters. Chase handed one pair to Jo and said, "You might want to put these on. Just in case we come across any rattlers."

Thank God she'd had the good sense to put on jeans and boots, which he'd completely forgotten to suggest to her.

She watched him as he slid a snake gaiter over his left foot, and then mimicked his movements.

"I've never seen something like these before. I'm

guessing they're effective?"

"Supposed to be."

"That's reassuring."

"Well, if they're not that's what the first aid kit is for," he grinned at her.

"Fair enough. We're a little ways from the hospital, though."

"Which is why we have a private runway, a small plane and licensed pilot on staff," he said and then winked.

"Y'all have thought of everything, haven't you?"

"We've had to. Like you said, we're about an hour and a half away from the nearest hospital, and our guests— which tend to be wealthy or friends and business associates of the wealthy— tend to expect things like private runways and easy access to the city and airport."

They finished fastening the gaiters and Chase grabbed the rifle from the gun boot before asking, "I know you've never hunted, but do you know how to shoot?"

She shot him a cheeky grin before turning around and lifting up the back of the flowy white cotton tank top she was wearing. He saw a brief flash of gun metal and pink tucked into the back waistband of her jeans, before she let the shirt fall back in place and turned to face him once again. "I realize my nine millimeter may not be super effective against a rattlesnake, but yes, I can shoot."

"Well I'll be damned. You're just full of surprises this weekend." Confusing, sometimes sexy surprises.

Jo snorted and joined him on the trail. "I live in Austin by myself. I wanted to be able to protect myself. And don't even act like you're not packing heat, too, cowboy."

He paused mid-stride. "How'd you know?"

"You leaned over earlier. Crossbreed holster. I didn't see your gun, though, if it's any consolation."

He laughed, resumed walking and then asked, "Do you ever find yourself in public, looking at people trying to determine if they're carrying?"

"All the time. Crossbreed holsters can be easy to spot sometimes, because of the crosses on the belt clips. Sometimes I'll notice a woman with a concealed carry purse, but rarely."

"Same here, although I can't say the same about the purse. I don't know if I've even seen one before."

"I'll show you mine later. They're not all the same, but some of them are made a certain way so that if you're paying attention you can figure out they're for concealed carry."

Of all the conversations he'd imagined them having, easy banter about holsters sure as hell hadn't been one of them.

Before he could respond, they rounded a curve in the trail and burst through a wall of mesquite shrubs and purple sage. Chase knew the minute Jo saw where they were by her quick, surprised gasp.

They stood on the edge of a cliff, overlooking the Devils River. Five hundred feet below them the river wound lazily through the ranch, and across from them was a wide expanse of gently rolling land dotted with scrub brush, cacti, mountain laurel, wild persimmon and oak trees. In the distance was a deep canyon, and then taller hills and plateaus.

"I always feel like I can see to the edge of the earth from here."

"It's beautiful, Chase. Absolutely gorgeous."

He scanned the area across the river and pointed. "Look, there, you can see a couple of bison."

She squinted and held her hand up to shield her eyes from the sun. "Where? I'm not seeing them."

Chase stood behind her and guided her hand up so that her index finger was pointing in the right direction. "There."

She looked again, stilled, and softly said. "I see them now."

He was standing close enough so that her blonde hair tickled his nose, the scent tormenting him in the best sort of way. His hand had dropped and settled on her hip. As they stood there, the sun starting to dip close to the horizon and paint the sky in shades of blue and orange, she leaned back into him, and Chase rested his chin on the top of her head.

"Beautiful," she murmured.

He wasn't looking at the sunset when he said, "Absolutely beautiful."

CHAPTER SEVEN

"You up for a beer?"

Two days after taking Jo out to Devils Ranch, Chase looked up from his laptop and the contract he'd been trying to read for the last thirty minutes and rubbed his eyes. Owen stood at his office door, his polo shirt wrinkled and dirty, his jeans looking no better, his red hair disheveled and a tired look on his face.

Chase asked, "Rough day at the office?"

Owen sighed, ambled over and flopped into a chair. "You could say that. Contractor hit a pipe while digging. Had to get that fixed. Then the cement truck broke down. Blew the engine. Took another two hours to get a new one out to the site. Two of my guys got into a fight and one of them ended up in the ER with a broken hand. Left the hospital about an hour ago, got a quarter mile away and blew a tire. It's been a perfect day."

"Wanna take a stab at translating legal jargon into plain English?"

"I'll take busted pipes, broken down cement trucks, broken hands and blown tires any day over legal shit."

Chase glanced at the time. 6:47. He vaguely remembered Kim poking her head into his office some time ago to let him know she was leaving for the day. He rubbed his hands over his face, knowing that the contract in front of him was going to continue to sound like gibberish to his tired brain, and closed the laptop. "I think I could definitely be up for a beer."

"Wings and Rings?" Owen asked, referring to their favorite place to grab a beer, some wings and unwind while watching a game on one of the many big screen TVs.

"Sounds good to me. Let me just shut everything down and I'll be there in a minute."

Owen got up and left, leaving Chase alone with his thoughts once more. He threw one more glance at his laptop, knowing that tomorrow he would have to force himself to focus and push Jo from his mind.

A man had to get some work done for crying out loud.

He vaguely thought about texting Jenn, seeing if maybe she and Jo would like to join them, and then realized he was acting like one of the teenagers Jo counseled. He dropped his head into his hands and muttered to himself, "For the love of tits, Roberts, you're a grown man. Act like one."

But the thought of tits made him think about Jo, and her breasts, and how amazing they'd felt pressed up against him when he'd kissed her that night at Owen's. The erection that had been at half-mast since he'd dropped her back off at her grandma's house two days ago—and partially the reason why he hadn't been able to focus on the stupid contract—stiffened completely.

He'd inadvertently chosen a really bad time to go celibate.

Not that he wouldn't change his mind if the opportunity presented itself. Jo wasn't someone just looking for a one-night stand. She wasn't looking to use him any more than he was looking to use her.

No, he would definitely not turn down that opportunity if it presented itself, no matter how much doing so would complicate things.

Shaking images of Jo naked and in his bed from his mind, Chase switched off his desk lamp before leaving his office, setting the alarm as he left the building.

In a few short minutes he was at Wings and Rings, making his way to his and Owen's usual booth in a quiet corner away from the noise of the bar, but with a big screen TV directly in their line of sight. As he approached, he saw that Owen wasn't alone.

Something in his gut tightened and then settled when he saw Jo and Jenn sitting there with Owen.

"Evening, ladies," he said as he reached the booth.

Jo's cheeks pinkened a little and she looked away quickly.

"Hey, Chase. Jo and I had just gotten here, then Owen walked in and invited us to sit with y'all. Figured you wouldn't mind," Jenn said in response.

"Why would I mind?" Chase took the only empty space left, which happened to be next to Jo.

He was pretty sure his friends were conspiring against him.

He wasn't sure if he minded all that much.

Their waitress came by, and he ordered a Shiner and his usual Xtra Hot boneless wings. Owen and Jenn were arguing about something, and Jo was oddly quiet beside him. He looked up at the TV and noted the score. The Wranglers were up 2-0 in the bottom of the third, and the camera panned to his brother in the dugout. His stat line flashed across the screen and Chase realized his brother was in the very early stages of pitching the Thing That Shall Not Be Named.

"Looks like he's pitching a good game," Jo said from beside him.

Chase nodded as the waitress returned with his beer. "That he is. Looks like he's getting some offense behind him, too."

No sooner were the words out of his mouth than Guzman belted a fastball out to Colt's Hill, which the Colt's Hill Kid promptly caught before dropping to the ground and doing The Worm.

"Three nothing."

Chase turned to Jo. "I didn't realize you were actually a baseball fan."

She shrugged and looked up at him. "More of a casual fan with a couple of favorite pitchers. I understand the rules and the basics, but not the minutiae or the strategy that goes into it. Gran, however, is a huge baseball fan, so I've watched a few more games than usual over the past few weeks. It's amazing how much you can pick up in such a short amount of time."

He wasn't about to ask her if she knew enough to realize that Matt was pitching the Thing That Shall Not Be Named, but he sure as hell hoped that if she did, she also knew not to call it by its actual name.

Some things really never did change, including superstitious tendencies.

Their waitress appeared with their food, and Chase watched the game as the inning ended and segued into a commercial break. Quiet settled over the table as everyone took that first bite of food. Too soon, the quiet was broken by Owen and Jenn going back to arguing over whatever it was they were arguing about.

"Do they always do that?"

Chase didn't even have to ask Jo what she was talking about; he'd gotten the question before. "Yes. It never stops."

Jo considered the two friends, chewed thoughtfully on her burger. Chase chuckled. "I know what you're thinking. And I'm pretty sure they really are a lot like brother and sister, but that doesn't mean people haven't wondered."

"Well, it is curious. I would think, though, that she would have said something to me if there was anything going on."

He leaned in, his mouth close enough to brush against her ear lobe, and lowered his voice. "Do you and Jenn tell each other everything?"

Jo turned her head, her lips millimeters from his jaw, and whispered, "Not everything."

Chase couldn't resist nuzzling his nose in her hair for the briefest of moments. Just long enough to torture himself.

She inhaled sharply and went completely still. He nuzzled her hair again, thinking about all the things he wished he could be doing with her right now, wondering what she was thinking, when her hand squeezed his thigh.

Hard.

"Chase!"

He jumped back like a kid caught with his hand in the cookie jar. "Sorry."

"No, no. Chase! Matt. He's hurt."

Jo's words were like having a bucket of ice water dumped over his entire body. He turned his attention back to the TV, realized Owen and Jenn had stopped arguing and were silently watching, too.

Their waitress passed by and Chase managed to ask her, "Can you turn up the game?"

She took a remote out of her apron and turned up the volume.

"Thanks."

On the TV, the announcers were silent. The entire ball park was silent.

And there was his brother, crumpled on the mound, the manager and the athletic trainers kneeling over him, concern plastered over their faces. The announcers finally started talking again, their voices hushed as they began to lead in to the replay of what had happened.

Chase watched it in a daze. As a former pitcher at a fairly high level, he knew the dangers of standing up on the mound and all of the various and sundry injuries that could happen.

This one was bad. Really bad.

The batter had hit a line drive, but instead of going out to center it had collided with Matt's head. The sound was sickening, like the bat hitting the ball all over again. His brother immediately fell to the ground.

Amazingly, the second baseman managed to catch the ball after it ricocheted off of Matt's head, effectively keeping the Thing That Shall Not Be Named in play.

Matt, however, wasn't moving.

"Come on, Matt. Get up. Get up." It was a litany. A prayer. Muttered under his breath as his stomach churned and his beer and wings threatened to make a return appearance.

Numbly, he felt Jo's fingers close around his, squeezing tight. He was thankful for the anchor.

"Get up. Dammit, Matt. Get up."

Matt wasn't moving.

And then he did.

Barely.

Chase released the breath he hadn't even realized he'd been holding. Matt was moving. He still wasn't sitting up, but he'd moved his hand.

The ballpark and their booth remained eerily silent as a stretcher was brought out to the field.

Was his mom watching the game? Oh, God, what if Mom was watching the game?

Panicked, he pulled out his cell phone from his back pocket saw he hadn't missed any calls.

Maybe Mom wasn't watching the game. He would wait, see what happened, and then call her and Dad.

This was just a precaution, right?

But he knew it wasn't. He knew it, deep in his gut. And while he and his brother had had their differences, and they'd had their fair share of arguments and yes, Chase had had his fair share of jealousy that his baseball career had ended with college, this wasn't supposed to have happened. Not to his big brother.

He felt sick.

Matt's body was gingerly placed on the stretcher. The EMTs strapped him down and then extended the stretcher to its full height before rolling him off the field and to the waiting ambulance. As they reached the baseline, Matt raised his hand a few inches and waved to the fans, which elicited a relieved cheer followed by muted clapping from the crowd.

The sound of his phone ringing jolted him, bringing everything into sharp relief.

Mom.

"Something's happened to Matt," his mom sobbed into the phone.

"I know, Mom. I just saw it. He'll be ok, Mom. It's Matt. He'll be ok." Chase wasn't sure if the words were meant to soothe his mom or himself.

His mom's sobs filled the line until his dad's voice became sharper. And then Dad was there and Chase felt his gut tighten again.

"You okay?" his dad asked.

"I think the more important question here would be is Matt okay?"

His dad sighed, and Chase could tell he was moving to another room, away from his mom. "I know, son. That didn't look good."

"That didn't sound good, Dad, much less look good."

"Your mama's gonna need you, you know that."

Chase pinched the bridge of his nose. "I know, Dad.

Just…give me some time. She doesn't need to see me worried, because if I'm worried she'll know that she needs to be worried."

"I know, son. Hold on. My phone's ringing. Let me get it real quick."

Chase listened as his dad answered the other phone, could make out bits and pieces of conversation. The words hospital, MRI, CT scan. Brain.

His dad hung up the other phone and came back on the line. "That was the team doctor. They're taking him in for an MRI. He's conscious but in some pain."

Chase could hear his dad's swallow over the phone line. "Chase, he's bleeding from his ear."

"Fuck."

"I'll let you know more as I hear things. I've gotta figure out how to break this to your mama."

"Be honest with her, Dad. She can handle it. We can all handle it." *We've gotten worse news before.*

"I know, son. I just worry."

"I love you, Dad. Give Mom a hug and a kiss for me. I'll be over in a little while."

"Love you too, Chase."

The call ended and Chase numbly set the phone on the table. He ran his free hand through his hair, his other one still entangled with Jo's.

Vaguely, he felt eyes on him. Owen, Jenn and Jo were all watching him. As was everyone else in the place.

They were trying not to, but they were. As Matt Roberts' little brother and a man who was firmly ensconced in Del Rio society, Chase was a subject of interest, and everyone in the restaurant had witnessed Matt's injury.

Jo squeezed his hand, and Chase finally spoke, quietly so that only the four of them could hear what he said. "That was Mom and Dad. Matt's at the ER and they're doing an MRI right now. He has some bleeding from his ear. That's really all anyone knows right now."

Their booth was silent for long moments until Jenn, in her typical wiseass way, broke the silence. "Well, I guess that dispels the theory that he has a skull full of rocks."

Chase laughed, thankful to Jenn and her sense of humor. It wasn't the first time she'd used it to make him feel better, and he doubted it would be the last.

At the sight of Chase laughing, the pace of the restaurant seemed to normalize. People still glanced at him from time to time, but their attention had gone back to their wings and their own dramas.

His stomach was still in knots, so he pushed his plate and beer away, knowing there was no way he could consume either right now.

"You gonna be okay?" Jo asked.

"I'll be fine, counselor." She stiffened beside him, and he realized his words had come out tersely. "I need to go, though, get over to Mom and Dad's."

Jo nodded and he unlaced their fingers, missing her warmth as soon as he stood. She looked up at him, worry in her blue green eyes, and he wanted nothing more than to grab her hand, pull her away from that booth and take her home so that he could bury himself inside of her and make this nightmare go away.

Instead, he tossed a twenty on the table and bid everyone goodbye.

CHAPTER EIGHT

"What do you mean, you want to come home and stay with me?" Chase asked as he paced the length of his brother's hospital room.

Matt sat in the hospital bed, looking ridiculous with half of his head shaved and the other, well, not shaved. Numerous MRIs and CT Scans had shown a skull fracture and internal bleeding from his brain, prompting emergency surgery to relieve the pressure. Thus the half-shaved head.

Now that the danger was past them and it looked like Matt was going to make a full recovery, Chase couldn't help but laugh every time he saw his brother's new hairdo. Chase wasn't laughing right now, though.

"I'm on the DL for an infinite amount of time, Chase, and the doctors have banned me from the ballpark. No bright lights, repetitive motions, loud noises for at least a few weeks. Mom's worried sick, and Dad's trying not to act like he is. And to be honest, the thought of going back to my condo by myself right now isn't very appealing. Figure I might as well come home for a while. That's what most guys do when they're put on the DL for an undetermined but way too long time, why would I be any different?"

There were so many reasons why he figured Matt would have been different. Instead of saying that, Chase sighed instead. "So your answer is to just move in with me?"

"Not for long, Chase. Just long enough to set Mom's mind at ease, and to get back to normal."

Chase stopped pacing and rested his hands on the rail at the foot of the hospital bed. "Matt, you know as well as I do that getting back to normal might take longer than you want it to. You took a line drive to the head less than two weeks ago. They clocked that thing at a hundred and ten miles per hour."

Matt shrugged. "I'll be fine in a few weeks, Chase."

Chase sighed, realizing that arguing was futile. Resigned, he asked, "What time do you get discharged today?"

Matt grinned, and Chase closed his eyes, wondering what the hell he was getting himself in to.

The great thing about being one of the highest paid players in the majors, Chase discovered later that day, was the ability to charter private flights at the drop of a hat, which had come in handy since their pilot out at the ranch was currently on vacation. As they descended into Del Rio, Chase once again mentally kicked himself for giving in to his brother so easily.

He liked his privacy, needed it, really, and was worried that his brother's presence would turn his usually quiet, peaceful home into a swinging bachelor pad full of noise and round the clock parties.

"No groupies or parties, Matt," he said as the plane bumped onto the tarmac.

Matt turned to Chase. "No loud noises, alcohol or repetitive motions, Chase. I think that pretty much nixes groupies and parties."

"You'd be the one to find a way to get around that."

Matt laughed, and the plane taxied to a gentle stop. Moments later, the door was opened and stairs were lowered, and they were met by an airport employee driving a golf cart. Chase tossed his wheeled carry-on bag onto the attached luggage trailer, and then grabbed Matt's suitcase and tossed it next to his bag. They climbed into the golf cart and the driver took off.

Less than thirty minutes later, they were in Chase's truck and heading towards his house. "Do you want to stop and see Mom and Dad on the way, or hold off?"

Matt stared out the passenger side window as they drove north on Veteran's Boulevard. "Can we hold off on it?"

As they left the heart of Del Rio, Chase wondered at his brother. He couldn't quite put his finger on it, but Matt was just *off*. Granted, having a near-death experience would probably make anybody a little *off*.

They made the rest of the drive to his house in silence, Chase not knowing what to say and Matt seeming unwilling to say anything. Chase pulled into the garage, and the brothers got out, retrieved their luggage and walked into the house without saying a word.

Winchester's muffled bark of greeting finally broke the silence as Chase closed the door behind them. The big Great Pyrenees ambled over, sniffing at legs and hands and crotches, his body wiggling in ecstasy as Chase gave him a brief rub down.

Chase squatted in front of his dog and asked, "Owen didn't give you too many treats, did he, Big Guy?"

Winchester licked Chase's chin in response, before changing the focus of his attention and nudging Matt's hand with his nose, his way of saying, "Pet me now, human." Chase stood.

Matt complied, scratching him between the ears. "Hey there, Win. Glad to see you still remember me."

"I'm not sure if he remembers you or if he's just being an attention whore," Chase said as he wheeled his carry-on into the living room.

Behind him, Matt wheeled his own suitcase. "I hear Jo's back in town."

Chase stopped, one foot on the bottom stair leading up to the second floor and his bedroom, and wondered where the hell that statement had come from. "Yeah. Has been for about a month."

He started back up the stairs.

Matt was right behind him.

"You seen her at all?"

Chase continued up the stairs. "A couple of times."

"And..?"

"And what?" Chase reached the top of the stairs and turned towards his bedroom. "Take either of the guest rooms, your choice," he said, hoping to escape without more of his brother's weird, sudden prying.

Matt turned in the opposite direction and headed towards one of the spare rooms. "You've loved her since she was in pigtails, Chase, and then she broke your heart. Was just wondering how being around her again was going, that's all."

Chase wasn't sure which part of Matt's statement shocked him more—the fact that Matt knew he'd loved Jo, the fact that he knew Jo had broken his heart, or his sudden interest in having a heart to heart. "Man, that ball really did fuck you up."

Matt shook his head, opened the door of his chosen room and rolled his suitcase in. "We don't get many chances at happiness, little brother."

"Okay, Yoda."

Matt turned around, his hazel eyes shuttered. But they were brothers, and even though they'd had a bit of a strained, competitive relationship their entire lives, they *knew* each other, in a way that only brothers could.

"I know I haven't always been the best brother, or

hell, even the best son to Mom and Dad, but that doesn't mean I don't care." He raked a hand through his hair. The unshaven side. Looked away, at something to the side. "Baseball is all I have, Chase. But you've always had… more, always wanted more."

"You could have more than baseball, Matt. You've just chosen to live life between the seams."

Matt swung his gaze back around, making eye contact and not letting go. "You have been, too. Your seams might be bigger than mine, maybe a little different, but you have, too. You may not play anymore, but you're still a pitcher. You'll always be a pitcher. And we're control freaks. We don't like losing control, because when we do shit happens."

"It's been a long day, Matt. I'm going to bed." Chase turned and opened his bedroom door, refusing to let Matt see that his words had bothered him at all.

Between the seams. Ha! What did Matt think he was? Some sort of baseball philosopher all of a sudden? Augie Garrido—the Longhorns' head coach who was known for his deep thoughts on baseball and life— he was not.

Chase left his carry-on at the foot of the bed before walking over to his dresser and turning on his iPod. He hit shuffle and Aaron Watson's "3rd Gear and 17" filtered through the surround sound speakers. At the sound of the tune about high school sweethearts going their separate ways and his dreams of playing pro ball coming to an end, Chase shook his head.

When the hell had his life turned into a fucking country song?

He'd just finished unpacking when the phone in his pocket vibrated.

Mom.

"Hey Mama."

"Did y'all make it home okay?"

Chase grinned. "Nice to hear from you, too."

Sarah huffed on the other end of the line. "Don't you give me a hard time, Chase Roberts. I just wanted to make sure y'all got home okay."

"Yeah, we did. About fifteen minutes ago."

Sarah paused on the other end of the line, and Chase sighed. "He's doing okay, Mom. No dizziness or anything like that."

Sarah's sigh of relief was so loud Chase almost thought she was beside him for a moment, rather than on the other side of town. "Good. Now how are *you* doing?"

Chase ran a hand over his face and sat down on the edge of his bed. "I'm fine. Tired. Missing my privacy already."

Sarah scoffed at that. "You'll live. Now, when were you going to tell me that Jo's back in town?"

"I, uh, didn't really realize it was all that important, Mom." Were there no secrets in this freaking town?

"Oh, honey, of course it is. That girl got the wrong end of a bad deal with the way her parents acted, not to mention she broke my baby boy's heart."

Chase sighed. Had his feelings been that transparent? "Mom, I really don't know why everyone thinks she broke my heart."

"Because she did. It was plain as daylight, Chase, how much you loved that girl."

"Mom, I was fifteen. Does anyone really know what love is at that age?"

Sarah's tone gentled. "Oh, honey, of course they do. It may be different at fifteen than it is at twenty-five or thirty or sixty, but love is love."

Chase ran his fingers through his hair and bit back a sigh. "Fair enough. Yes, Jo's back in town. Yes, we've seen each other. No, there's nothing going on."

Well, okay, maybe that last part wasn't completely

true. But his mom didn't need to know every little detail about his love life.

Or lack thereof.

Frustrating lack thereof.

"That's not what Dorothy Johnson told me."

"Dorothy Johnson?" She was a long-time friend of his mom's and known as a bit of a gossip. "Why would Dorothy tell you something was going on between Jo and me?"

"She saw y'all at Wings and Rings the day Matt got hurt. Said y'all looked pretty cozy right up until Matt got hurt, and that she held your hand 'til you left."

Good God, there wasn't anything sacred in this town. Absolutely nothing.

"Mom, I'm not sure what Dorothy thinks she saw. But yes, we were holding hands. I was worried about Matt and she was comforting me. She's a high school guidance counselor for crying out loud—that's what she does." *Keep telling yourself that*, his conscience whispered.

"You should bring her to supper some time. Your dad and I would love to see her again. It's been years."

Chase was pretty sure the thought of sitting down to a family meal with his parents would make Jo fairly uncomfortable. Then again, it could also help Jo—and to be honest, himself—to move on from the past. To appease his mom he said, "I'll ask her and see what she says. But she's pretty busy taking care of her grandma."

"Just promise me you'll ask her, honey."

"Sure, Mom. I promise."

After he and Sarah said their goodbyes and Chase had hung up his phone, he stared at the wall for long moments. What was it George Bernard Shaw had said? If you couldn't get rid of the skeletons in the family closet, you might as well make them dance? Problem was, he didn't think Jo was up for making any of her skeletons dance.

CHAPTER NINE

"Such a shame, what happened to that Roberts boy." Gran shook her head as the current game's producer decided to once again replay the line drive that had hit Matt in the head almost two weeks ago.

Jo stood up, gathered her and Gran's plates off of their TV trays, and took them into the kitchen. Every time they showed it, she saw Chase's face, heard his muttered pleading with his brother to get up off the mound. She'd never seen him so scared, not even as a kid and he'd had to go through yet another surgery, and witnessing his emotions that evening had shaken her.

She hadn't known what to say then.

She didn't know what to say now.

Not that she'd had an opportunity to say anything. He'd left the restaurant that night and she hadn't heard from him since. Logically, she understood—they hadn't even exchanged phone numbers or email addresses. Weren't friends on Facebook, didn't follow each other on Twitter, weren't connected on LinkedIn.

The only things they'd exchanged were heated kisses and old emotions.

Nothing to see here. Moving right along.

She slammed a plate into the dishwasher with a little

more force than necessary, and forced herself to take a mental step back.

His brother had just had a near-death experience from what little she'd been able to gather from Jenn, who *had* talked to Chase.

He could call Jenn, but not the woman he'd been flirting with just seconds before things went to shit?

Jo felt the sharp edges of jealousy clawing at her gut and slammed the dishwasher door closed.

Fuck.

She needed to get out of this house.

"Gran, I'm gonna go for a run. I'll be back in a little while," she yelled from the kitchen before heading to her bedroom to change into workout clothes.

Yes, a run sounded good. Not as gratifying as deadlifts or back squats, but maybe it would help improve her mood, if not relieve some of the tension she'd been feeling.

Once she'd changed into her running clothes, she strapped her Bulldog fanny pack to her waist, grabbed her STI Elektra off the nightstand, did a quick press check, and fastened it with the Velcro loops on the inside of the pack. She dropped an extra magazine into a different zippered pouch, along with her driver's license and concealed handgun license. Her phone went in the front pocket, along with some earbuds just in case she decided she needed music.

Out on the sidewalk, Jo looked around, taking note of her surroundings while going through a series of warm-up stretches. She then set off at an easy pace, allowing her body to get into a rhythm before pushing herself a little more.

It grated that she was jealous of Jenn. She knew she had no reason to be, really had no right to be jealous. But it was there, simmering under the surface. It irritated her that for all these years, Jenn had been right there, such a big part of Chase's life.

Never mind the fact that Jo had been the one to throw it all away. Cutting off ties with Chase had been her choice and no one else's.

Not for the first time in the past eighteen years she wished she hadn't made that decision.

It was easy—too easy—to imagine how their lives might have been different had she not thrown their friendship away. Somewhere, in the part of her heart that wanted marriage and babies and a dog, there was a picture of the two of them together, a baby on one hip and a toddler chasing that imaginary dog around the backyard. The kids had his hair and smile. Her eyes. The toddler—a boy—was already showing signs of being the best pitcher the world had ever seen. And the baby? Well, she adored her daddy.

Despite the fact that Jo had ended their friendship right at that age when girls started thinking about those happily ever afters with specific boys in mind, and despite the fact that she'd never truly acknowledged her feelings, she'd longed for him. As the years had flown by, she'd longed for him even more. The high school sweetheart love story. The long-distance phone calls and weekend visits while in college. The well-timed marriage proposal right after graduation, and the June wedding a year later.

She didn't deserve those things, though. Didn't deserve *him*.

How could she, when she'd so stupidly thrown it all away?

He'd been her best friend, and she his. And she'd thrown it away out of fear and confusion and disgust with her mother and a sense that doing so was the only way to protect him and his family.

Jo ran, her legs and arms pumping hard and fast, until she was sprinting down the sidewalk, yards and cars and people and children's toys a blur. Her thoughts pushed, crowding in and shouting so loud they were drowning each other out.

Why the fuck hadn't he called?

~~*~~

7:23.

The numbers stared back at Chase, and he vaguely registered the time.

He'd been at work since just before six that morning, needing to get back to the office and real life. Matt had been in his home less than twenty-four hours and Chase was already wanting to climb the walls or punch something.

Matt's Yoda routine last night, along with just *being* there, had set him on edge. Chase liked his space, needed his privacy. In a town of roughly 36,000 people, he often straddled the line between public and private. On one hand, Del Rio was just big enough to afford some modicum of anonymity. On the other, it was just small enough that everyone knew who he was, even if they didn't actually know him.

Thus, the need for a safe haven.

He read over his emails again. A local reporter had reached out to him regarding the uptick in commercial real estate sales and construction the area was currently experiencing. He suspected the reporter probably wanted the scoop on Matt more.

For such a private guy, he sometimes wondered how his name ended up in the news so often. Then he would remember that he'd inadvertently caused that to happen. As the city's top commercial real estate broker—not to mention his relation to Matt—it wasn't a huge shocker that people would reach out to him or that his name would appear in newsprint. He was well-respected by town leaders and local businessmen, sponsored the local Little League teams and held a pitching clinic in the fall.

Living life between the seams? Ha! Whatever the fuck that meant.

He decided a response could wait until tomorrow, and shut down his computer. Knowing he probably needed to leave the office but not yet willing to go back home and hang out with his brother and endure yet another Yoda routine, Chase debated calling Owen or Jenn to meet up for a quick beer.

He'd pulled up Owen's number and was in the process of texting him when he realized it was Friday night. Odds were Owen had a date and Jenn was probably doing... something. Knitting or reading or making lesson plans, since Chase couldn't remember the last time Jenn had gone on a date. Now there was someone who lived life between the seams, or whatever you wanted to call it. Jenn spent her Friday nights knitting.

Knitting!

Whereas he spent his...hanging out with a dude in a bar, having one beer and then going home and spending the rest of the time with his damned dog.

Screw Matt and his sudden I-care-about-you routine.

Feeling adrift, he set the alarm and locked up, climbed into his truck, started it and stared at the front of the office building. Without really thinking about it, Chase threw the truck into motion.

Thirty minutes later, lost in a fog of exhaustion and frustration, he realized he'd inadvertently driven to Nellie Westwood's neighborhood. He shook his head and groaned. What the hell was he doing to himself?

He slowed as he passed Nellie's house, debated stopping and ringing the doorbell. He hadn't seen or talked to Jo since the night of Matt's injury. Oh, he'd thought about her, probably far more than any man sitting by his brother in ICU should have, but he hadn't spoken to her.

Not having her phone number had helped with that, he

thought wryly. Then again, it wasn't like he couldn't have gotten it from Jenn.

Instead of stopping, though, he continued down the street, feeling slightly angry at the clawing need that hadn't gone away ever since he'd run into her that night at Walmart. Had that really been almost a month ago? In some ways, it seemed like years, and in others like it had been yesterday.

Chase continued to drive slowly down the street, watching for children and toys as the late evening sun cast deceptive shadows over the neighborhood. He turned a corner, and another, circling back while deliberately avoiding Nellie's, houses now on his left and a small park on his right.

That's when he saw her, standing on the edge of the grass, just inside the park, bent at the waist, her body shaking as if she couldn't get enough air.

He veered to the curb, slammed the truck into PARK before killing the engine, grabbing the keys and exiting the truck as if it were on fire. He ran the ten yards to her, worried and scared at the way her lungs were heaving.

He reached her in seconds, placed a reassuring hand on her upper arm, and was greeted by having his hand ripped of her arm and a kick to the shin.

"Get your hands off of me!" Jo yelled as she stood up, and Chase realized that her right hand was going for the fanny pack at her waist.

Having no desire to find himself at the wrong end of what he suspected was in that fanny pack, he calmly said, "Jo! Jo! It's me, Chase!"

She stopped, hand poised over the black pouch, blinked her eyes and sunk to the ground, her legs crossed Indian-style. Her forehead smacked into her hands as she continued to cry.

Gingerly now, clueless and just a little scared, Chase

crouched down beside her. Jo had always been pretty even-tempered as a kid, so the few times he'd been around her when she'd been upset he'd been completely clueless as to how to make her feel better. Funny how in that regard things really hadn't changed—he still had no clue what to do to make her feel better.

But he wanted to try.

~~*~~

Jo tried desperately to get her breathing under control and to make the tears stop as she sat there on the ground, Chase mere inches away from her.

Why wouldn't they stop?

No matter how many deep breaths she took, the shaky feeling in her insides wouldn't go away, and the tears wouldn't stop flowing.

She'd almost shot him.

Rationally, she realized that she hadn't known it was him when she'd felt a man's hand on her arm. She'd been bent at the waist, trying to calm herself down from the panic attack that had gripped her while she'd been running. She'd been thinking about him and bitching and moaning to herself and *bam!* Panic attack.

Jo hadn't had one in years, not since after Ray— the one boyfriend she'd actually loved—had broken up with her after finding out he was being shipped off to Afghanistan. Panic—over being alone, over the thought of him being killed—had gripped her and sent her over the edge. Even then, though, it hadn't felt like this.

And then, to make things even better, she'd almost shot him.

Shot him!

Her body started shaking, and oxygen seemed harder and harder to come by. Numbly, she registered Chase's hand on her shoulder, then smoothing her hair. And then she was in his lap and his arms were around her and he was saying something to her in a really soft voice. She couldn't understand it, but it sounded nice and comforting.

Air.

Slowly, but surely, she found air.

Jo wasn't sure how long she sat there in his lap, vaguely realized anyone could be staring at them and the odd tableau they made. Stupidly, because she felt something needed to be said, she said the first thing that popped out of her mouth: "Why haven't you called me?"

She felt his muscles tense slightly before relaxing again, and felt stupid and childish and selfish for even asking such a thing.

"I'm sorry, Chase. I shouldn't have asked you that. You've been dealing with your brother, I know. Jenn's mentioned it. I've just been…"

Worried, she'd been worried, dammit.

"So you almost shot me because I hadn't called you?"

She heard the teasing tone of his voice, but couldn't keep her body from tensing. *She'd almost shot him.*

"Oh, God, Chase. I almost shot you!"

"It's not your fault, Jo. I should have said something rather than just grabbing your arm. I know better."

She shook her head, knowing that he was right, but still feeling panicky over the entire situation. "I should have known it was you."

"How, Jo?"

Her hands fluttered at her sides, as if searching for answers. "I don't know. I just should have."

"You and I both know that's a load of bullshit. I approached you without warning, without saying anything and grabbed your arm. You were protecting yourself." He paused. "If anything, we need to work on your fighting moves and your draw time. Had I been a real threat I could have taken you out before you'd even been able to think about grabbing your gun."

She shook her head, but felt some of the tension drain from her body. "I still can't believe that just happened."

"What *did* just happen?"

"Other than me almost shooting you? Oh, just a mild panic attack." The pitch of her voice raised on the last two words, making her sound and feel almost hysterical again.

Jo closed her eyes and breathed deeply through her nose.

In.

Out.

She seemed to do a lot of deep breathing exercises around him.

"I think a bench might be more comfortable, what about you?" Chase asked.

Jo took another deep breath and nodded. "Probably."

They got up and found a bench that afforded them some relative privacy, sitting in silence for long moments as Jo got her breathing under control.

"I didn't call because we hadn't gotten around to exchanging phone numbers." He sighed as they both looked straight ahead, as far apart from each other on the bench as they could get. She saw his Adam's apple bob out of the corner of her eye. "We're…are we even at the part where we exchange numbers? Is that what this is? Is that what we're doing?"

She considered his words for a moment before answering. "I'm not sure what we're doing, Chase. I hadn't planned on any of this happening. Honestly, when Gran asked me to stay with her over the summer I was scared to death of seeing you but figured it was bound to happen. I hadn't really allowed myself to think about it beyond that."

"I," his voice was tight when he finally spoke again, "don't know what to think about that."

Jo sighed, her emotions in that weird place between high alert and frayed. "About what?"

"About all of it." He sounded angry, and she chanced a look at him.

Yup, he was angry. Pissed, was more like it.

"Chase, we haven't spoken in years, and while that falls mostly on me it falls a little on you, too. I've been back here and there—and we both know you knew when I was in town, because Jenn knew and Jenn will tell us anything and everything as long as she's not sworn to secrecy—and you've never once tried to talk to me."

"You--"

She turned so that she was facing him and cut him off. "And that's just as much on my shoulders as it is yours. Like I said, more on mine than yours, since I was the one who ended things all those years ago. So no, Chase, I hadn't planned on seeing you or talking to you or kissing you or any of the *whatever* this is we've been doing. But we did see each other and talk to each other, and you did kiss me and I did somewhat drunkenly spill my guts. We can get mad about it—God knows both of us probably have enough stored up anger with each other to burn this town to the ground—but it is what it is, Chase. It just is what it is."

He'd turned his body during her tirade, angling it towards hers so that their bent knees were touching. She could feel energy and anger and tension coursing through his body, could see it in the way he held his mouth and his shoulders. As a boy, he hadn't shown much anger, even though God knew he'd had more than enough reasons to. It figured that as a man, he would hold it in check, tense with it and probably angry that he was angry.

Same, but different. The words whispered through her head.

"Anger, Jo? What do you have to be angry about with me? You're the one who ended our friendship. You. You just stopped talking to me. And then you left town. So please, Jolene, tell me what *you* have to be angry about."

"I wanted you to fight for me!"

The words were ripped from her before she could snatch them back, loud and angry and clear as the laughter from the kids playing tag some fifty yards away. The truth, which she'd long denied even to herself, lay there between them, her angrily yelled words like a living breathing thing.

They stared each other, breaths harsh as though they'd both just run a marathon, long moments of charged silence hanging heavy in the air.

Finally, he spoke. "You sure had a funny way of showing it."

"I was fourteen, Chase. I'd just figured out that I wanted you to kiss me. I didn't know what I was feeling or what I wanted, only that I was embarrassed by all of it and felt like everything was somehow my fault."

He considered her for long moments. "For what it's worth, I wanted to fight for you, but I didn't think you wanted anything to do with me. So I didn't."

"We've both screwed up, Chase."

He nodded in concession. "Yeah."

"We were kids."

He nodded again, looked away. Breathed deeply before saying, "I was in love with you. While we're at confession, I guess I should throw that out there too along with the rest of this mess."

Jo had been prepared for lots of different confessions from Chase; that he'd hated her, that he'd had a crush on her, that he'd wanted to kiss her that day beside the pool, that he wished she'd never come back. This one, though, took her breath away and caused her insides to feel jittery, like a bag of popcorn in the microwave. "Chase...I... when?"

"Somewhere in the seventh grade." He said it nonchalantly, but she still knew him well enough to realize he was anything but nonchalant. The importance of that piece of information was not lost on her either. Seventh grade. He'd definitely wanted to kiss her that day by the pool, she was pretty sure of that now.

"Oh, God. I really did break your heart." Hers felt like it was shattering into a million tiny pieces.

He smiled, but it didn't quite reach his eyes. "Just bruised it a little bit, I think."

"Chase—"

"Jo, it's in the past."

"No, it really isn't, Chase. Whatever this is that we've been doing? It's all tangled together. You and I both know that. And you have to know that I never, ever meant to hurt you like that. I thought I was doing the right thing, and fuck did the right thing hurt like hell. You were my best friend. The first boy I wanted to kiss. My first real crush. In some ways you were my first love. So it might be in the past, but all that…" she searched for the right word, finally settled on, "shit has helped make us who we are today."

She turned and flopped against the back of the bench, tired and lonely, sad and still a little angry. Logically, her counselor's mind knew that they could only let things build for so long and that they'd both reached a boiling point. She knew it wasn't healthy—for either of them—to keep so many secrets and emotions locked inside. As a woman, though, she almost wished she didn't feel all of the things she was feeling, because life would be so much simpler without all those pesky emotions she'd been feeling ever since she'd run into Chase almost a month ago in the feminine hygiene aisle.

"How is it that even at our ages, we can still make each other feel like awkward, overly emotional teenagers?"

Jo chuckled. "If there's one thing I've learned, it's that no matter how old you get, somewhere inside of you lives an awkward teenager. Emotions are hard, and I don't know that any of us are well-equipped to deal with them in a not-awkward way. And we never really got to go through that phase together. I guess we're making up for lost time."

"If it's any consolation, you make me feel like a teenager in other ways, too."

Jo turned her head and looked at him. "What?"

He raked his gaze over her sweaty body and she blushed.

"Oh. Fair enough." She fought a giggle. "You make me feel like a teenager, too, for what it's worth."

Chase smiled. "Well, I guess that soothes my ego at least a little bit."

They sat in silence. Jo had no clue what he was thinking, but her thoughts were a mess of memories and wishes and emotions. At least the panic had loosened its grip on her.

"So how's Matt?" They couldn't avoid the emotional land mines forever, but there was no reason why they couldn't take a short break from them, either.

Chase huffed out a frustrated breath. "He decided he wanted to live with me for a few weeks."

"You sound thrilled."

"Absolutely. I mean, I am thrilled that he's okay and that he's going to be okay. I'm just not thrilled about him crashing at my place for so long."

"Understandable. Y'all always had a bit of a competitive relationship."

He snorted. "To say the least. We just got back last night. By the time I left the house before six this morning he was already driving me crazy just by being there."

"I'm sorry."

"It's not your fault."

"Not the Matt stuff. Although, I am sorry he got hurt like that. And I'm sorry he's imposing on you and making you uncomfortable. But what I meant was that I'm sorry for dumping more emotional crap on you, when you've already had a pretty rough past couple of weeks as it is."

Chase wrapped his hand around hers and squeezed. "Don't apologize for the honesty, Jo, or the emotions. I've been carrying around the anger and the hurt for so long now I almost take them for granted. I know it isn't the manly thing to say, but we needed to clear the air."

"We did." She swallowed. "So what is this that we're doing now?"

Chase stilled beside her, long enough that she began to worry she'd said the wrong thing yet again, when he finally asked, "Can I have your number?"

Jo smiled and let hope bloom. Maybe everything was going to be alright between them.

CHAPTER TEN

The words of Del Rio's own Radney Foster poured through the bar's sound system as people all around him laughed, talked and knocked back shots. Secretly, Chase had always loved "Nobody Wins." It probably wasn't the manliest song, but he'd liked it the first time he'd heard it on the radio back in junior high.

Chase sipped his beer, quiet. The bar wasn't packed since it was a weekday, but with tomorrow being the Fourth, there were enough people to provide a lively atmosphere. On the other side of the table, Matt steadily greeted fans and well-wishers. He still hadn't fixed his hair; the half-shaved mess had apparently become a badge of honor.

Or, knowing his brother, an attempt at picking up chicks. Against doctor's orders.

Chase rolled his eyes as yet another woman stuffed into a too-small shirt and too-tight jeans sauntered up to his brother. They were like moths to a goddamned flame.

Apparently the half-shaved look was working for him.

After Girl Number Fifty-Seven left, Matt swiveled his chair towards Chase. And just sat there. Staring.

"What is up with you here lately?" Chase asked, exasperated.

If Matt hadn't been perfecting his Yoda routine, he'd been jonesing to get out of the house and be around people. In his clearer, less irritated moments Chase understood that his brother was dealing with a lot of stuff, grappling with a near-death experience and the future of his career. Baseball was all his brother knew. Hell, Matt *was* baseball, and Chase didn't envy him any of the shit he was dealing with right now. But damn was he getting irritated.

Matt shrugged. "Just wanted to say thanks."

"For what?" Chase muttered.

"Getting me out of the house. I was starting to go stir crazy."

Matt still hadn't been cleared to drive, and probably shouldn't have even been at a bar three weeks after having brain surgery, but when he'd threatened to steal Chase's truck keys and find something to do on his own, Chase had finally relented. They were both active guys, not used to spending a lot of time sitting still and doing nothing.

In that way they did have a lot in common.

So Chase had finally given in and brought him to April's, a little bar he, Jenn and Owen enjoyed for the relatively cozy atmosphere, dim lights and usually a lack of singles on the prowl. It was a country bar through and through, with the set list comprised mostly of Texas country artists except for Friday nights, when the set list opened up a bit.

Just his kind of place.

"I still can't believe I let you talk me into bringing you to a bar."

Matt grinned. "Glad to know I can still push your buttons, little brother."

Chase sighed, and was about to respond when Owen walked up. Thank God. Reinforcements. Matt and Owen shook hands in greeting before Owen took a seat and ordered a beer from a passing waitress.

Once his beer had arrived, Owen sat back and said, "I invited the girls."

"Girls, huh?" Matt asked, almost lasciviously.

"Jenn and Jo. Figured we could save Jenn from a night of knitting and get Jo out of her grandma's house for a while," Owen said.

Matt wiggled his eyebrows at Chase. "That clarifies things."

"Don't even start, Matt," Chase warned.

Owen looked from Chase to Matt and back again before laughing. "Oh, this is good. Do we have another member of the Chase Needs to Make a Move club?"

"Absolutely," Matt answered.

"I didn't realize you cared," Chase drawled, irritated. Since when had his personal life become so interesting to his best friend and his brother?

"Not so much caring as getting tired of your moodiness," Owen said. "You're worse than a woman the past few weeks."

Matt choked out a laugh. Chase glowered. "It's none of your damned business."

"If she's as pretty as she used to be, can I have her, then?"

Chase narrowed his eyes at Matt. "I *will* hit a man who just had brain surgery."

Owen and Matt both hooted with laughter, damn them.

~~*~~

"Should Matt even be at a bar, all things considered?" Jo asked Jenn as they walked through the door.

Jenn shrugged. "Probably not. But you know Matt."

"No, not really. I mean, I know him, but not like I do Chase. He was always playing select ball or little league or high school. He wasn't around much."

Jo thought she heard Jenn mumble "Lucky you" under her breath, and wondered what her best friend's dig against

Matt was. Before she could ask, though, Jenn spotted Chase, Matt and Owen and waved.

The three men turned towards them, and Jo's body felt on fire as Chase's gaze caught hers before perusing her from head to toe and back up. She fought the urge to pull down the hem of her skirt or tuck a strand of hair behind her ear.

They hadn't seen each other since that day in the park, almost a week ago, but they'd talked. He'd called her a few times, she'd called him a few times. They'd exchanged texts. Nothing earth-shattering, but they'd definitely been feeling each other out and rekindling their friendship (among other things).

Jo was learning that the boy she'd known was still there; he'd just turned into a somewhat complicated man. Same enough to be somewhat comfortable. Different enough to be damned intriguing. It was a heady mix of old and new, tangled up with all those old emotions and this new attraction that had firmly gripped her and refused to let go.

He hadn't kissed her since that night at Owen's house when she'd somewhat drunkenly spilled her guts. They'd teased and flirted, along with holding hands that night at Wings and Rings, sat close to one another and touched.

But he hadn't kissed her again.

As they stared at each other from across the bar, she almost desperately wished he would walk over, sweep her into his arms and kiss her like his life depended on it.

Instead, he stayed firmly planted on his barstool, and she made her boot-clad feet move towards him.

It wasn't until after they'd reached the table that Jo realized Matt was sporting a hairdo more likely to be seen on 6th Street in Austin than in a little bar in Del Rio. Her laugh was unexpected, but she couldn't hold it in once it had come out. "Oh my God, Matt. Your hair!"

"Nice to see you too, Jolene." He winked at her.

Matt had always been a good-looking charmer, and even with the crazy ass hairdo that still held true.

"I guess the Bigs don't pay as much as I thought if you can't even afford a decent haircut." Jenn's comment, which Jo figured was supposed to have been teasing, came out sounding almost mean.

Some of the twinkle left Matt's hazel eyes, and Jo looked at Chase, her eyebrows raised in a silent question. He shrugged, apparently as lost as she was.

Jenn chose to sit between Owen and Chase, leaving the barstool between Matt and Chase open. Jo took it, and shortly a waitress appeared to take their orders. Jenn ordered a margarita and Jo followed suit.

Conversation flowed. Mostly. The banter was easy and fun—except between Jenn and Matt. Jo knew her best friend well enough to know that something was up, but had no clue as to what that something was. There was just a general discomfort between the school teacher and the major league pitcher.

Jo had the niggling feeling she'd missed something while living in Austin.

Owen and Chase decided to go play a game of pool, and Matt followed, promising Chase he would just "sit there and look pretty" and not exert himself. Table to themselves, Jo turned to Jenn and asked, "Okay, spill. What is going on with you and Matt?"

Jenn fidgeted, twirled a red curl around her finger. Sighed. "Nothing."

There was a lot more to that sigh than "nothing." Thoughtfully, Jo tilted her head to the side. "Are you sure about that?"

Jenn gulped her margarita. "Oh, I'm absolutely sure there's nothing going on between Matt and me. Unlike you and Chase."

Jo let the change in subject slide, knowing she'd get back to it sooner or later and not wanting to press Jenn too much. "I don't know what's going on between Chase and me."

"He looked like he wanted to eat you up with a spoon when we walked in." Jenn giggled.

He kind of had, hadn't he? Jo thought.

"To be honest, I'd probably let him."

"What's holding you back?"

Jo sighed. "I have no idea. The past, I guess. The future. The present."

"Jo, I know better than anyone that the two of you had a lot of air clearing you needed to do. From what little the two of you have told me—you're both being incredibly tight-lipped, which is really annoying, by the way—it sounds like you've at least laid most everything out there on the table. At some point y'all have got to stop focusing so much on the past and start paying attention to the here and now."

From where she was sitting, Jo had a clear line of sight to the pool table. Owen racked, then dropped his first two shots before missing his third. "I think we're getting there, Jenn. We just have to get to know each other again. We're different people now."

Jenn snorted. "Not that different. Sure, you've both had relationships, you live in different cities now and have your own careers. But deep down? He's still Chase and you're still Jo. Just grown-up versions."

Same, but different.

Abruptly, Jenn stood. "I've gotta go to the ladies' room. Be right back."

While Jenn was gone, Jo watched Chase over the salted rim of her margarita glass. He threw back his head and laughed at something Owen said. His smile was genuine, causing warmth to unfurl in her stomach.

His fingers were curled around the pool cue, and not for the first time in the past few weeks, Jo was fascinated. Those big pitcher's hands were rough and masculine and strong. She'd spent a few nights on the phone with him, fantasizing about those hands. Holding them. How they would feel on her skin, her breasts, between her legs.

Warmth spread through her body, pooling at the juncture of her thighs. Absently, she looked down at her margarita. She'd only taken a couple of sips.

No, this was all Chase making her warm and tingly.

Just as it had been for the past month or so.

Chase leaned over the pool table, setting up his shot. As though he could feel her gaze on him, he looked up. Their gazes caught. He looked back down, took his shot. Missed. Owen made quick work of the remaining balls, and Jenn stepped up to challenge him. Chase handed her his pool cue before heading back across the bar to Jo.

And then he was there, those big palms *thunking* down on the table. Leaning forward so that their noses almost touched, his voice barely above a whisper, he said, "You look a little lonely over here."

"Do I now?"

He nodded his head. They stared at each other for long moments, the tension between them so thick Jo wondered how they were both still breathing. It was like being under water for too long, still feet away from the surface, wishing you could just breathe deep.

She wasn't sure she liked it, but she wasn't sure she didn't like it, either.

The DJ switched songs, to a slow romantic number that had couples young and old swaying out on the dance floor. Slowly, tentatively, Chase reached for Jo's hand.

"Dance with me?"

Her throat too tight, still struggling for air, she nodded and allowed him to lead her out onto the dance floor.

Chase's big hands wrapped around her waist, pulled her as close as their clothes and propriety would allow. As they swayed along with Honeybrowne's "Texas Angel", Jo found herself once again mesmerized by those melted chocolate eyes.

She'd dreamt about those eyes as a teenager. They were amazing.

She wanted to lick him up, like chocolate that had melted on her fingertips.

The thought made her blush, but the look he gave her made her wonder if maybe he wasn't thinking similar thoughts.

He tucked a curl behind her ear and settled his head against hers. "You're killing me, smalls."

"Hmmm?" she murmured, her eyes half closed as she simply enjoyed the sensation of being held in his arms.

"If you keep looking at me like that, I might have to do something about it."

Jo pulled back slightly, enough so that she could see his face. She raised her eyebrows, blinked innocently and asked, "Looking at you like what?"

"Like I'm dessert and you have one hell of a sweet tooth."

Desire churned in her stomach, dropping and swirling and stirring up parts that hadn't been stirred in quite some time. "Well, I do like dessert. Especially chocolate."

"Chocolate, huh?"

She nuzzled his neck, half-drunk from the smell of his skin alone. "Like your eyes. They remind me of melted chocolate."

Jo felt more than heard his unsteady intake of breath followed by a slight stutter to his step. Instead of speaking, he pulled her in closer, and suddenly she was all too aware of the fact that Chase Roberts apparently wanted her as much as she wanted him.

They swayed together, silent, tension pulled tightly between them like fresh guitar strings. Jo could feel her heart thumping in her chest, an unsteady, almost too fast rhythm. She could see his pulse throbbing in his neck, could feel every ragged intake of breath as their thighs brushed.

The last strains of "Texas Angel" filtered through the smoky bar, and Jo slowly felt reality intrude into their intimate little bubble. The DJ deftly segued into another song, this one slightly more up tempo. She tried to move away, put some space between them, but Chase's grip on her waist tightened and he held her in place.

A crooked grin curved those lips she'd been thinking about way too much here lately.

"I think I should have listened to this song first."

Jo swallowed past the lump of desire in her throat and asked, "Why's that?"

Chase tilted his head towards the DJ booth. "Listen to the words. You'll understand."

They stood there on the dance floor, a few couples still moving around them, and Jo listened, belatedly recognizing Jon Wolfe's "I Don't Dance."

She looked into his eyes and asked, "So you're the sneak out at three a.m. type, huh? Never would have guessed that about you."

Despite her teasing words, desire had punched her—hard—in the belly at the thought of going back to her place...or rather, probably his place, considering she was currently staying with her grandmother.

"Generally, no. And not with you. Definitely not with you."

Their bodies continued to sway together, almost of their own volition, and Jo realized that the words held a ring of truth. One dance wouldn't be enough, couldn't be enough.

His fingers dug into her hip and his breath was ragged in her ear. "What are you thinking?"

She lightly, almost imperceptibly, rubbed her cheek against his, her already frayed nerves sparking at the feel of his stubble against her skin. And she took a chance, decided to be bold and follow Jenn's advice to live in the present rather than the past. "That I really, really want you to kiss me."

Jo felt the slight stumble her words caused, and smiled.

Chase pulled away from her, tunneled those long pitcher's fingers through his hair. "I need some fresh air. How about you?"

Suddenly feeling unsure, Jo tucked her hair behind her ears and bit down on the inside of her cheek. "Um…sure?"

Chase grabbed her hand and led her through the bar to the back entrance, which opened up to a patio area where folks could enjoy food, conversation, or just escape from the crowd inside. Tonight, it was empty. Everyone was inside, wanting a piece of Matt.

Without warning, Chase turned, grabbed Jo's other hand and pushed her up against the back wall of the building. The fairy lights strung around the edges of the patio cast his face in shadow. Her heart rate picked up, slammed against her chest as if she'd just finished sprinting towards the finish line. He pressed his lower body into hers, pinning her against the wall.

She idly wondered if she should be scared at this new, unseen side of Chase, but was absolutely thrilled instead.

Dimly, her gaze focused on nothing but his face, every part of her body *aware* of his body pressed against hers. Josh Abbott Band's "Oh, Tonight" floated through the air, muted by walls and doors and the bubble of desire wrapped around them. Chase softly sang along with the song, reciting lyrics about being kissed on the mouth and fighting feelings for a long time.

Before she could formulate a thought—much less a response—Chase claimed her mouth with his own. Hard. Hurried. Like she was water in the middle of the desert and he'd been walking for days. She kissed him back, met his tongue thrust for thrust.

Jo's fingers dug into his shoulders, holding on for dear life.

Too much. It was all too much. His lips. His tongue. The feel of him, hard and ready and apparently big pressing her between her thighs.

She was drowning. She needed air.

Was she sure this was what she wanted?

His fingers tunneled through her hair, grabbed hold at the base of her head.

She'd never been one to enjoy hair pulling, but holy hell just like that she felt her body go up in flames.

My God, we really are going to set the world on fire.

Jo's hands drifted from Chase's broad shoulders to his chest. Around to his back and then to his stomach, which was flat and taut through his t-shirt. Back around, where they settled on his ass and grabbed, trying to pull him even closer.

Chase's hands unwound themselves from her hair, smoothed over her neck to her face, which he cupped with both hands. They fed on each other's mouths, desire pooling and aching between her legs, in her belly. Her breasts felt full, tender and heavy, her nipples hard and too sensitive against the cups of her bra.

He backed her up fully against the wall before reaching down to pick up her boot-clad feet and guide them so that they were wrapped around his waist.

Pinned fully against the wall with her legs locked around that taut waist, her sundress bunched around her hips, the only thing between their bodies was a flimsy pair of panties and the denim of his jeans.

His hands cupped her bottom, helping to hold her up while his mouth left hers to trail hot, wet kisses along her jaw and then along her neck. He rubbed against her, the bulge behind the denim creating a delicious friction that only left her wanting more.

Chase sucked on her neck, bit down lightly and pushed against her harder. Jo gasped and moaned, too lost in sensation to care if anyone heard her.

The friction against her clit, his hands on her ass and his mouth at her neck were too much. Not enough. God, she wanted more. Needed more. She needed his hands all over her, that amazing mouth on her breasts and him deep inside of her.

His hips tilted against her again, and she could feel the pressure building, but didn't want to go there alone.

"Chase." His name came out on a breathy moan.

"Hmm?"

Jo swallowed, trying to clear her head long enough to tell him what she wanted. He pushed his hips against her again, and slipped one hand under the elastic of her panties. Her broken thoughts scattered as his thumb played at her entrance, swirling and dipping, teasing as his denim clad cock continued to rub against her clit.

He captured her lips again, thrust his tongue into her mouth in a way that could only make her think of his hard length thrusting into her. His thumb pressed inside, thrusting in time with his tongue and his cock against her clit. She wrapped her arms around his neck, grabbed his thick brown hair with her hands as her body moved in time with his.

Her tongue met his thrust for thrust, her body moved with his pelvis and thumb, falling naturally into a rhythm together. His thumb pressed deeper, swirled before being replaced with two different fingers, which pressed into her, stroking, coaxing.

A new pressure built, one she'd never felt before with anyone else.

Too much. It was too much.

Oh, God.

Her orgasm broke, spasms that gripped his fingers and that she felt from the top of her head to her toes. Her scalp tingled. She felt like her entire body was on fire, exploding and pulsing as liquid heat rushed from her body and soaked his hand and her panties.

Stunned, Jo opened her eyes and met Chase's gaze. Those melted chocolate eyes looked like they'd been sprinkled with cinnamon—hot and sweet.

He kissed her again, long and hard, and her body tightened against his fingers again. Her breath hitched, and he pulled his mouth away. His gaze roamed over her face, unfulfilled desire etched across it.

"Are you gonna come for me again?" he whispered.

Her inner muscles convulsed again. Once. Twice.

"Not without you, Chase."

His eyes darkened and the hand still cupped around her ass flexed.

"Are you sure?"

She nodded. "Take me home with you."

He brushed a sweet, hesitant kiss over her lips and nodded. "Do you want me to go grab your purse, or do you want to?"

"I'll get it."

Slowly, reluctantly, they pulled apart from each other. Jo set her feet back on the ground, her knees wobbly and thighs shaky. For long moments they just stood there, staring at each other before Jo finally broke the spell and said, "I'll go get my purse and meet you in the parking lot."

Chase nodded and grinned. "Make it quick."

Jo couldn't hide her smile as she walked back into the bar on unsteady legs.

CHAPTER ELEVEN

Chase drew an unsteady breath and ran his hands over his face, Jo's scent still on his fingers. His dick grew harder, which he hadn't known was possible.

The heavy July air settled around him, and he tried to strike a casual pose against the driver's side door of his truck as he waited for Jo to join him.

A lethal combination of nerves and desire gripped him, churning in his stomach and tossing around in his brain.

Chase *thunked* his head against the window behind him.

Breathe, Roberts. Breathe.

He couldn't remember the last time he'd wanted a woman so much. Jo did something to him, twisted him up inside until he didn't know which way was up or down. Twisted him up so that he lost his head and did stupid, erotic things in public.

How they hadn't been caught was anyone's guess, but he wasn't going to look a gift horse in the mouth. The last thing they needed were headlines about a local businessman (and Matt Roberts' little brother) and the daughter of the town's formerly best-known adulterer getting caught doing the hanky-panky behind a local bar. He had a reputation and business to think about, and she had a grandmother she didn't want to disappoint. Not to mention if word got back to her school he was pretty sure she could lose her job.

Chase glanced down at his watch.

Where was she?

He looked back to the entrance of the bar, willing her to walk out while at the same time wondering what the hell he was doing. This was Jo. His childhood friend. First love. Only love, if he was being honest with himself. The girl who'd one minute been his best friend, and the next would barely look at him.

Suddenly, she was there, walking towards him, and all of the crap from their past didn't seem to matter so much. Her flimsy cotton sundress fluttered around her knees. Brown, embroidered cowboy boots lovingly caressed her calves. His palms itched to replace those boots; she had amazing legs. Legs he'd fantasized about ever since that day at the lake. Her full, firm breasts strained against the buttons that marched from her cleavage to her waist. His fingers twitched involuntarily as he raked her body with his gaze.

And then she was in front of him, her breath a little less uneven and her color not quite as high, but in the dim lights of the parking lot he could barely make out the hardened peaks of her nipples pressing against the blue cotton of her dress.

They stood there for long moments, staring at each other. Lust and uncertainty played across Jo's face, and Chase was glad he wasn't the only one feeling those things.

"You rode here with Jenn, right?"

Jo swallowed and nodded.

He inclined his head towards his truck and smiled. "Hitch a ride with me?"

"Sure."

Chase followed Jo around to the passenger side, opened the door and held it as she grabbed the oh shit handle and hoisted herself into the big, black pickup. He closed the door and circled around to the driver's side.

Once enclosed in the relative privacy of the cab of the truck, he turned to look at her, knowing that everything he was feeling was written all over his face.

Jo reached out and cupped his cheek. "You okay over there?"

Chase snorted. "Isn't that supposed to be my line?"

Jo laughed and leaned towards him so that she could brush her lips over his. He felt the light touch all the way to his groin.

Her lips were gone almost as soon as they touched his. "Take me home, Chase?"

He turned the key in the ignition and threw the truck into drive without waiting to make sure the glow plugs had warmed up. Hell, it was still ninety-five degrees outside. He wasn't sure they had much warming up to do.

Chase pulled out of the parking space he'd backed in to and made a left out of the parking lot. They made the trip in silence, the radio the only sound. As he turned on to Veteran's Boulevard he reached over and grabbed her hand, needing the feel of her to anchor him in reality.

It had been a long time since he'd taken a woman home. The last one had been well over a year ago, and had blabbed about it on some internet message board where sports groupies went to swap stories. After the chastising phone call from his mother and the teasing text from his brother, he'd made the decision to no longer take women to his place. Instead, he went to their's—until that had ended, too.

Now here he was, speeding through the night towards his house with a beautiful, eager woman beside him. Nerves once again pushed, threatening to ruin his night.

This was Jo. No need to be nervous. Except he couldn't help but be nervous. Usually, he didn't care about the scars. They were there and had helped make him the man he was today. He knew some women saw them as a turn-off, while others thought of them almost as exotic. Others felt sympathy. Those were the ones that really grated.

What would Jo think?

Sure, she knew about his childhood illness, or at least of it if not the down and dirty details. But she'd only seen the scars that one time, the summer before everything went to hell. Would they turn her on? Weird her out? Would she feel sorry for him?

Reflexively, his hand tightened its grip on hers at the thought of Jo being grossed out, and then looking at him with pity from those big blue green eyes.

He could feel those eyes on him now as he made the turn into his neighborhood by the lake. Instead of addressing any sort of concern, she commented, "Nice neighborhood. Movin' on up a little, huh?"

Chase grinned. "Just a little. Not that I don't love the neighborhood we grew up in, but the places here have bigger yards."

"Privacy?"

He glanced at her quickly before making the turn on to his street. "How'd you guess?"

"You're a fairly private man, Chase Roberts, and I can't say I blame you."

They reached his house, and he hit the garage door button. The door rolled up, and he pulled his big truck into the garage.

"How the hell did you manage to get this thing in here?"

"Custom garage. When the house was built, I asked them to increase the dimensions on the garage so I could park in here."

"Privacy again?"

"That and thieves. No use leaving a big truck out where it's easy pickings. Tailgates and trucks both vanish pretty quickly in a border town." He turned off the truck and hit the button to lower the garage door. As it went down, Chase got out, rounded the hood of the truck and opened Jo's door for her.

"Such a gentleman." She smiled down at him.

"You might not be saying that later."

She blushed, swung her legs out of the truck so that her toes rested on the running boards and said, "I hope not."

Desire punched him in the gut again, and Chase couldn't help but assist her out of the truck. Anything to put his hands on her.

Jo's body slid along his as he helped lower her to the ground, the friction causing her dress to slide and bunch up around the tops of her thighs. Slowly, Chase stepped back, deciding that maybe distance would be a good thing—at least until they got inside and there was a proper surface available. Preferably a horizontal one.

He took her hand, turned and led her into the house. The garage opened into a large utility room. On a panel beside the door an alarm tone sounded. Chase punched his PIN into the number pad and the buzzing stopped.

He opened the door that led from the utility room and almost tripped over Winchester.

The three-year-old Great Pyrenees lifted his big head off the cool floor, shot him a baleful look, sighed and *thunked* his head back onto the floor.

Chase nudged Winchester with the toe of his boot. "Come on, Win. Up and at 'em."

Sighing, Winchester heaved all one hundred and twenty-three pounds of muscle, fat and fur, took three steps into the kitchen and away from the door and plopped down again.

Chase heard a chuckle from behind him. "He's quite

the character, isn't he?"

"You have no idea," Chase said as he led her into the kitchen. "Sometimes I swear he thinks he's a human rather than a dog."

"Is it okay if I pet him?"

"Absolutely. You'll probably end up with a friend for life."

He watched as Jo walked over to where Winchester was sprawled across the floor, drool already puddling under his big snout. She squatted and held out her hand. Winchester lifted his head and reached out to nudge her palm with his nose.

Slowly—because Winchester rarely did anything quickly—the big dog got up and stood so that he and Jo were eye to eye. He gave her a once over, sniffed a few times and then wagged his tail seconds before placing his big paw into Jo's still outstretched hand.

"Oh, he's giving me paw!"

"He doesn't do that with just anybody."

Jo looked up and over at Chase. "So you're saying I'm special, huh?"

Chase nodded, and Winchester decided he wasn't getting enough attention, so he nudged Jo's other hand with his nose until she turned her attention back to him.

"Insistent, aren't you big guy?"

Chase chuckled. "I'm pretty sure he thinks the world revolves around him." He reached out and scratched behind Winchester's ears, coaxing out his big doggy grin.

"Such a happy boy. You're just a big happy boy, aren't you Win?" Jo buried her fingers in Winchester's double coat. Winchester, apparently in doggy heaven, did something he rarely did to anyone other than Chase— licked Jo's chin.

"Oh, thank you, Win. Thank you for the kisses. You're such a sweet, handsome boy."

Win snuggled closer and buried his head in Jo's chest. She laughed as she lost her balance and gracelessly ended up sitting on his kitchen floor. Win, never one to miss a prime opportunity, snuggled as close as he could before plopping his big body into Jo's lap. He let out a contented sigh, and looked up at Chase as if to say, "Ha ha. Snooze you lose, buddy."

Jo laughed and stroked her fingers through Win's thick fur. "He's definitely a charmer. Aren't you, Winchester? You handsome boy, you." The dog's tail thumped once. As Chase stood there in the middle of his kitchen, staring down at this woman and his dog, the words from the song that had been playing back at the bar, "Oh, Tonight," filtered through his head, the part about it being too late because the singer had already fallen in love.

While he didn't think he was there yet, he was man enough to realize he was treading in dangerous waters here.

"Do you need anything to drink?"

Jo looked up at him and grinned. "Some water would be great. If you could help me get up it would be appreciated; while I'm very much head over heels for Winchester here, this floor isn't exactly comfortable to sit on."

Chase laughed and then clapped twice. Winchester lifted his big head and glared. "Come on, big guy, gotta get up and move."

Winchester sighed—again—and hefted his big body up. Sensing that Chase wasn't playing around, he made his way to the gigantic dog crate in his corner of the kitchen, entered it and flopped back down.

The dog taken care of, Chase reached down and offered Jo a hand. She took it and used it to help herself up off the floor.

Chase pulled open the door of the fridge and reached in and grabbed a couple bottles of water. He handed one to Jo before asking, "So do you want the full tour now or later?"

He wasn't sure where the abruptness of his question came from, but Jo didn't seem to mind.

"How about we do an abbreviated tour right now?"

Chase nodded, took her free hand in his and led her through the kitchen and into the living room. "This is the living room."

"Mmm. Nice."

He gestured toward a closed door to the right. "That's the formal dining room. It gets used maybe once a year."

"As is the case with most formal dining rooms."

"Yup."

They turned and started up a curved staircase, which opened up to a large loft area.

"This is the loft." He gestured to their right. "Those are the guest bedrooms and my home office." He turned them left and led them to a closed door. He reached out, nerves dancing in his stomach again.

Get a grip, Roberts, it's not like you're a virgin bringing home a girl for the first time.

"And this is my bedroom."

As he crossed the threshold the lights came up until the room was diffused with a warm glow.

Jo wandered further into his bedroom, and he clicked the door closed; if he didn't, Winchester would decide to intrude.

Chase walked over to his iPod docking station, turned on some music and watched as Jo explored his bedroom. Placed her purse on his dresser. Touched the smooth oak that was stained a dark, rich brown. He watched as she sauntered over to his king-sized bed, with its light green coverlet and tan sheets and wondered what she was thinking.

Instead of asking, he simply continued to watch her movements, realizing that he liked the look of her here.

Jo trailed her fingers over the green coverlet before turning and walking—slowly—back to him. She stopped inches away.

Randy Roger Band's "Kiss Me in the Dark" filtered through the in-ceiling speakers that were connected to the iPod dock, and Jo wrapped her arms around his neck. "Dance with me?"

Chase lifted an eyebrow. "This is kind of an odd song to dance to, beat and all."

"I know." She smiled, and suddenly all of her bravado was gone. "I get the impression that both of us are dealing with some hella nerves right now, though."

"Is that right, counselor?"

She nodded. "I know why I'm nervous, but what about you? What's got you so tense?"

Instead of answering he pulled her into his arms and began to sway their bodies. It wasn't in time with the music but he didn't care—he just needed something to stall.

He turned her question back on her. "What has you so nervous all of a sudden?"

She shook her head. "Nu uh. I asked first."

He sighed. "It's, uh, been a while and I don't want to disappoint you?"

Jo pulled back enough so that she could see his face. "How long is 'a while' for you, cowboy?"

"About a year."

She stumbled slightly before regaining her composure. "Seriously? But you're so…a year, really?"

Curious about what she'd been about to say, Chase asked, "I'm so what?"

He could feel her swallow against his shoulder. Long seconds ticked by before she finally whispered. "Hot. You're so hot."

Pleasure and surprise coursed through him, and suddenly the scars didn't matter to him and he got the sense they wouldn't matter to Jo, either. And she sure as hell wasn't some jersey chaser hell-bent on spreading his secrets.

"So what has you so nervous? I shared mine, now you share yours."

She chuckled. "It's been a while for me, too."

"How long's 'a while' for you?"

He could feel the hesitation in her grip. "Um, about two years. I'm, uh, kind of picky."

He dropped a kiss on the top of her head. "So it's been a while for both of us. If we screw it up the first time we have all night to get it right."

Jo's laugh was teasing tinged with nerves. "All night, huh? Now there's some of the confidence I'm used to."

Chase stopped dancing, just stood there with every nerve ending on fire. His words came out in a gravelly whisper. "I want you, Jo." Had always wanted her, really.

She looked up at him with those blue green eyes, more green than blue at the moment. "I want you, too."

Slowly, Chase moved in to kiss her, watching those aquamarine eyes grow greener and greener the closer his lips got. Behind the bar had been the time for hot and heavy. Now, though, he wanted—needed—to take his time, worship every inch of her luscious body and claim her as his own. Finally.

Their lips met and he kissed her slowly, thoroughly, until he felt her start to melt against him. When her fingers dug into his shoulders he went all possessive caveman, picked her up and carried her to the bed.

Chase gently placed Jo on the edge of the mattress and melded his mouth with hers again. Their tongues tangled, the rhythm growing faster and more impatient. In an effort to slow things down he broke the kiss and began trailing his lips along her jaw, the sensitive place behind her ear, down her neck.

He nipped lightly at her shoulder. Laved her collar bone with his tongue. The slight bump he felt reminded him that she'd broken it in high school while cheering during a football game. He'd stood there on the sidelines, helmet in hand as he watched her climb into the ambulance and ride away.

Now, he kissed it, like he'd wished he could do back then.

He pushed the memory away and continued to work his mouth down her body. She hummed almost like a cat when he kissed her exposed cleavage. He felt her hands tangle in his hair and smiled.

Just as slowly he began to unbutton the bodice of her dress.

One.

He kissed the skin that had been exposed.

Two.

Chase ran his tongue along the open seam, making Jo squirm beneath him.

Three.

He revealed her bra and a small patch of skin under it, which he kissed.

Four.

He nipped at her belly.

Five.

He swirled his tongue around her belly button before pushing the unbuttoned fabric aside.

Chase nibbled and kissed his way across the exposed skin of her belly, loving the way her muscles jumped with every touch. She squirmed beneath his mouth and she tugged at his hair with her fingers.

He looked up at her face, tense with a desire that took his breath away. His pulse quickened and his cock twitched behind his jeans. Determined to take this slow, though, he moved up and feathered a kiss on her lips before slowly dragging one spaghetti strap off her shoulder. He'd waited eighteen years to do this, he was damned sure going to take his time.

He dragged the other off her shoulder before murmuring, "Sit up."

Jo did as he asked, her unsteady breathing threatening to push her breasts from her bra.

Chase slid the dress straps down Jo's arms until the entire bodice was pooled around her waist. Watching her face instead of her body, he reached around and slid the three hooks of her bra free.

The garment teetered, clinging to her body for long, tortuous seconds before gravity lent a hand. It fell away, dropping to her lap, and Chase *had* to look now.

His gaze slowly dropped to the prettiest pair of breasts he'd ever seen. Full, firm, with dusky pink nipples that hardened as he watched.

He slowly circled a hard nipple with an index finger. Jo's breath hitched.

"You're beautiful."

She smiled. "Touch me, Chase."

He nearly came undone at her whispered plea. Somehow, though, he managed to reign in his stampeding desire.

"Stand up."

She did as he asked, and he—maybe a little faster than he'd planned—peeled the rest of the dress off of her. She stood there in nothing more than a pair of purple lace panties and cowboy boots. It was the hottest thing he'd ever seen.

Slowly, reverently, he slid those purple panties down her thighs, her calves, her boots, until they pooled on the floor around her ankles. He kneeled and steadied her as he slipped them off one ankle and then the other.

Deciding the boots were simply too hot to take off for

now, he kissed his way up her legs, his big hands gripping her hips. When he reached the apex of her thighs he feathered kisses in the middle of her triangle of golden hair, the place where her pelvis and thigh met, her belly, the tops of her thighs, until he felt her squirm slightly in his hands.

His mouth resting just below her belly button, he gently pushed her onto the bed until her back was against the mattress and her legs hung over the edge.

Still feathering kisses along her stomach, he reached out with both hands, grabbed her boot-clad ankles and brought them to his shoulders. Open for him now, he sat back just slightly so that he could look at her.

She was beautiful. Deeply pink and swollen. Wet. He had to taste.

Chase lowered his head, gently spreading her lips with his thumbs, and flicked his tongue over her clit. Her hips jumped and settled, and he did it again before running his tongue along the entire seam. He played at her entrance, thrusting in and swirling his tongue, teasing her.

God, she tasted good. Better than he'd ever imagined

His cock twitched again and his balls tightened. They would have to wait. He had more important things to do right now.

Chase's mouth settled over Jo's clit, his tongue laving the hard nub. She pushed against his mouth, and Chase slowly slid a finger inside of her.

Jo's moan was so quiet he could barely hear it, but then she was pumping her hips against his face, moving in time with the finger he had inside of her.

Chase twisted his hand so that the pad of his finger was pressing up against the spongy spot he'd found during their make out session behind the bar. He applied pressure, stroking the swollen spot as he did so, while his mouth sucked at her. With his free hand he reached up and palmed one of her breasts before lightly rolling the hard nipple between his thumb and forefinger.

"Oh, God. Chase!"

Liquid flooded over his hand and his chin as Jo's inner muscles convulsed around his finger. Gentler now, he licked at her clit, then down so he could get a better taste of her.

She tugged at his hair and squeezed her thighs around his head. "Too…" *pant* "much."

Chase smiled, kissed her pretty pink lips one more time and stood up. She watched him through slitted eyes, and because it turned him on and he sensed it would turn her on, he brought his finger up to his mouth and sucked her juices off of it.

By the way her chest trembled and her eyes darkened, he figured he'd been right.

She sat up and pulled him closer to her. "I think it's time we got you naked, too."

He grinned. Jo unbuckled his belt, fumbled briefly with the button of his jeans before popping it open. She slid the zipper down as he grabbed the hem of his t-shirt and drew it over his head.

She pushed his pants down, and he let her. They pooled at his ankles, and his boxers followed, caught by his boots. Jo looked up at his face before touching his chest. "My turn," she whispered.

Chase stood there, his cock hard and throbbing and stiff like a soldier, wanting nothing more than to be buried inside of her.

Instead, Jo reached out and trailed two fingers over the scars that sliced across his abdomen.

"Do they hurt?"

He shook his head. "Not anymore. They haven't since I was in high school."

She leaned forward and kissed them, her lips barely there against the puckered skin. No woman had ever done that—most of the time they were afraid to even look at them much less touch and kiss them. But Jo was doing just that, and Chase now knew for certain that his nerves had been for nothing.

Jo's hands and mouth continued to explore. When he felt a fingertip slowly skim along the underside of his dick, though, he grabbed her hand and pushed her back onto the bed. "If you touch me like that I'm really not going to last long."

She pouted, but he could tell that a smile wanted to break free.

Chase toed off his boots, jeans and boxers, and Jo did the same with her boots. Completely naked, skin to skin, he kissed her again.

Jo's hands gripped his shoulders as their tongues tangled and lips devoured. The air grew heavy and languid, and Chase could feel the steady *thump, thump, thump* of his heart. Their breathing quickened, and he slid a hand down her belly to that heavenly place between her thighs. She was hot, wet and ready. He teased her clit with his thumb until he felt her breath hitch and her hips move impatiently against his hand.

Blindly, he reached into the second drawer of his nightstand, found a foil packet and withdrew it. He broke the kiss, tore the packet open and rolled the condom on. Jo opened her thighs for him and he pushed against her entrance.

She wrapped her legs around him and slowly, tortuously, Chase slid all the way home. He stayed there, suspended and still, as much for himself as for her. She was hot and tight and fit him like a glove.

He moved his hips, and together they found a rhythm all their own. He lowered his head and caught one of her nipples with his mouth. He suckled, nipped lightly and moved to the other one. He felt her muscles twitch around him and suckled harder between taking the turgid tip with his teeth and applying pressure while flicking his tongue over the very tip.

Her fingers dug into his shoulders and her hips urged him to go faster.

"Harder, Chase. Harder."

Still biting at her nipple, Chase thrust harder. A thin layer of sweat covered their skin, causing their bodies to make a faint sucking noise every time they pulled apart. The sound only served to turn him on more.

He lifted his head and whispered, "How close are you?"

She gasped as he thrust into her—hard. "So…close."

"Tell me what you need."

Instead of saying anything, she placed one of her hands between them and touched herself.

"Oh, God, Jo. Do you have any idea how hot that is?"

She smiled and gasped out. "Play with my nipples."

Chase did as she asked—not that it was really a hardship—and sucked at her nipple before biting down again. As he alternated between sucking and biting, he could feel her muscles tightening around his cock. Her hand between their bodies moved faster and faster, and her breaths grew shallow. Sensing she was *right there* he bit her nipple a little harder than he had before, and he was rewarded with a very guttural, "Chase!" followed by the feeling of her orgasm pulling at him.

He pumped his hips harder, faster, and watched her face as convulsions continued to wrack her. She opened her eyes and he was gone. His own orgasm ripped through him, bursting in waves as he pumped his hips once, twice more before stilling.

Chase dropped his forehead to hers, lightly kissed her on the mouth, and waited for his heart to stop pounding in his ears.

He felt Jo's hands caressing his back and smiled.

"We're definitely going to have to do that again," Jo said, her breathing still a little harsh.

Chase reluctantly pulled out of the warm cocoon of Jo's body. He rolled over so that they were side by side, searched for and grasped her hand, reveling in the feel of it. He turned his head so that he was looking at her and said, "We are *definitely* going to do that again."

CHAPTER TWELVE

Chase was dozing, his body curled around Jo's after making love for a second time, when he vaguely heard the sound of footsteps coming up the stairs.

He jerked up into bed, senses on alert.

Winchester wasn't barking, he realized dimly.

Jo stirred beside him and he gently placed a finger over her lips. He was reaching for the gun in his nightstand when he heard Matt call out, "Don't worry, Chase. It's just your brother. Y'know, the one you left at the bar without saying anything to him."

Chase and Jo looked at each other, and Jo's eyes widened.

"Oh my God. We're awful people," she whispered.

Chase choked back a laugh before getting out of bed, putting on his boxers and leaving the bedroom.

Matt was standing in the loft, but he didn't look pissed at least.

"Sorry, Matt. Something, uh, came up." You could say that.

Matt didn't even have the decency not to laugh. "She still here?"

Chase nodded. Matt held up his hand for a high five. "You're so juvenile."

Matt dropped his hand, but the grin didn't leave his face. "Just wanted to see what you would do."

"How'd you get home anyway?"

The light in Matt's eyes dimmed slightly, but the smile stayed in place. "Jenn."

Chase raised an eyebrow. "I can't figure out why you two dislike each other so much."

Matt shrugged before opening his bedroom door. "It's nothing, little brother. Get back in there with your woman."

Chase started to reply with, "She's not my woman" but then stopped himself, as the thought occurred to him that he wanted her to be his woman. The click of Matt's bedroom door closing jarred Chase from his thoughts, and he turned back to his own bedroom and Jo.

His woman.

He liked the sound of that, he thought as he walked back to his bedroom, closed the door behind him. Jo sat in the middle of his bed, her hair a riot of messy waves, sheet tucked around her chest and under her armpits. She looked rumpled, well-loved and sexy as hell.

He shucked off his boxers and crawled onto the bed, stealing a kiss once he'd reached her. She sighed into his mouth and tangled her tongue with his own. God, he loved kissing her. Almost as much as he loved making love to her.

Almost. But not quite.

Wordlessly, he eased her back down onto the bed and loved her body the way he wanted to love the rest of her.

Completely.

~~*~~

Jo woke the next morning in stages, slowly becoming aware of her surroundings as her brain clicked into gear. Sunlight filtered through a strange window, and warm sheets caressed her naked body. She stretched, felt the tug and pull of well-used muscles and smiled.

Chase.

Who knew the man had moves like that?

Speaking of…she propped herself up on her elbows and watched him as he slept. His face was relaxed in sleep, breathing deep and even, his limbs sprawled like he was in constant motion. The sheet and coverlet were draped across his hips, leaving his torso bare.

Good Lord but he was sexy. Toned and taut in all the right places, his skin golden and perfect. Her gaze traipsed down his body. Dark nipples. Mostly hairless chest. Flat stomach. Belly button. Happy trail. Scars.

In the light of day, and without him watching, she looked at them. There were several. Six biopsies and two surgeries, if she remembered correctly. Eight heart breaking procedures he and his family had endured, not knowing if this would be the one that finally got the some answers or fixed his broken kidneys.

His parents had put one foot in front of the other through every single one of them, always there for their son, loving him unconditionally. She'd been there for the aftermath of most of them, sitting by his bed playing card games, helping him with homework so he didn't fall behind. She hadn't fully understood what was wrong, but she'd known her friend would be okay for a while, then get sick and end up in the hospital yet again. As they'd gotten older she'd lain awake some nights praying and crying for him, scared to death of losing him.

Funny how she'd been the one to push him away.

Chase stirred, and her gaze moved over the rest of his torso, lower when she noticed the erection tenting the covers. She looked back up at his face, saw his grin and smiled back.

She kissed him lightly on the lips. "Good morning."

"That it is," he said as he wrapped an arm around her, bringing her closer. Their lips and tongues tangled and Jo felt her body tighten in response, heat pooling between her thighs and her stomach performing somersaults.

Chase moaned when Jo nipped his earlobe, groaned when she swung her leg over his hips to straddle him. The head of his penis rubbed against her opening, slick and hard and hot. She teased them both as they kissed, rotating her hips so that their most intimate parts rubbed together with constant friction. Slow. Tormenting.

She broke the kiss and gently laid her lips on his nose. Forehead. Jaw. Neck. Shoulder. Collarbone. Other shoulder. Other collarbone. She trailed slow, sweet kisses down his torso, communicating in the only way she knew how at the moment. Without words, but with slow, sweet kisses and soft touches and gentle sighs and moans.

Jo paused at Chase's nipples, taking turns giving them attention, learning that he liked it when she nipped just slightly at them. She spent time lavishing kisses on his chest. His sides. The puckered skin that made her heart both ache and swell with pride for the boy he'd been. Dipped her tongue in his belly button. Kissed her way along his happy trail and she scooted down his legs.

The sheet had tangled around his ankles at some point, leaving his sex uncovered, hard against his pelvis. She kissed the underside, teased with her tongue before moving on to his thighs.

Even the man's legs were sexy, all ropy muscles and coarse with dark hair.

Slowly she made her way back up, noting that while his breaths were coming harsher and faster now, he didn't seem to be in any hurry, either. She grinned, feminine power coursing through her veins.

It was a heady thing.

She took him in her hand, lightly stroking up and down. Cupped his balls with her other hand, gently squeezing. He arched his hips off the bed and sighed, the sound more like a moan.

She kissed him again, small, feather light kisses along his hard length, before swirling her tongue around the head and taking him in her mouth. His hips gyrated, urging her forward. She took him completely, his length filling her, before moving her head back, then forward again.

"Oh, God, Jo."

She felt his hands on her head, lightly threading through her hair, before they settled on her shoulders. She loved him slowly, completely, enjoying the feel of him in her mouth and the sound of his moans with every swipe of her tongue.

His fingers dug into her shoulders before moving down to her breasts to toy with her nipples. She moaned, the sensation sending sparks of pleasure straight to her core. Chase pinched them, causing her to gasp. He slid out of her mouth, and hooked his hands under her armpits, gently hauling her body up so that she was straddling his wet erection.

Their gazes collided, and she was entranced, at his mercy and every whim.

He arched his hips, rubbing the head of his cock along the seam of her sex. Her hips responded, almost involuntarily, rubbing against him in turn. They rocked against each other for long moments, gazes still locked as pleasure built.

Chase grasped her hips, his fingers applying gentle pressure, the head of his penis pushing into her entrance, teasing and tormenting.

She quietly answered the question she saw in his eyes, wanting the same thing. "Clean as a whistle, on the pill since I was eighteen. You?"

"Not on the pill, but clean." His voice was husky and hoarse. Sexy. "You sure about this?"

Jo nodded. "I trust you, Chase."

Their hips moved together, him sliding into her as

much as she slid onto him, taking him to the hilt. He bumped against her cervix, slid along nerve endings she hadn't even realized she'd had.

Chase. Completely bare. Inside of her.

Too soon the thoughts and the feelings were too much. Jo felt like she was bursting at the seams, all light and heat and emotions.

It had never been like this. With anyone.

Her orgasm broke, feminine muscles clenching and milking as she came on a low gasp. Chase's hands tightened on her hips as he arched into her, her name a moan on his lips.

She fell forward, allowed herself to nuzzle her nose into the crook of his shoulder and breathe him in. Kiss him lightly as unspoken words pushed at her throat, begging for release. His arms came around her and he breathed, a shaky sound that made her heart both soar and plummet.

I love you.

She wanted to shout those words. Whisper them. Write them on his heart like a tattoo.

Instead, she slowly disengaged their bodies and lay down beside him. He reached for her, guided her head onto his chest and rubbed her back in silence. Dropped a kiss on the top of her head.

She snuggled closer, wrapped an arm around his middle.

I love you, Chase.

~~*~~

Never in her wildest dreams could Jo have seen herself doing the walk of shame into her grandmother's house at, oh, 11:32 the morning after, oh, the greatest, most soul shattering sex of her life.

But here she was, not even bothering with an attempt to sneak in.

Gran looked up at her, and then went back to doing her

daily therapy exercises.

Jo just stood there, wearing the same dress she'd left in yesterday, her wild hair pulled back in a messy ponytail, no makeup, and a slight case of whisker burn across her chest.

Thank God Gran couldn't see the love bite Chase had left on her stomach just an hour ago. Or the whisker burn on the insides of her thighs.

Dear God, she was going to go up in flames.

Long moments of silence passed while Jo tried not to fidget and Gran finished the current set of exercises. Long moments where Jo felt equal parts guilty and giddy, which really was an awkward combination.

"Jolene, you're a grown woman and owe me no explanations."

Jo released a breath she hadn't realized she'd been holding, but still felt embarrassed at the thought of her grandmother even remotely suspecting what she'd been up to last night and this morning. Hopefully Gran just thought she'd had a little too much to drink and spent the night with Jenn. She'd opened her mouth to offer up just that explanation—not that she liked lying to Gran, but there really were some things grandmothers were better off not knowing—when Gran spoke again.

"It's about time you and Chase made up and figured out you belong together." And then she winked. Actually winked.

"Uh...um..."

"Oh, don't act so shocked, young lady. I was young once, too. I remember what it's like to be in love, and you and Chase have been in love with each other since before you stopped believing in the Tooth Fairy. And I may be old but I'm not blind—Chase Roberts is what I believe you youngsters would call 'eye candy'."

Jo's mouth opened into an "O," and she was unable to make anything remotely resembling an intelligent statement. How did Gran know the term "eye candy" anyway?

Jo shook her head as if to clear it, grasped for something to say rather than standing there and looking like an idiot. "But you called the physical therapist a hussy the other day for drooling over Matt."

Gran tossed her a withering stare. "And she is a hussy. Not because she found the man attractive, but because of the way she talked about him, like he was a piece of meat and she was the grill."

Jo wasn't entirely sure how any of that made sense to Gran, much less how it was supposed to make sense to her.

"It's one thing to be attracted to a man and respect him and like him and act on those feelings. It's another thing entirely to look at a man as nothing more than an object. That's why she's a hussy."

Gran apparently wasn't familiar with twenty-first century hookups, but Jo wasn't in any hurry to be the one to explain *that* one to her. Instead, she said, "Fair enough. I still should have called and let you know I wasn't coming home rather than worrying you."

The older woman raised a gray eyebrow. "I wasn't worried about you in the least, Jolene. Why would I be? You're a grown woman. Besides, I've seen this one coming for years. Just surprised it took this long."

Jo really did wonder if one could die from embarrassment. "Well, still, Gran. It was irresponsible of me and won't happen again."

Gran's snort was anything but ladylike. "Now that I don't believe for a second. And for the record, I won't worry when you don't come home tonight, either."

She pulled out a resistance band for her next set of hip exercises before saying, "I imagine you want a shower and some lunch before you go back out with Chase. You'd best hurry if you don't want to be late."

Torn now between embarrassed and bemused, Jo nodded her head in agreement. "I think I'll go take a shower."

Minutes later, as she stood under the warm spray of the shower, Jo finally allowed herself to freely think about everything that had happened in the past twelve hours. As her hands soaped up her body, every muscle twinge and sensitive spot served as a reminder of last night's activities.

In other words, it was impossible *not* to think about what had happened between her and Chase.

It had been incredible. More so than she'd even begun to imagine. Chase had dedicated himself to her body much like he dedicated himself to everything else in life—fully, intently. Completely.

Even though the post-orgasmic glow still flowed through her veins, Jo couldn't help but wonder about what the future held. She'd been truthful the other day when she'd told him she hadn't planned on any of this, hadn't thought they would spend even a small amount of time together much less find this very adult…*something*… blossoming between them. But now, it was there and just seemed to be growing.

She wanted to encourage it, to nurture it, to allow herself to feel all the things she was and could feel for Chase. Unfortunately, the truth of their situation could not be ignored: she didn't live in Del Rio anymore, hadn't for years. In about a month she would have to go back to Austin and prepare for the new school year, meet with teachers, parents and students regarding class schedules and college decisions. She couldn't pick up and move back no more than he could pick up and move to Austin.

Jo massaged conditioner into her scalp, as much to cleanse as to ease the tension that was trying to creep into her body and stir up a headache. Odds were she was jumping the gun on the future anyway. While Chase wasn't exactly a man whore, she wasn't naïve enough to think that he was thinking beyond today in regards to their relationship.

She rinsed the conditioner from her hair then turned off the shower with a decisive flick of her wrist.

No more worrying about the future. Just live in the here and now and enjoy it while it lasts.

Unfortunately, Jo had a feeling that was going to be much easier said than done.

CHAPTER THIRTEEN

Later that day, Jo pulled up to Chase's house at a quarter past five, parking in the empty space in his driveway. From the looks of it, Jenn and Owen were already here, if the two other vehicles out front were any indication.

Leaving the change of clothes and toothbrush she'd brought with her—just in case—in the car, she grabbed the bottle of wine and bowl of potato salad from the front seat and made her way up Chase's front walk.

In the late afternoon sun, Chase's house was gorgeous. Two stories. Limestone. Dark blue shutters and trim with windows that sparkled in the sunshine. The front yard was wide, with xeriscaped beds populated by yucca and purple sage. A palm tree stood sentinel next to the garage, and a large oak tree invited people to sit under the shade in the front yard.

It looked warm and welcoming, like the man who lived there.

She reached the front door, rang the doorbell and waited, not sure what the protocol was for entering someone's home after having hours of wild monkey sex with them that ended less than twelve hours prior. Did she wait until someone answered, or wait a few seconds and then just walk in? She shifted from one foot to the other, hating how she'd gone from being a confident, single, professional woman to anxious schoolgirl seemingly overnight.

Seriously.

And then the door was opening and Chase was there, his brown eyes warming at the sight of her and a smile curving the lips that had touched her in places that were currently going all warm and tingly. He leaned over the threshold, caught her mouth with his for a long, slow, *hello there* kiss.

Jo was pretty sure she felt her ovaries throwing a party.

"Hey there gorgeous," Chase said, his voice low and full of promise as he stepped aside to let her in the front door.

"Hey there yourself." She lifted the wine and potato salad. "I, uh, brought stuff."

Brilliant, Jo. Had she really paid tens of thousands of dollars for a master's degree?

"You didn't have to do that. There's plenty here," Chase said as they made their way from the living room to the kitchen.

This afternoon, with the haze of lust and nerves slightly dulled, Jo was able to pay more attention to her surroundings. His home was big without being ostentatious, with an open floor plan that flowed from space to space. A big leather sofa sat in the middle of the room, facing a rustic entertainment center showcasing a huge flat screen TV airing the ball game.

The Wranglers were currently beating the Marlins, she noted.

"Does the game being on bother Matt?" she asked as they passed through to the kitchen.

Chase shook his head. "I don't think so, since he's the one who turned it on. But I never can really tell with Matt, especially the past couple of days."

They stopped at the kitchen island, where Jo set down her packages. It looked like they were alone in the house, and she could hear laughter coming from what she guessed was the backyard. So she asked, "Is he okay? I mean, obviously he seems to be doing as well as someone could physically after something like that. But is he *okay*?"

Chase smiled and grabbed her hand, pulling her to him until their bodies were flush with one another. "You planning on diving into my brother's psyche, Counselor?"

His eyes sparkled, and Jo couldn't hide her smile. "If he needs to talk, I'm willing to listen, but I don't know that I could be impartial considering I've known Matt as long as I've known you. He's like an annoying brother in some ways."

Chase chuckled, nuzzled his nose against the side of her neck. Jo's eyes closed of their own volition, warmth flooding through her body. "As long as I'm not like an annoying brother."

Jo sighed. "Impossible."

And then his lips were on hers and all thoughts of Matt and his possibly fragile psyche scattered. As if from far away, she heard more laughter and a dog barking. Water splashing. The rapid *pop pop pop pop pop* of someone setting off a row of Blackcats.

Vaguely, she thought she heard the sound of a door opening, but the feeling of Chase's lips and tongue and hands were overpowering her brain cells.

"Well then."

Startled, Jo broke the kiss, her cheeks flushed with embarrassment on top of desire. She watched as Chase blinked a few times, as if trying to clear his head, before saying, "Looks like we've been found out."

Jenn's laugh rang out, filling the kitchen. "I knew it!"

Jo snorted and turned to her best friend. "Knew what?"

"That y'all had hooked up last night! Headache my

right pinky toe."

Jo recalled telling Jenn that Chase was giving her a ride home because she'd developed a sudden migraine. Apparently she'd done a poor acting job. Oops.

"Um…"

Jenn walked over and hugged them both. "I'm so happy for you guys."

Jo and Chase looked at each other over Jenn's head, Jo feeling decidedly awkward considering there had been no discussion of the future or even the present. "Thanks."

Chase winked at her, and Jenn pulled away, almost bouncing on her toes. "I love you guys, and I'm so glad y'all finally admitted you love each other."

Jo looked anywhere but at Chase and Jenn. The floor. The ceiling. Winchester's dog crate. Chase cleared his throat, and Jo could feel his body shift beside hers.

"Oh hell. I just stuck my big foot in my big mouth, didn't I?"

Jo opened her mouth to respond—with what, she didn't know—but before she could even form a thought Chase said, "It's okay, Jenn. No harm, no foul."

No harm, no foul? Now there was a stunning declaration of love.

Not that Jo expected Chase to even remotely make a stunning declaration of love. Affection, maybe. But love? They were still feeling each other out.

And up.

Jenn blushed. "Sorry, guys. Didn't mean to embarrass you. So. Um. Yay. How 'bout them Cowboys?"

Jo laughed. She couldn't help it. "It's okay. We're just…um…yeah."

Chase choked back a laugh beside her. She elbowed him in the ribs. "Ow! What was that for?"

"For laughing at me. Isn't this awkward for you, too?"

He shrugged. "Maybe. A little. But not really. I mean,

we're all adults here."

Jo turned and faced him. "It doesn't make you feel awkward that we got caught making out like a couple of high school kids, or that the person who caught us happens to be our mutual best friend who mistakenly assumed we're in love with each other?"

"Well, when you put it that way…" he paused, as if thinking about it. "No, not really. Why do you feel awkward?"

"Because, ah…" she stammered, "we…um…we don't…ah…know what we're doing here?"

Chase wiggled his eyebrows and gave her his best smile. "Oh, I think we know what we're doing, Jo."

Her ovaries wobbled.

"As fascinating as this is, I think we might be venturing into TMI territory here."

Oh hell. She'd forgotten Jenn was standing there. What kind of best friend forgot that her best friend was standing *right there*?

The kind of best friend who's lady parts are still shocked and awed and giving a standing ovation.

"Sorry, Jenn." Chase grinned at their friend, and those aforementioned lady parts tingled.

Good Lord, the man was potent.

Jenn's blush had finally faded. "No problem. Normally I would ask Jo for all of the down and dirty details anyway."

Chase raised an eyebrow.

"But I don't think I'll ask her this time. It would be like asking my brother about his sex life. Eww."

"Not that I would tell you anyway. Because, yeah. Awkward. And stuff." Jo said.

The back door opened again, and Owen stepped through this time. "Nobody told me the party had moved in here."

"We were just about to go outside," Jo said.

"After they finished making out," Jenn added.

Owen wiggled his eyebrows and raised his hand for a high five, which Chase did not return. "Too soon?"

Chase shook his head, Jo snorted, and Jenn grabbed a couple of beers from the fridge.

There's no place like home, Jo thought to herself as Chase snagged her hand and the four of them walked outside.

She almost stumbled when she realized the backyard wasn't empty. Matt was there—which she had expected—but so were Matt and Chase's parents. She tried to let go of Chase's hand, but instead of complying he just tightened his grasp.

She tugged.

He squeezed.

She wanted to glare at him but instead forced a smile on her face as Sarah Roberts approached and wrapped her in a hug. Of course, Chase let her hand go *then*.

She was going to kill him for not warning her.

"Jo, it's so good to see you," Sarah murmured into Jo's hair. "We've all missed you."

Jo's eyes stung at the warmth and sincerity in Sarah's voice, and for the first time she realized that Chase may not have been the only one who had been hurt by her actions. His parents had always been incredibly affectionate with her, and she'd returned that affection. In all her confusion and anxiety about Chase, though, she hadn't allowed herself to miss his parents, too.

Tears clogged her throat, and she was afraid that if she spoke she would fall apart, so she nodded instead and squeezed Sarah in return.

"Don't hog her, Sarah!" Bo Roberts' tone was gruff and teasing, causing Sarah to step back and slap at his arm before he, too, caught Jo up in a hug.

"We've missed you, Jolee Girl."

At the sound of the nickname only Bo had ever called her, Jo almost did lose it then. Luckily, Chase and Matt had gotten their height and size from their dad, and her face was buried in the older man's shoulder, hidden so that no one could see her composure slipping. She nodded, squeezed him back hard, and fought to regain her composure.

By the time he pulled back, she'd managed to pull herself back from the precipice and had plastered a smile on her face. She caught Chase watching her, noted the worry in his eyes and her smile softened into something that felt more natural.

Sarah and Bo stepped back, and Jo blindly reached for Chase's hand, needing something solid to keep her in the here and now rather than transporting her back twenty years to happy times and bittersweet memories.

"It's good to see y'all too." She smiled at his parents, meaning the words in a way she wouldn't have just five minutes earlier. It *was* good to see Sarah and Bo, and their warm, heartfelt greeting had quickly helped heal some of the bruises on her soul that she hadn't even acknowledged existed.

Awkwardly, she realized that Owen and Jenn had jumped into the pool and were apparently trying to give them some privacy. She didn't miss Jenn's smile or wink, though, before Owen pushed her under water. Matt was paying attention to something on his iPhone, but Jo didn't doubt for a second that he'd observed every second of that little exchange.

Chase's parents settled into chairs around a big, wooden table, and for the first time Jo was able to actually look at Chase's backyard. It was huge, with a high wooden privacy fence and lush greenery all around the edges. More privacy, she assumed. The deck they were standing on was raised a few feet above the ground, with steps leading on either side down to the yard. The pool was directly in front of the deck, and was a bit of a marvel in and of itself.

Rather than being surrounded by smooth concrete or tile, it was edged by the same limestone as the house. Kidney shaped, one end featured a diving boulder, and the other featured a waterfall that flowed into a separate, slightly elevated and smaller pool that Jo assumed was probably a hot tub. Banana plants and hibiscus surrounded the waterfall and hot tub, creating a shaded oasis that cried relaxation.

Even with the large pool, there was still plenty of yard—and green grass—for Winchester, who at the moment seemed perfectly content to snooze under the shade of the deck's covering.

The yard sloped downward towards the back, and to the right Jo could make out the vivid blue water of Lake Amistad. To her left, she could just see the peaks of the Sierra del Burro mountains across the border in Mexico. The view alone had been worth her earlier discomfort at seeing his parents.

Jo thought back to the conversation she and Jenn had had at Chili's a few weeks ago, and Jo realized Jenn hadn't been lying—Chase really had done well for himself.

She chose an empty deck chair and sat, enjoying the view and the ebb and flow of conversation around her.

"Penny for your thoughts." Chase leaned over and said quietly in her ear.

She smiled. "This is one hell of a view, Chase Roberts."

"It is, isn't it?"

He was looking at her rather than the lake or the mountains, and Jo felt a flustered blush creep up her neck. She nodded and he chuckled.

"You two really need to get a room," Matt muttered under his breath, never once looking up from his iPhone.

Chase kicked him in the leg, causing Matt to look up and glare before rolling his eyes and turning his attention back to his phone.

Jo was wondering how to subtlely ask Matt if everything was okay when Sarah reached out and took the phone from Matt's hands.

"Mom!"

"Matthew Tyler Roberts, you're putting this damned phone away right now and speaking to your friends and family rather than ignoring us."

Matt's expression turned flat, but even Jo could see the barely leashed tension that vibrated through his body. From the pool, Jenn snickered and said, "Matthew Tyler Roberts, huh? Somebody's in trouble."

Matt didn't look at Jenn, just got up and stormed inside. Jenn's expression clouded over briefly before she turned around and dove under the water. Sarah and Bo looked slightly uncomfortable, Chase looked confused, and Jo was torn between worry for Matt and his odd behavior and wanting to shake Jenn for being uncharacteristically bitchy. She squeezed Chase's hand and murmured, "I'm gonna go grab something to drink. You want anything?"

He shook his head and she got up and went inside. Matt was sitting on the couch, watching the ballgame. Jo grabbed a couple of Dr. Peppers from the fridge and headed into the living room, holding a cold maroon can out as a peace offering.

"These still your favorite?"

Matt looked up at her, took the can and mumbled, "Thanks."

"No problem." She hesitated, trying to figure out how to offer an ear without coming across as pushy.

"Jo, whatever it is you want to say, just say it."

She took a breath, studied the can still in her hand, before saying, "I know I have no point of reference for what you're dealing with right now, Matt, but if you need an ear I'm a pretty damned good listener."

For a second he looked almost angry, before once again sliding the mask over his face. "Thanks, Jo, but I'm fine."

No, you're not. She nodded her head. "Fair enough. The offer stands, though, Matt. And if not me, try to find someone to talk to."

"I'm not a fucking woman, Jo. I don't spend time sitting around talking about my goddamned feelings."

She barely refrained from rolling her eyes. God save her from emotionally stunted males. "Somehow that doesn't surprise me. By the way, when the hell are you going to get your hair fixed? You look like you should be coming out of a bar on Sixth Street."

Matt snorted, but his posture relaxed, which was what she'd been aiming for. "I don't know. I kinda like it."

"Going for the sympathy fuck, hey?"

Matt finally laughed out loud at that. "Honestly? No. My sense of humor's just fucked up enough that I find it funny."

"Oh, it's definitely funny. Anyway. I'm going to go back out. Maybe you should join us and apologize to your mom for being a dick."

"When did you get such a potty mouth?"

"Oh, somewhere between my senior year of college and dealing with teenage boys on a daily basis."

He shook his head. "You're braver than I am. You couldn't pay me to deal with teenagers all the time."

"It's definitely challenging. Anyway, I'm gonna go back outside. Enjoy your coke."

Matt looked down at the still unopened Dr. Pepper in his hand, at the TV, up at Jo and then back to the cold can in his hand. "I'll be back out in a few minutes. Just need to cool off a little bit."

Jo had a feeling he wasn't talking about from the heat, and wondered yet again what was going on between Jenn and Matt.

CHAPTER FOURTEEN

The next evening Jo found herself sitting around a limestone fire pit on the patio of the boys' ranch, a glass of wine in one hand and Chase's hand in the other. A feral hog was roasting in some sort of box called a Cajun cooker—Chase had explained to her how it worked, but she was still skeptical—and somewhere in the distance she heard the *yip yip yip* of a coyote.

Once again, she was struck by how beautiful it was out here. Growing up in the area, she had a love and appreciation for this part of Texas, where the Hill Country began to fade into desert and mountains. Living in central Texas had given her a love and appreciation of the greenery, water and rolling hills that defined Austin and the area surrounding it.

But there was just something about this area that called to her.

Jo leaned her head against the back of the wooden Adirondack chair, and looked up at the sky. The sun had dipped below the horizon, shades of purple and orange and black announcing its descent. The moon had begun to rise, and stars were starting to peep out. Already, there were hundreds upon hundreds of them. The sight took her breath away.

"Whatcha lookin' at?" Chase whispered in her ear.

"The stars. You don't get views like this in Austin."

She felt more than saw him shake his head. "No, you don't."

He leaned back, rested his head against the back of his chair, and squeezed her hand. She squeezed back.

"Did you like it? Living in Austin for college?"

Chase snorted. "What college kid wouldn't enjoy living in a place like Austin? Hot chicks, Sixth Street, live music all the time, great food. It was fun, I got to play ball for my dream school and got a top-notch education in the process. I actually stayed for a while after graduating, worked for a couple of IT startups. I got in with a commercial real estate firm, helping out with marketing and stuff. The more I learned, the more I enjoyed the business. I got my real estate license, learned a lot, stayed there long enough until I could take the broker's exam. Once I passed it, I moved back home and started my own commercial firm. What about you?"

"What about me?" Her tone was teasing.

"Do you like living in Austin?"

She shrugged and continued to look at the stars, which were increasing in numbers as the last bit of light left the sky. The fire crackled and popped, and she could hear Jenn, Owen and Matt inside the ranch house, laughing and arguing over a game of pool. "It's a beautiful city—as you know—and there's always something to do. I readily admit that I enjoy the convenience of having an HEB or a Walmart within a mile or two, and a Central Market or Whole Foods within reasonable distance. There's the food—Austin really does have some amazing restaurants. I love my women's shooting league, and working with kids and helping them."

"I sense a 'but' in there."

She smiled. "Yeah, I guess you could say there's a

'but'."

"So what is it?"

Jo sighed. "Honestly, the place gets on my nerves sometimes. Hell, most of the time. Traffic sucks. The cost of living keeps going up. The City Council's comprised of a bunch of idiots who don't listen to their constituents. And the city that used to actually be weird just isn't any longer, at least not organically. Any weird that exists is a bit manufactured at this point. And don't even get me started on the state of the public school system."

"I thought you loved your job."

"I do. Or, I love the kids. I love helping the kids. And I like most of my coworkers. It's the people at the top." She blew out a breath, took a drink of her wine. "I always have to keep my mouth shut about this stuff, y'know?"

He squeezed her hand. She rolled her head to the side, saw that he was looking at her. "So what has you so frustrated?"

She drew her brows together, trying to figure out where to begin. "Well, for one, it's getting more and more difficult to do my job. There's so much fear now of a lawsuit that all of us are working with one hand tied behind our backs. There's also the fact that the administration's become bloated. There are more administrators and non-teaching personnel than teachers and counselors. I'm talking admin assistants, marketing and PR folks, accounting, stuff like that. The superintendent keeps telling the community and the teachers that the coffers are dry, that there's no money for teacher raises, and it's been that way for the past four or five years. But then they turn around and remodel a football stadium or want to give iPads to high school students. Meanwhile, principals are trying to stuff thirty-five kids into a classroom that should only hold about twenty-five. We're losing teachers—good, veteran teachers—and the kids are suffering because of it. I just…I just keep putting one foot in front of the other and doing what I can to help my kids and to make sure they get out of there with clear goals for the future. But some days, especially the ones when I hear the superintendent on the radio or the news begging for more money, those days I get really, really tempted to walk."

"Why haven't you?"

Now there was a question she'd asked herself more than once. "Because I love the kids. I'm in a pretty good high school, we don't have the problems that some of the other schools in the area do with violence, drop outs, low test scores, etcetera. But we have our issues. I know the kids, know their families. I've been there long enough that I know a lot of their older siblings, their parents. Most of the time I'm helping them with class scheduling and college prep, but there are always the students who just need someone to talk to, or the trouble students that need someone to care. We had three kids commit suicide last semester. Three. There were days then that I wanted to walk away because my heart was breaking, but I couldn't. The kids needed me, and I guess in some ways I needed them. I also have good friends that I work with, some really great teachers. Besides, with this economy I've been a little scared to walk, especially since I've had job security, even if I have had one hand tied behind my back."

"And here I thought high school counselors just helped kids fill out scholarship applications." His tone was teasing.

She smiled. "Oh, I do plenty of that, too. Believe me. And I celebrate with every student and share their excitement when they get a scholarship offer or admission to their number one college. That's the fun part—helping the kids figure out what their goals are and how to get there."

Chase rolled his head so that he was once again looking up at the sky. She studied his profile, drinking in the angles and curves of his face, the dark stubble that shadowed his jaw.

"Have you ever thought about moving back home?"

Jo looked back up at the night sky, contemplating the stars and his question. "Until my parents died, not really. I had no desire to be anywhere near them. In the past few years the thought's kind of been there, especially with Gran getting on up in years. But I haven't really given it any serious consideration, even though Jenn's begged me more than a few times."

"So what exactly happened with you and your parents?"

She shrugged, felt a tinge of sadness where once she'd felt nothing but anger. "I left for college. At that point I had a full understanding of the type of person my mother was, and I'd never been close to Dad. Mom would call me every now and then, bitch about how Dad wasn't paying attention to her, ask me if I'd gained the Freshman Fifteen and what I was doing to make sure I didn't. She would sometimes send me care packages, but they weren't your typical care packages. Instead of homemade cookies and photos from home, or even laundry detergent and quarters, her care packages would be stuff like the latest fad diet book, a box of diet pills and a picture of the Super Model of the Day. She always wrote 'Perfection equals success!' on those damned pictures.

"I would throw the diet pills away—I'd tried some before and it was like I turned into Jessie Spano from that episode of Saved by the Bell. But by that point I was pretty deep into disordered eating, so I would read the stupid books. The pictures, I would hang up on my wall. I stopped talking to Mom a couple of months into therapy. I'd realized she was enabling the disorder, encouraging it, really. I tried to talk to her about it a few times, but she wouldn't listen, didn't realize that her behavior was damaging herself and me. We were on the phone one day, and she was laying into me pretty good, piling on the guilt trip and trying to push my buttons. I lost it, just got fed up, told her where she could stuff her diet pills, diet books and perfection, and that if she didn't make some changes and get help herself that we were done. She hung up on me, and I'd never felt so free in my life. I was a little sad, but mostly it was like I could breathe for the first time in a long time. We never spoke again after that. Gran came to my graduation, but that was it. I don't know if Dad even knew what had happened, since he never really talked to anyone. How those two met and got married and managed to create me I'll never know."

They sat there in silence, looking up at the stars. After several long moments she felt a wet nose nudging at her elbow. She looked down at Winchester and smiled, set her wine glass aside and scratched him between his ears. He rested his chin on her lap, his body wagging as he gave her puppy dog eyes.

Chase tugged on her hand, brought it to his lips and kissed her knuckles. "I'm sorry you had to go through all of that."

His simple gesture made her heart flutter in her chest a little bit. "It was what it was, and it's made me who I am today. In some ways, it makes me a better counselor."

"Still, though. I'm sorry you had to go through that. It sounds like you could have used a friend or two."

Her smile was tinged with regret as she turned her head and looked at him. "I could have, yeah. That was on my shoulders. I had Jenn, but she was up at North Texas, so we were relegated to talking on the phone and instant messaging each other. I had a couple of friends at Baylor who I trusted enough to let them know what was going on. Katie and Rebecca were really a good support system, and good roommates. We were all in the same program, so they kind of watched out for me, knew what to look for to make sure I wasn't going back down the ED rabbit hole."

"What exactly did you do? You said you didn't do diet pills. The most I know about eating disorders is anorexia and bulimia."

"It goes beyond those two, but they're the ones that get the most coverage, I guess you could say. For me, I started out bulimic, but hated puking. So I turned to restricting, and over exercised. Basically, I counted calories and was obsessed with the macros—carbs, proteins, fats. I was eating about nine hundred calories a day, and exercising for at least two hours a day. Every now and then I would lose it and go on a binge, which would sometimes make me sick. I would feel so guilty about the binge I would go right back to restricting and amp up the exercise." She shook her head at the memory of herself in high school and college.

"I was sick. I looked awful. My hair was falling out and I stopped having periods, which is probably more than you want to know. I *felt* awful, physically and mentally. Logically, I knew I was slowly killing myself, and in a way I didn't care. Therapy showed me a lot of things, including the fact that at that time, I truly didn't care. It wasn't that I wanted to die, or that I was suicidal, but that I wasn't sure why I should care about living. I was depressed, to say the least, along with having some anxiety issues. I'd felt out of control since junior high, or rather, that life was out of control. I was ashamed of my parents, and there really was no control of any sort in our household. If it wasn't for Gran, I honestly don't know what would have happened to me as a teen. She was the only stability I had. But I could control what I ate, and how much I exercised. Until I couldn't control it anymore, which was when I would binge. And that was probably way more than you ever wanted to know about the crazy inside my head."

Chase tugged on her hand. "Come here."

She lifted an eyebrow. "Where?"

"Just get up and come here."

She did, and he pulled her down, moved so that she was lying on her side next to him in the oversized chair. He ran a big hand up and down her back, dropped a kiss on the top of her head. She felt him breathe in and out, could hear his heartbeat under her ear. "I'm okay, Chase. I've dealt with all that crap and moved on. I haven't fallen into the trap of disordered eating in over eight years, and I'm healthy as a freaking horse."

He dropped another kiss on the top of her head. "I know."

"I appreciate the comforting, stud, but I don't need it," she said, keeping her tone light while trying to draw his thoughts out of him.

"I know you don't. But I do."

She raised an eyebrow and asked into his chest. "And why is that?"

Jo waited long moments while Chase inhaled and exhaled. She could almost hear his brain working. "All this time, I've been really pissed at you. I don't think you have any idea how mad I was at you when you stopped talking to me all of a sudden. I was a kid, and you'd hurt my feelings and that made me mad. I tried to hate you, but I couldn't. But God, Jo, I was so mad at you. There were so many times in high school, and especially in college, when I almost reached out to you. Those few times we saw each other in college? I was pissed. It seemed like everything was great for you and you were happy and didn't need me or our friendship. I was a chickenshit, and instead of asking you a question I didn't want the answer to, I acted like everything was fine, too. But it wasn't fine for either of us, I don't think."

Jo swirled the tip of an index finger over the soft cotton of his t-shirt, turning his words over in her brain. "The last time we saw each other in college, I'd been in therapy for a few months. At that point I'd been refeeding and was starting to get healthy again. My therapist had been gently nudging me for a few weeks, trying to get me to open up to people who didn't know about the ED. She knew about you, because in some ways the day I heard my mom on the phone with your dad was the straw that broke the camel's back, and she firmly believed I needed to talk to you and explain to you what had happened. When we bumped into each other that afternoon, I wanted to tell you everything. But I was scared, and there was some girl with you, so I didn't. I knew my therapist was right, but I couldn't get over the thought that telling you would mean losing you again."

He tightened the arm he had wrapped around her. "To be honest, I still have to fight not being pissed at you sometimes."

His words stung just a little. "I guess that's fair."

"It is and it isn't. You walked away, but I didn't put up any sort of fight, and I had plenty of chances."

"Chase, I've said it before and I'll say it again—we were dumb teenagers, and God do teenagers make really stupid mistakes."

He sighed. "That they do. I just wish I would have been there for you. I can't imagine what it must have been like going through that."

"And I wish you would have been there, too. But things happen for a reason, and life has a funny way of working itself out. We end up where we're supposed to be, when we're supposed to be there."

They cuddled in the chair for long moments, the silence broken only by the laughter of their friends from inside the house, and the sounds of nighttime in the desert around them. Overhead, millions of stars shone in the sky, and Jo could see the glow of the Milky Way. A sense of melancholy settled into her heart. She loved it here, not only on this ranch with Chase, but in Del Rio. In a month she would have to go back to Austin, start preparing for another school year, meet the new students that had transferred in, help others with scheduling. The thought made her heart feel heavy.

"I wish you didn't have to go back next month."

Had he been reading her mind? She snuggled closer, silently vowed to make the most she could out of the next month, and said, "Me too."

CHAPTER FIFTEEN

Chase rolled his head and glanced at the glowing numbers of the alarm clock beside the bed. 2:17.

Jo's warm body snuggled against his hip, and she sighed in her sleep. Trying not to disturb her, he sat up and rested his back against the head board. He'd slept in this room at the ranch multiple times, but tonight was the first time he'd ever had a woman in it.

He looked down at Jo, her blonde hair spilling in waves across the dark blue pillow case, illuminated by the moonlight filtering through the window. He knew that if he reached out and touched it, sifted a lock between his fingers, that it would be soft and silky to the touch. The citrusy scent of her shampoo teased his nostrils.

God, even her hair turned him on.

She shifted in her sleep, rolled over on to her back. Her breasts pushed against the tank top she'd put on before falling asleep. He grew hard. Just like that.

Chase looked away from Jo, stared into the darkness in front of him, and gently thumped his head against the headboard. His dick throbbed and his heart hurt. Hell of a combination, that.

He kept replaying their earlier conversation in his mind, the cool, almost detached way she'd talked about the past, and the completely not detached way he'd reacted. As he'd listened to her story, he'd felt such a mixture of emotions. Sadness for the young woman she'd been, dealing with demons he couldn't even begin to imagine; even though he'd had his own crap to deal with, he'd at least had a supportive family to help guide him through it. Sadness because her relationship with her parents had been even worse than he'd imagined. He couldn't understand how a parent would say or do the things her mom did, and couldn't fathom having a father so out of touch with reality and his family that he was completely clueless as to what was going on in his daughter's life or what his wife was doing behind his back. A little bit of anger.

To be fair, the anger had begun to fade the first time he'd kissed her, and by now it was pretty much gone. Every now and then it would rear its ugly head, but now it was more that he was angry that they were in a situation that was emotionally tricky at best. She had to leave in a month and go back to Austin—even though it seemed like she didn't exactly want to.

That alone was hellish, but when he added to it the fact that there were some things she probably had a right to know before they got in even deeper with each other… yeah, this situation was quickly spinning out of control.

He'd avoided Jenn's comment about he and Jo being in love, even though he'd known after the first time he'd kissed her out on the lake that his heart had been hers since he was fifteen. Hell, if he was being completely honest with himself, he'd loved Jo for as long as he could remember.

The organ in question almost ached at the thought of what she'd been through, the fact that in a month she would be gone again, and that if the distance didn't kill their relationship his secrets could. Her leaving he could respect; she had a career in Austin and couldn't exactly leave at the drop of a hat (not that he'd ever ask her to do that to begin with).

And then there were his secrets. Once he opened up and fully let her in, he wasn't sure what the future would hold for them, or if they could even have a future together. Sure, everything was all fun and games and hot sex right now, but what about six months, a year, two years down the road when things got bumpy?

Because it was going to get bumpy. It was going to happen whether he wanted it to or not, and it wouldn't be fair to drag Jo down that bumpy path alongside him. Would having someone to lean on be nice? Absolutely. But it wouldn't be fair, especially since he had absolutely no clue what the future had in store for him beyond the next few weeks.

His scars ached—phantom pains that sometimes popped up when his anxiety levels ratcheted up—and he rubbed at them, as much to sooth the ghost pain as himself.

Jo stirred beside him, opened her eyes and blinked a few times before sleepily asking, "You okay?"

Chase grabbed her hand and wrapped his fingers around hers. "Yeah, just couldn't sleep."

She sat up and rubbed the sleep out of her eyes, yawned. "Anything you want to talk about?"

I don't know how.

"Always the counselor, huh?" he forced himself to tease.

"It's hard to turn off. But right now I'm asking as your friend, not a counselor. What's wrong?"

"Come here." He tugged on her hand until she scooted towards the headboard. Jo rested her head on his shoulder, her back against the headboard. She fit beside him perfectly, which should have comforted him but instead scared the shit out of him.

They sat there like that for long moments, the silence of the night broken only by their breathing.

"So tell me, Chase Roberts, why can't you sleep?"

"I was just…thinking. That's all. Having a hard time getting my brain to shut up."

I'm going to lose you, and I don't think I can do that again.

"That happen often?"

"Often" would be an understatement.

He nodded, even though she couldn't see it. "Yeah. Has since I was a teen. I would get pretty bad insomnia sometimes, and would just stay awake at night thinking and worrying about things."

"Anxiety?"

"Correct." He was somewhat more comfortable talking about the past than the present and the future. At least the past was a known entity. "When Mom figured out what was going on with me, she marched me to the doctor and then a therapist—which I hated, by the way. The therapist diagnosed me with Generalized Anxiety Disorder and suspected I had a tinge of PTSD thrown in, which seemed stupid to me at the time. PTSD was for people who fought in wars and shit, not some kid who really had it pretty damned good, all things considered."

Her breath brushed against his chest when she spoke. "PTSD happens to all kinds of people who experience traumatic and frightening situations. After all the surgeries you went through as a kid, I can't blame you for having some anxiety issues and a little bit of PTSD." She snorted. "I probably didn't help much, either."

"My therapist thought that was the switch, so to speak, that flipped it all on. To this day I don't quite understand it. I survived six biopsies, two surgeries, and a fairly frightening medical diagnosis. I was fine through all of it. You stopped talking to me and it was like my world just stopped or something."

"Our brains don't always work in ways that make

sense. We have an amazing survival instinct, and do a great job protecting ourselves from the really bad shit. And then something that's bad, but not as bad as the real trauma, triggers a reaction and the floodgates open so to speak."

He twisted a lock of hair around his finger, memorizing the feel of the silky strands between his fingers, just in case he didn't get to do this for forever. "Yeah. So I started having panic attacks and was just constantly anxious. Couldn't sleep. Luckily we were able to do cognitive behavioral therapy to get it under control. I kind of refused to take meds, didn't want it screwing with my baseball career, especially since the only time my brain was quiet was when I was on the mound."

Not to mention the fact that the very unknown future had always loomed just there on the horizon, a grim shadow reminder of everything he could eventually have to face. Baseball—and the pitches he made—was the one area of his life where he felt he had any semblance of control.

She looked up at him. "Sports are amazing like that, aren't they?"

His eyes met hers. "Yeah, they are."

"So what has you feeling anxious tonight?"

"Who said I was anxious?"

She sat up. "Please. You don't have to hide it from me or act all macho. If anyone understands crazy, it's me."

The words were there, pushing at his brain and his heart, lying in wait on his tongue, waiting to be spoken. As he looked into those clear green eyes he felt as though he were falling, falling, down into a fathomless ocean and only she was there. In her eyes he saw understanding, compassion, friendship and what he hoped like hell was love.

The words got stuck, though, and Chase hated himself just a little bit for not being able to say them, to tell her the truth and lay it all out on the line—the good, the bad, and the really fucking ugly. But she was leaving in a month. What good would it do to spill his heart and have it broken again?

Still, though, if he was too chickenshit to tell her all of the words, he could at least show her some of them.

~~*~~

Jo saw the change in his eyes, felt it in the tension coiling through his body, seconds before his lips were on hers. Firm, insistent and yet oh so patient. She knew what he was doing, resorting to sex to deflect talking about his feelings. She couldn't exactly complain about it, though, since in a way she'd been doing the same thing for the past few days.

So she kissed him back, tangled her tongue with his, let him draw her leg over his so that she was straddling him. Those hands that she was so utterly fascinated with drew her tank top over her head and tossed it somewhere over her shoulder. When his mouth closed around one of her nipples, all of her thoughts scattered and the only thing that mattered was his mouth and his hands and him.

Chase.

She sighed his name as he teased her breasts before trailing kisses back up her chest to her neck, along her jawline. His hands cupped her hips, the fingers sliding under the waistband of her panties. He guided her back, so that she was lying down, her head at the foot of the bed, before he slowly drew the scrap of pink lace down her legs and off her body.

He touched her everywhere. Slowly. Reverently. Kissed her slowly, thoroughly, like she was a dessert he wanted to savor. She could feel her heart beating, like the slow, seductive *thump thump* of a sexy love song.

Moonlight filtered through the window, casting Chase's body in light and shadow as his mouth moved from hers and down her body. He watched her face as he gently palmed her breasts. His melted chocolate eyes were intense, filled with an emotion Jo knew all too well.

"Oh, Chase." She reached out and palmed his cheek. He closed his eyes, drew in a breath. She didn't know what kind of demon was chasing him, but she had the overwhelming urge to make it all better, whatever it was.

Jo sat up, so that they were face to face. She kissed his nose, his forehead, his jawline, pressed her lips to his before simply sitting there, forehead to forehead, nose to nose. Blindly, she reached for his hands, tangled their fingers together.

He kissed her again, and she let him, even though there were so many things she wanted—needed—to say. Chase untangled a hand from hers, brought it up to cup the back of her head, gently at first and then harder as his fingers dug into her scalp.

As if in a dream, she vaguely heard music coming from somewhere down the hall. Apparently they weren't the only ones who couldn't sleep, she mused as the strains of a fiddle filtered into their bedroom, followed by lyrics filled with longing for a lover's touch. A little longer. Just a little bit longer.

He kissed her again as the music softly played somewhere in the house, the far away sound combined with the ethereal moonlight filtering in through the window, making Jo feel almost as if she were in a dream. She rose up onto her knees, scooted forward so that she was straddling his hips. She could feel his erection straining against his boxers and she rubbed herself against him, wanting, no, needing more.

She really couldn't get enough of him.

Somehow he managed to get his boxers off without breaking their kiss. She teased them both, rubbing against him, her body on fire and heart racing. He broke the kiss and caught her gaze with his own before taking matters into his own hands and guiding his length into her.

Slowly, she sank down, taking him inch by tortuous inch until he was buried to the hilt. Their position made hard, deep thrusts impossible, but the way that he tilted his hips slowly against hers was a friction better than anything she ever could have imagined. She dug her fingers into his shoulders, wrapped her legs around his waist as his hands gripped her hips and moved her body with his in slow, sensual strokes.

Her orgasm built slowly, like a wave gathering force as it neared the shoreline. Her eyelids fluttered closed, and Chase murmured, "Stay with me. Look at me, Jo."

She opened her eyes, looked into his and broke.

~~*~~

Chase lay there, wrung out, emotionally if not physically drained. Jo's head rested on his chest, her even breathing a soothing balm. God, she had him tied up in knots.

She feathered a kiss against his chest, her lips warm and soft on his skin.

I love you.

She glanced up at him.

Had he said that out loud?

Apparently not, since she snuggled back up against him, her eyes no longer searching his face.

"I love you, Chase."

Her whisper was so quiet he wasn't sure she'd actually said it. His heart skipped a beat, all the same.

"Did you just…"

She sat up and looked at him. "Yeah, I did."

He reached out, tucked a strand of hair behind her ear. Kissed her forehead and exhaled slowly, no longer able to hide this particular truth that had been staring him in the face for weeks…hell, years. This, at least, he could admit to, even if it was unfair to both of them. "I love you too."

She smiled, kissed him briefly and then burst into tears. What the fuck?

"Um, Jo? Don't cry, honey. You're not supposed to cry when a man tells you he loves you."

She swiped at the tears streaming down her cheeks and chuckled. "They're happy tears. Well, happy and a little sad. Kind of bittersweet."

"Okay, happy tears I can deal with. I think." Maybe. Despite having Jenn as a best friend all these years, tears were something he'd never quite been good at dealing with.

She reached across his body and snagged a tissue out of the box on the nightstand before blowing her nose. "I'm sorry. I didn't mean to freak you out."

He rubbed her back, trying to comfort her while trying to calm his racing heart at the same time. Maybe he shouldn't have told her, even though the words had been there, pushing to get out. Maybe it was unfair of him to want to keep her for forever, considering he wasn't exactly sure what his forever entailed. And maybe this was the woman who'd been made just for him.

The anxiety had returned, but he forced himself to focus on Jo. She was more important right now than his stupid panicky brain. And even though he'd never told another woman he loved her, he was pretty sure this was one of those Really Big Moments that needed to be handled just right.

For the first time in a long time he wished he had a baseball in his hand and a pitcher's mound under his feet. He knew what to do in that situation. But this? In this he felt a little clueless.

"You just scared me a bit. First time I tell a woman I love her and she bursts into tears. It's great for the ego," he teased.

She laughed and mopped at her eyes with a fresh tissue. "I don't know why I started crying like that, it's just…fuck, Chase, what are we going to do?"

God, she had no idea what she was asking, did she?

Chase wrapped an arm around her and drew her to his side, kissed the top of her head. "We'll figure it out. We're adults, not stupid teenagers anymore. We can figure it out."

I hope we can.

"I don't want to lose you again."

Oh, God, you're killing me here.

"Me either, honey."

CHAPTER SIXTEEN

Over the course of the next two weeks, Jo acted like a woman possessed. Her time was split pretty evenly between Gran and Chase.

During the day she stayed with Gran, keeping her company and helping as needed. Fortunately, Gran was mending quite nicely and didn't really need Jo around anymore, and had actually encouraged her to spend more time with Chase.

Then there was Chase. Evenings and nights were spent with him. Sometimes they would meet Owen and Jenn somewhere for supper or drinks, but for the most part once they got home—weirdly, that's how she was thinking of Chase's house these days—they didn't leave until the next morning when Chase had to go to work and Jo went to go see Gran. They talked, made each other laugh, and made love. Everywhere.

But when Matt walked in on them fooling around in the kitchen, Jo took it as a sign that maybe they should be a bit more discreet.

Or at the very least, maybe they should only make use of the big kitchen island when they knew for certain that Matt was not in the house.

"Jesus, you two, get a fucking room," Matt muttered as

he backed out of the room.

Chase rested his forehead against Jo's and chuckled. "Well, that's embarrassing."

Jo could feel her cheeks turning pink. "To say the least."

Chase backed away from the kitchen island and helped Jo down. She straightened her clothes and pulled her hair back into a ponytail as Chase turned to the stove and the pot of pasta that was dangerously close to boiling over.

"You need help with anything?" She asked as she wrapped her arms around his waist from behind.

Chase turned his head and pecked her on the lips before turning back to the pasta. "This is almost done."

The sound of the front door slamming reverberated through the house, and Jo raised an eyebrow. "I guess Matt *is* done."

Matt had finally been cleared to drive the Monday after the Fourth, but hadn't seemed to be enjoying his newfound freedom as much as they'd expected. Instead of taking off and getting out of the house like everyone had figured he would, Matt had continued to stick to Chase's, iPhone glued to his hand or his ear. The only time he really seemed to leave was in the evenings, when Jo was at the house, and they had no clue where he'd been going. They had, however, been grateful for the privacy.

Chase shrugged. "He needs to get out and stay off of Twitter. I even threatened to throw his phone and laptop in the pool the other day. He just laughed."

"I take it the rumors aren't getting any better?"

Over the past couple of weeks, rumors about the future of Matt's career had been coming fast and furious. He'd tried to keep them to himself, but the team had had to address the news reports at some point. Matt hadn't been told by the team that he'd been let go, but it had become obvious that someone was feeding information to national sports news outlets.

"Unfortunately, no. I think that's partially why he's stayed cooped up. Love him or hate him, Matt's a proud guy and baseball is his life."

Jo stepped away and grabbed plates from a cabinet. "He's thirty-five, though. He has to realize his career's almost over."

Chase lifted the pot of pasta off the stove top and took it over to the sink. As he dumped it into a strainer he said, "You would think so. But I don't know how much thought Matt's given it."

Jo heard the worry in Chase's voice, and was worried herself. It was hard not to—she'd known Matt as long as she'd known Chase, and he *was* a proud man. She couldn't imagine what it must be like, having your entire career and future dissected and discussed in such a public manner. "He has to have given it some thought. He's not stupid."

Jo watched as Chase dumped the drained pasta into a bowl, added homemade meat sauce and stirred.

"No, he's not stupid."

Chase grabbed a serving spoon from the crock beside the stove, and Jo could feel tension radiating off of him in waves. The sudden change was disconcerting. "You okay?"

Chase scooped pasta onto his plate and sighed. "I'm fine, Jo. Just frustrated. Matt's future isn't the only one up in the air. It feels like everything is up in the air."

"Right. It feels like something else, though. You were fine until we started talking about Matt and his Twitter woes."

Chase hesitated, and Jo's counselor's brain kicked into high gear. She knew Chase. Loved him. Was absolutely certain that something about all of the false—or at least false-for-now—reports about Matt was bothering him.

"I just...I know how tough it can be, having a bunch of false and negative crap out there about you. The internet's a great thing, but lots of people will use it for evil, to spread lies, to make themselves feel better, with no regard to how their words and actions will impact the people they're lying about." He picked up his plate and moved to the back door and the patio, where they ate supper most evenings.

She scooped some pasta onto her own plate, grabbed her drink and followed him outside. "You sound like you have some personal experience with that."

Chase snorted, wouldn't meet her eyes. Suddenly, Jo remembered a conversation she and Jenn had had when she'd first gotten back to town. Jenn had suggested that Jo should Google Chase, but she'd never gotten around to it, hadn't had the time nor the inclination.

"I do."

"So if I were to Google you, Chase Roberts, what would I find?" she asked casually as she took her seat. Chase almost choked on the water he'd just swallowed.

Jo could see the internal debate in his eyes, knew he was deciding what to tell her and how. After a couple of minutes that felt more like an hour, he finally answered. "It would depend on how deep you dove, honestly. The first page or so of search results is the stuff I want people to see—my business website, professional and personal social media accounts, a couple of YouTube clips of me pitching in college, that sort of thing. The second page is good stuff, too. Old news articles, reviews, interviews, some stuff from when I pitched in college. Once you get to the third page, though, things start to get dicey."

He grimaced, and Jo squeezed his knee, casually chewed and swallowed before asking, "What's on page three?"

"It's embarrassing, really. Do you know what a jersey chaser is?"

"Uh, no."

Chase gave up all pretense of eating and set his fork

down before continuing. "Well, a jersey chaser is someone who's only interested in athletes. Kind of like groupies for baseball or football, soccer, lacrosse."

"So like a buckle bunny?" Jo asked, referring to women who chased after bull riders.

"Yeah, like a buckle bunny. These women can be very forward, to put it mildly, and very vocal about their exploits. The infamous Brett Favre cell phone photos? Those are nothing compared to some of the details jersey chasers share with the world.

"At any rate, when you're an athlete you get kind of used to chicks hanging around all the time. It starts in high school, really, and just gets worse from there, especially if you play a high-profile position."

"Like a pitcher," Jo said.

Chase nodded. "Like a pitcher. And if you happen to have a sibling who's also a well-known athlete, the jersey chasers somehow seem to get even worse. I'd seen it with a couple of my friends in college, managed to stay away from it myself. When Matt made it to the Bigs, though, suddenly there was this spotlight on me for my entire senior year of college. Nevermind the fact that I knew I didn't have a future in the majors, and had no desire to spend the next ten years in the minors barely getting by, the girls still chased after me."

"I'm pretty sure they would have chased after you anyway, baseball or no. You're kind of hot, babe."

Chase laughed, tunneled his fingers through his hair in embarrassment. "Thanks, honey. So, yeah. I'll admit that I made some not so great decisions in college."

"Isn't that what college is for?" she asked.

"Partially, yeah, I guess. I figured I should enjoy the ride while it lasted, y'know. I was in my early twenties and knew that the attention and women throwing themselves at me wouldn't last. So I had fun while I could and figured that was that."

"There's nothing wrong with that, y'know."

"I know. The college stuff was…whatever. It was college. It's the stuff that happened *after* college that's been embarrassing."

Jo raised an eyebrow. "Did they keep chasing after you?"

Chase leaned back in his chair, sighed. "Yes, especially while I was in Austin. I don't know if you've noticed this, but Austinites—especially Texas fans—tend to love their former athletes. There's definitely a bit of hero-worship going on, and to be honest, I'm not complaining since my name and my status as a former athlete helped me get my foot in the door. I worked my ass off and that helped me become successful, but I'm not stupid enough to think that my name had nothing to do with it. The problem is that a lot of women also love and hero worship former athletes. There's a certain segment of women who don't care what your status is—third string, retired, starting quarterback— while there's another segment that will only date the elite guys."

"I'm guessing you're using the word 'date' loosely?"

"Absolutely. More like wham bam thank you mam, let me go post this all over the internet now."

Jo winced. "So what happened after you graduated?"

"You know the important parts. There were the women, though, more right after I graduated, and then slowly dwindling in numbers as time went by. Every time Matt would make the news, though, there would be this weird surge in attention on me. It was strange, and it took me a while to put two and two together. Even after I moved back home, it continued. Thankfully, the attention wasn't as bad, but after the World Series run a couple of years ago it was like I couldn't chase them away. For months I had women hitting on me, stopping by the office, even had a couple show up here. Poor Kim kept opening mail and finding panties and suggestive notes. I didn't respond at all, except to call the cops a few times to have women removed from work and here, but a couple of them decided to go ahead and blab online and claim they'd had sex with me. It was raunchy stuff, too. I'd been seeing someone at the time—for a while, off and on, nothing serious. She knew about the jersey chasers, didn't seem to care. And then the pictures happened."

"Oh, no." She reached out and took Chase's hand, twined their fingers together and squeezed. She had a bad feeling where this was going, if the tone of his voice and the grim set of his jaw were any indication.

He squeezed her hand back, sighed. "Yeah. She took some video with her cell one night. I didn't know, didn't see it and wouldn't have ever suspected her of it. She'd also been taking pictures of me for a while, again, without me knowing, mostly because she would take them while I was asleep or in the shower. She went to one of the more popular blogs that sports groupies follow and gave them all the dirty details, video and pics included. It wouldn't have been so bad if the story had stayed confined to that one website, but it didn't. It got tweeted. A couple of the photos were posted to Instagram. The video was uploaded and shared. For some stupid reason *Deadspin* picked it up. I guess maybe because I'm Matt Roberts' little brother, or maybe because their writers have a weird fascination with athlete's dicks, but they picked it up and made the rounds again. After that, a handful of women started posting to message boards and blogs, claiming they'd also had sex with me—even though they hadn't and I'd never even met them—and used the original pics to back their stories up. One of the pics had a good look at the scars, and a few of them really focused on that. One of them claimed to have been turned off by them, but said she fucked me anyway because she felt sorry for me. Another said they were a turn-on, and this one chick…God, she was a piece of work…she intimated that I'd gotten them while she and I had been participating in a particularly rough BDSM role-playing session."

Chase shook his head, pinched the bridge of his nose with his free fingers. "It was all so ridiculous. I hired an attorney, pressed charges. We were able to get the video and photos taken down, and some of the websites took the stories down after we threatened to sue. After some digging, we found out that the same women who were claiming to have slept with me had been trying to screw Matt and had been unsuccessful. Well, one of them had been successful, and apparently just wanted go for a double."

"That's disturbing and disgusting."

"Tell me about it. The whole thing rattled me for a while. It took me almost a year to go on a date, and that was with someone Jenn set me up with who had no interest in sports, didn't know who Matt was and had never watched a baseball game in her life."

"So what happened to her?"

"One of her friends found out she'd gone on a couple of dates with me and decided to show her a couple of the websites that are still active. She ended it, said she couldn't date an amateur porn star."

Jo laughed, couldn't help it, really. "Amateur porn star? Please. You were a victim, not a porn star."

"I know. It wouldn't have lasted with her, anyway. She was nice and all, but the…spark, I guess…just wasn't there."

She smiled and winked. "Well, I'm glad for that part at least. As for the other stuff? It sucks, but I know you're not that guy. Maybe in college and in your younger and wilder days. But now? You're not that guy."

"It's just embarrassing, more than anything. My mom saw some of those websites, for crying out loud."

"Seriously?"

"Yes. She had a Google alert set up so that any time there was news about Matt she got it—I'm still trying to decide if that's weird or just a really loving mom who cares about her kid, by the way—so when the *Deadspin* article broke she opened it, never thinking I and my dick would somehow be involved."

"That must have been quite the shock for your mom."

"Oh yes. That was a particularly uncomfortable phone call."

They sat in silence, neither of them moving to finish their now cool suppers. Jo thought about her students, how easy it would be for some girls to get caught up in chasing after the star quarterback or the hotshot basketball player, and how cell phones and social media have made public humiliation much easier.

"Over the past couple of years I've had to take professional development courses on how to handle revenge porn cases. What happened to you sounds eerily like that, but not quite."

Chase leaned forward and grabbed his fork. "Revenge porn?"

Jo nodded. "Basically, with so many people having cell phones and social media accounts these days, teenagers— and adults, to be fair—have found it easier to share private photos with one another. You know how it goes, girl and guy are dating, guy asks girl if he can have some nude photos of her, girl sends guy said nude photos, guy shows said photos to his friends, girl gets upset, Daddy gets pissed, and guy and girl break up. There have been some cases where the guy has gone on to post those photos to amateur porn sites, social media accounts, stuff like that, without the girl's consent. The guy's mad at her, or just an immature douche, or both. The problem is that a lot of times the guys will share personal information about the girl—her name, phone number, social media accounts, email and physical addresses. All kinds of stuff. I've had a couple of students who have been victims, and it's been hard, seeing them deal with it. They're young, y'know, and teens don't always think through to the consequences of their actions, and they sure don't expect to have their trust broken like that. I've seen families spend thousands upon thousands of dollars to get the photos and information removed, but as I'm sure you know, it's almost impossible to completely erase anything off the internet."

"The internet is forever," Chase murmured.

"Exactly. I can't imagine having my trust betrayed like that. Then again, I also can't imagine what would drive someone to do something like that in the first place. These women—they'll seriously go that far?"

"Unfortunately, yes. There are some that will stalk guys on social media, at the ballpark or the stadium—wherever and whatever sport—find out their home addresses, hit on them in bars with their husbands present. It's unsettling."

Jo had picked up her fork, and set it back down. "Wives will literally hit on athletes in front of their husbands? What kind of marriage is that?"

"Not much of one." He sipped his beer. "I'm not going to get into those stories—I'm not privy to a lot of them, honestly—but if you ever get a chance to meet Matt's agent, Darrin, he has a ton of stories he could tell you."

"I'm not sure I want to hear them."

Chase laughed. "Honestly? They're so disturbing all you can really do is laugh, and thank God your life is normal."

CHAPTER SEVENTEEN

Normal.

Six letters.

A fairly simple word.

Something his life had kind of been just a week ago.

Something his life would never be again.

"We've known this was coming, Chase. Your BUN and creatinine have been slowly climbing over the past year. Your GFR's dropped dramatically—from forty to twenty-eight over the past six months. Your blood pressure's slowly crept up and you're anemic."

Chase nodded. This was nothing he and Dr. Gupta hadn't talked about in the past, and shouldn't have come as such a shock. He'd had a feeling it was coming, had known he'd been pushing himself a little harder than he should have been and had been a little more tired than usual.

"So what's next?"

Not that he didn't know, but it helped to discuss the game plan with his nephrologist.

Dr. Gupta sat down on his stool, clasped his hands on his knees and sighed. "Well, you're officially in stage four Chronic Kidney Disease. The double-edged sword here is that it's not as bad as it could be, but it does mean we need to begin discussing dialysis and transplant options, so that we're fully prepared by the time you're in end stage renal failure. You won't be eligible for a transplant until your GFR drops to twenty, so we'll need to monitor that closely over the coming months. The good news—if you want to look at it that way—is that you don't have to be completely in end stage renal failure in order to be eligible for a transplant, which means you may never have to go on dialysis."

Chase swallowed past the lump on his throat. He'd known this was coming—they'd known this was a possibility since he was a teen and he'd had two ureteral reimplantations to fix the connection between his ureter and his kidneys. They'd discovered the scarring on his kidneys when he was fourteen, and the doctors had warned him and his parents then that Chronic Kidney Disease and eventually End Stage Renal Failure were very real possibilities.

Unfortunately, CKD was a possibility that had become a reality. Shortly after he'd graduated from college, he'd had an annual check-up and had found out then that he was in stage two Chronic Kidney Disease. He'd been able to manage it and slow the process over the past ten years with diet and exercise, but over the past year his body had apparently decided to take a turn for the worse.

"So what are my immediate next steps?"

Dr. Gupta nodded. "I know you have all of the literature, and that we've talked about this before, but as for immediate next steps, I would say that I would like to get you in with a dietician. I know you eat healthy and that you're very active, you're still urinating so I'm not going to restrict your fluids just yet. But I would like you to meet with the dietician just to go over the renal diet so that you have some basic guidelines. That being said, your potassium and phosphorus levels are still in the okay range, so I'm not going to put you on any binders or tell you start restricting those things just yet."

Binders were pills that basically helped your body balance out your phosphorus levels. He knew that because, yeah, he'd done his research.

"I'm guessing I do need to start watching other stuff, though, like Gatorade, beer, etc.?"

"Yes, stay off the Gatorade. One beer every now and then probably won't hurt you at this point, just listen to your body. How much do you drink on a regular basis now?"

"Maybe three or four a week." He almost always limited himself to one beer at a time. Just the one, and then he switched to water.

Dr. Gupta nodded. "Good. Good. How about we drop that down to one or two a week?"

"I'm fine with that."

"No calcium supplements, or anything that has added calcium in it—your parathyroid seems to be working okay right now, but if your phosphorus levels start to increase added calcium could cause a lot of problems. The dietician may advise you to adopt a slightly lower protein diet, so that a lot of protein waste isn't building up in your body, since your kidneys aren't filtering protein anywhere near as well as they were even six months ago. Again, follow her advice but listen to your body—you're a lot more active than the typical CKD patient, and that will end up working in your favor, I think."

Chase fought to grab one of the many thoughts spinning through his head at the moment. "So I know we've briefly talked about this before, and as you just said, I may not even have to go on dialysis if I can get a kidney transplant fairly quickly, but do you think I should go ahead and prepare for not being able to find a live donor? The stats I've been seeing say that the wait time in Texas is currently over five years if you're on the transplant waiting list."

"The time varies depending on blood type, but yes, the average is just over five years, which is just one of the reasons why we always encourage a live donation if possible."

"Right, but what if I can't find a live donor?" Furthermore, how did he even *ask* someone to just give him a kidney?

"Then we would need to look at dialysis options. If you choose hemodialysis I would suggest going ahead and getting a fistula before you need dialysis—catheters can be dangerous and are not optimal."

"I guess there's no point in asking if you're sure I'm heading towards a transplant?"

The doctor smiled thinly and shook his head, removed his reading glasses and set them aside. "Unfortunately, no. You'd been doing very well, but the rapid decline of your kidneys over the past six months points towards a slide to end stage renal failure."

"Any idea what's caused them to decline so suddenly?"

Dr. Gupta shrugged. "It's very hard to tell. You do all of the right things, so this is nothing that's your fault. Your kidneys have been fighting since you were a child. You're now thirty-three. They can only take so much."

Chase nodded.

"I would also like to start seeing you every three months. A week before you come in the next time I'll need you to have bloodwork done, along with a twenty-four hour urine collection."

Great. He hated peeing into those damned urinals.

"Any other questions?"

"Not really, Dr. Gupta. I've been researching this for years."

How do I break the news to Mom and Dad? Shit, how do I break this to Jo?

~~*~~

"You okay? You seem like you're a million miles away," Jo asked over dinner.

Chase's smile didn't quite reach his eyes. "Yeah, sorry. Just have a lot on my mind."

She reached across the table and took his hand. "Anything you want to talk about?"

He looked down at the table and blew out a deep breath. A sense of foreboding snaked up her spine.

"Chase, what's wrong? You're kinda making me nervous here."

"What happens when you go back to Austin?"

"What do you mean?"

"I mean, what happens when you go back to Austin? How do we know the long distance thing will work? Hell, we haven't really even talked about what happens come August. I think I've just assumed we would stay together and work something out."

"Why wouldn't we stay together and work something out?"

He shrugged. "I don't know. But I don't know that we could, either. I mean, what's our game plan?"

"To be honest, I haven't really thought that far ahead."

"Is that necessarily what we want to do? Just let things go where they may with no planning or thought?"

"It's a relationship, Chase, not a baseball game. This is you and me, not the bottom of the ninth with one out and a runner on third while down by one."

Chase leaned towards her, palms pressed flat on the tabletop, his eyes frantically searching her face as he quietly said, "You don't think I don't know that, Jo? I've already lost you once, I don't think I can do it again."

She reached out and cupped his cheek. "Chase, honey, you're not going to lose me again."

"How do you know that?" The desperation in his voice

made her want to cry.

I don't.

~~*~~

Three days later, Chase found himself more grateful than ever for Owen's unexpected arrival in his office.

"What's up?" he asked.

Owen collapsed into the chair on the other side of Chase's desk, groaned and tipped his head back before running a hand over his face.

"It's been the shittiest of shitty weeks."

Tell me about it.

Chase tossed his pen on to his desk and leaned back in his chair. "What happened?"

"More like what didn't happen. I swear, it's been the summer of shitty shit. Seems like every week it's something new. Broken hands from fighting. Blown tires. Lost loads. Contractors not delivering supplies on time. This week my foreman was out for a few days after his wife had baby number four. Whatever. We knew it was coming and had prepared. What I hadn't prepared for was two of my guys quitting with no notice and finding out another had completely forged his ID, right down to the fake social security card that looked real. Imagine my surprise this morning when I found out he was sitting in jail after trying to flee from border patrol with a truck full of people who did not have fake IDs yet."

"Jesus. Sounds like you've had almost as bad a week as I have."

"Oh? What's up with you?"

Chase shook his head, not sure where to start or if he really even wanted to. "Well, I found out on Monday I'm in stage four CKD and will need a transplant sooner rather than later. Oh, and Jo and I haven't talked in three days."

"Okay, first, I'm sorry, man, about the transplant. Even though you knew it was coming, that can't be easy to hear.

Second, why aren't you and Jo talking? Last I saw the two of you were stuck to each other like frickin' glue."

"I don't know, really. The transplant thing has me freaked out. The long-distance thing has me worried. Either of those two alone isn't exactly great, but you throw them together and it's just one big clusterfuck. So I've been doing the manly thing and avoiding her because, hey, I don't know what else to do."

Owen shrugged. "You'll figure it out. But it sounds like you need some R&R just as much as I do. You up for going up to the ranch and slinging some lead? The crew's at a standstill until next week anyway."

It was on the tip of his tongue to say "no," but then Chase thought about it and said, "Why not? Let me text Daniel and see if he needs us to grab anything for him before we head out."

Owen nodded before standing. "I'm gonna swing by the house, take a shower and throw a bag together real quick. Meet at your place in an hour?"

"Sounds good," Chase said, his hand reaching for his phone to shoot Daniel a quick text. Done with that, he stared at his phone for long moments before pulling up Jo's name and messaging her, too.

~~*~~

Chase: Going up to the ranch with Owen for a day or two. Get in some range time. Love you.

Jo looked at the message from Chase and sighed. Well, at least he was texting her now.

Her heart in her throat, she responded to Chase's text.

Jo: Have fun. Love you, too.

That was simple and breezy and no pressure, right? Right?

She thunked her head against Gran's refrigerator. Jesus, she was acting like a seventeen-year-old.

She shook her head in an attempt to clear it, and then

decided to text Jenn.

Jo: Apparently Chase and Owen are going up to the ranch for a couple of days. Girls' night?

Jenn: Sure. Miguel's then drinks somewhere not public?

Jo shook her head. She wasn't entirely sure what was going on with Jenn, but maybe tonight she'd finally get some answers.

Jo: No problem. You wanna come over to Gran's? We can figure out something from there.

Jenn: Or we could just party with Gran. ;-) Be there in a few.

Jo snorted. Party with Gran? Because that was her idea of fun.

Like having your boyfriend distance himself and virtually ignore you for three days is your idea of fun, too.

~~*~~

About an hour later, Jo and Jenn were seated at a corner table at Miguel's.

"Alright, so why don't you want to have drinks somewhere public?" Jo asked without preamble.

Jenn sighed and blew a curl out of her eyes. "Because people are driving me freaking crazy."

"Like who?"

Jenn dropped her head into her hands. "Everybody."

Jo lifted an eyebrow. "Everybody?"

Her best friend groaned. "Okay, not everybody. Mostly my parents and Matt."

Jo wasn't sure where to begin, but since worrying about Jenn's life seemed like a much better idea right now than worrying about her own, she asked, "What's up with your parents?"

Before Jenn could respond, their waiter arrived to take their drink order. They both asked for sweet tea. Jenn waited for the teenager to leave.

"I think I taught him a few years ago. That makes me feel old."

Jo laughed. "Nuh uh. You're not getting away with changing the subject."

Jenn rolled her eyes. "Fine. My parents are just…" Jenn's hands fluttered in the air. "They're crazy. Mom called me this morning to tell me they'd been contacted by that Doomsday Preppers show and they're thinking about filming an episode. What would my principal think if he found out my family's a bunch of nut job preppers?"

"Wait." Jo held up a hand. "They're that far into it?" Last she'd heard, the McDonnel's had moved out towards Sanderson after selling their family home and purchasing five hundred acres in the middle of nowhere. She knew they were worried about the economy and were worried about an economic collapse, but she hadn't realized they'd gone that far down the rabbit hole.

Jenn nodded, her expression one of misery. "Unfortunately, yes. It's gotten steadily worse over the past year. They're at the point where they have weekly drills and play renegade soldier."

Their waiter returned, set their teas down and took their order. Neither of them bothered to look at the menu— this was clearly a conversation that called for enchiladas. As soon as the teenager was gone, Jo asked, "Weekly drills?"

Jenn groaned. "Yes. They get out their guns, dress up in desert camo and act as if their compound is under siege."

"Compound as in Branch Dividian or compound as in Kennedy?"

"Compound as in off the grid shipping container fortress. They have a landline and satellite cable and internet. That's it."

"Wow. I didn't realize they'd gone that far off the deep end."

"Yeah. It's ridiculous. Mom keeps ordering emergency food kits and other survival stuff and sending them to my house. I've just been stashing it all in the spare bedroom, figuring I'll ship them to Mom and Dad eventually, or use them as a science experiment or something. Matt happened to be there one day for the latest shipment, and it was embarrassing to say the least."

"Wait. Matt knows your family's a bunch of preppers? What was Matt doing at your place? I thought you guys hated each other."

Before Jo could get an answer, their waiter returned with their food. Instead of answering Jo's question once he left, Jenn dove into her enchiladas.

"Seriously? You're going to drop that on me and then not answer my question?" Jo asked.

Jenn swallowed before saying. "Sorry, I'm hungry, and don't know where to begin."

"How about, I don't know, at the beginning?"

Jo watched as Jenn took a deep breath and clearly tried to gather her thoughts. "I don't know that Matt and I hate each other. There was just some…animosity there."

Animosity or something else? Jo wondered. Jenn wasn't Matt's usual type, and Matt wasn't Jenn's usual type, but stranger things had happened.

"At any rate, he's been coming over to my place in the evenings here lately, so you and Chase can have some privacy. He was there that day and now he thinks it's funny to give me a hard time about it."

"So that's where he's been going," Jo murmured.

"Yeah. He says he wants to give you guys some alone time, and that he doesn't want to hear all the wild monkey sex going on when he's not getting any."

"That's oddly sweet."

"Matt, sweet? Yeah, right."

"So you and Matt have managed to hang out

together—alone—and not kill each other? I'm impressed."

"Oh, I almost stabbed him with a fork the other night."

Jo laughed. "What'd he do to deserve that?"

Jenn looked away before saying, "Nothing, really. He was just being a jerk."

Jo had a feeling there was more to the story than that, but decided to let it slide.

"So what's up with Chase? I've called him a couple of times this week and he hasn't answered. He's barely responded to text messages. That's not like him."

Now it was Jo's turn to dive into her enchiladas.

"Uh oh. What's going on? Y'all didn't break up, did you?"

"Not that I know of. We had a pretty serious talk the other night, and Chase seemed like he had a lot on his mind, really worried about something. I tried to get it out of him, but all he would do is ask me what our plan was for once I go back to Austin."

"And what is the plan? I love you guys, and obviously y'all are meant for each other, but even soul mates can't survive distance for too incredibly long."

Jo shrugged, misery settling into her bones. "I know that. He knows that. Part of it's my fault—I haven't exactly wanted to talk about it, even though I know we need to."

"Uh, yeah." Jenn took a sip of her tea before continuing. "What I don't understand is why you've been avoiding the inevitable. Just rip the damned bandage off already."

Jo pushed her enchiladas around her plate. "I know, I know. I'm just so scared of the what-ifs, and the thought of losing him. I think by avoiding having that particular conversation, it's been easier for me to keep reality at bay."

Jenn shook her head. "You counselors really can be some screwed up people."

"Tell me about it."

"Oh, I can if you really want me to."

Jo snorted. "No, thanks. I'm well aware of just how messed up I am. But seriously, I just get the feeling that there's something else bothering Chase, that it's not just the distance thing. I just can't come up with any ideas."

Jenn shrugged. "I really don't know. I mean, the distance thing is kind of a big one, y'know. And knowing Chase, he's probably scared to death to let you in all the way, because even though he's one of my best friends and one of the nicest men on the planet, he also has some issues and has a really hard time letting people in."

"Yeah, thanks to me," Jo said bitterly.

"Partially, maybe. But I don't think it's just you. Chase tells me most everything, but I know there are things he keeps pretty close to the vest." Jo watched as Jenn dragged her fork through the remaining enchilada sauce on her plate, making swirly patterns with the tines. "I know he tells Owen more than he does me, and Owen would never divulge state secrets, so to speak."

"How exactly did Owen and Chase and you become friends to begin with? I don't remember him from high school."

"Really? He moved here like our junior year, I think, but he was pretty quiet. Junior ROTC. Graduated a year ahead of us. After he graduated he joined the National Guard and moved to Houston for a while. Came back to Del Rio oh…nine years ago maybe? At any rate, he came back here and opened up a construction business. Chase moved back not long after that, and with him being in commercial real estate they ended up working together a lot, and then ended up doing a lot of the same community events. They just became friends really quickly."

"So you became friends with Owen by proxy then?"

Jenn shrugged. "Kind of. More like, Chase started inviting Owen to go to the lake with us or come over to his place or to April's, and before I knew it I suddenly had two hot guy friends who unfortunately both treated me like I was a sister."

Jo snorted. "About that…was there seriously never anything between you and Owen?"

Jenn laughed. Loudly. "Oh, God, no. I mean, did I think he was hot? Obviously. Even a blind woman could see that. But there simply wasn't any chemistry, and at the time I honestly wasn't looking for a boyfriend or even sex. It was a very easy slide into friendship. Anyway, though, enough about me. How about we get the check and head back to Gran's for some ice cream and alcohol?"

"Ice cream *and* alcohol, huh?"

Jenn signaled for the waiter and said, "Just feels like that kind of a night."

~~*~~

"Hey, boss, got something to show you." Daniel approached Chase's truck almost as soon as he and Owen pulled up to the ranch.

"What's up?" Chase asked as he and Owen made their way into the office, Winchester on their heels.

Daniel walked around the desk and pulled out a white envelope. "Got this in the mail today. Not sure why it didn't go to the P.O. Box in town rather than coming here."

Chase opened the flap and slid out a piece of paper, opened it and began reading.

"You have got to be shitting me."

"What's up?" Owen asked.

Chase handed him the piece of paper and raked his fingers through his hair. This really was shaping up to be the shittiest of shitty weeks.

"Oh, come on. They can't do that."

"I know, right?"

They both sat down and then looked at the letter Owen had thrown on to Daniel's desk. Daniel sat on the other side of the desk, his expression of disbelief mirroring Chase and Owen's.

Dear Landowner,

It has recently come to our attention that West Texas Water Company, LLC has submitted a proposal to the state that will dramatically impact water levels in Val Verde County. We have cause to believe these plans will especially affect the Devils River, where the differences between groundwater and surface water are negligible.

Walter Johnson, owner of West Texas Water Company, LLC, has submitted a proposal to the state that would pipe billions of gallons of water from the Edwards-Trinity Aquifer to other areas of the state, most notably San Antonio. It is one of three proposals to help the state deal with the water shortage we're facing due to the severe drought.

As you are most likely aware, the Devils River is fed by underground springs that bubble up from the Aquifer and then disappear under the surface. All of us landowners work hard to preserve the beauty, habitat and quality of the Devils River and the springs that feed it. For a lot of us, those springs and the River also play an important role in providing water for livestock and wildlife, and there are other landowners along the river whose livelihoods are impacted by ecotourism.

Preliminary research shows that West Texas Water Company's plans would remove close to 50 billion gallons of water from the River basin. Considering the drought we've been experiencing, it's unlikely that those 50 billion gallons of water could ever be replenished. Not only would this dramatically decrease the water in the River basin, but it would also decrease ground water in the Aquifer— groundwater which we all depend on for our wells.

West Texas Water Company's plan would also affect

*San Felipe Springs in Del Rio, meaning the Rio Grande in
and of itself would be impacted by this proposal. All of us
in Southwest Texas depend on the Aquifer and its rivers and
streams in one way or another. Please join us in fighting
West Texas Water Company and this dangerous, reckless
plan.*

Sincerely,
Devils River Conservation Association

"I knew the water situation across the state was bad,
but I didn't realize it was this bad," Daniel said.

Chase shrugged. "Well, in Wichita Falls they're saying
they'll run out of water within two years and have started
recycling wastewater and putting it back into the public
drinking system. I don't know that you can get much
worse than drinking filtered toilet water that's already been
flushed."

"That's just disgusting." Owen shuddered.

"Yeah, but they're doing what they have to do," Chase
said. "Everyone who lives in Texas is aware of the drought
and how it's affecting the water supply. And we all know
desperate times call for desperate measures. But this?"
he gestured towards the letter on Daniel's desk, "This is
robbing Peter to pay Paul."

Owen pinched the bridge of his nose. "The way I
see it, this won't just hurt the Devils River or San Felipe
Springs or Del Rio—this will hurt Lake Amistad and
the Rio Grande, which means cities all the way down to
Brownsville will feel the pain of having their water supply
diverted to other parts of the state. I don't see how anyone
in good conscience could think this is a good idea."

"Apparently this Walter Johnson doesn't have much of
a conscience to begin with," Daniel said before turning to
his computer. "Anyone who would suggest this is a good
idea is either an idiot or simply doesn't give a shit. I'm

leaning towards both after finding his Facebook page. The guy's a douche."

Daniel turned his monitor so that Chase and Owen could see the Facebook profile Daniel had pulled up. On it were dozens upon dozens of posts about the proposal, along with some images and content that was at best bigoted.

After reading one particularly bad post, Chase shook his head in disgust. "I think calling him a 'douche' is giving the guy too much credit."

Daniel closed the tab and turned the monitor back towards him. "Probably, but the guy's not exactly someone you'd want to be friends with, and he obviously has some questionable beliefs."

"How's that going to help fight his plan to drain us of our water, though?" Owen asked.

Chase responded. "It's not, not really, other than the fact that the state would hesitate to get in bed with someone who very publicly expresses his opinion that being white makes him far superior to anyone who isn't white."

"Anyone think there's a way we could get a picture of him at a Klan rally and send it to the important folks in Austin?" Owen joked.

At least, Chase thought he was joking.

Daniel snorted. "Do they even have Klan rallies anymore?"

"I'm sure they do somewhere," Chase shrugged. "Not like those are exactly on my calendar."

"This is all well and good—so the guy's an asshole, obviously—but what do we do next?" Owen asked.

"Well, we need to bring Matt and Darrin up to speed, all things considered. I'm not sure how much either of them will get involved or even really care, but since they are co-owners they need to know. And we contact the Devils River Conservation Association, see what we can do to help. That's really all we can do."

Daniel and Owen both nodded in agreement.

"Anyway. I'm gonna go throw my bag in my room and grab a bite to eat." Chase stood and looked at Owen. "You up for some hog hunting tonight?"

Owen grinned. "I'm always up for hog hunting."

CHAPTER EIGHTEEN

Later that night, Chase lay in his bed at the ranch, his mind a tangled mess of thoughts and emotions.

Hog hunting had helped a little; there was just something therapeutic about sitting outside on a clear night, with nothing but the sounds of wildlife around you. No cars. No airplanes. No ringing phones. Just locusts and moths and bats in the air, deer and hogs moving around under cover of darkness.

It hadn't helped enough, though. He was no closer to having any answers than he'd been three days ago.

So far, the only person he'd told about the latest Chronic Kidney Disease diagnosis had been Owen, and they hadn't talked about it beyond his offhand admission that things were getting worse. He needed to tell Jo. He needed to tell his parents. Hell, he needed to tell Jenn and update Matt, too, all things considered.

All were fraught with all kinds of emotional land mines he wasn't looking forward to dealing with.

His parents had already almost lost both of their sons; Chase, as a child when the vesicoureteral reflux had led to multiple surgeries and kidney scarring, and Matt just a month ago with that freak line drive to the head. Sure, they were both still alive, and Matt seemed to be on the mend, but Chase's reality wasn't one he would imagine any parent wished for their child to go through.

On one hand, they'd known for twenty years that he would most likely need a transplant one day. On the other, it had been far too easy to fall into a bit of a lull, thinking that the day his kidneys failed was some far-off time in the future. As long as he ate healthy and exercised, watched his blood pressure and kept up with his nephrology appointments, he was fine and had been fine.

Until he wasn't.

It was one thing to know that needing an organ transplant was a possibility, another to find out it was your reality. And while he was beyond grateful that he—and his family—had literally had decades to prepare for this reality, it was still difficult to process.

Why now?

Why had his body decided to finally start the too-fast downward slide now, after he and Jo had found something that he knew deep down was special? Furthermore, how could he do this to Jo?

She'd already been through so much in her life. Sure, she'd come out stronger in the end because of it, but he loved her enough to not want to ever cause her any sort of pain or distress. If he could shield Jo from all of the bad in the world, he would.

Considering he'd been giving her the cold shoulder the past few days, he realized he wasn't exactly sparing her one of those bad things, it was just that he didn't know what to do. She didn't deserve to be with a sick guy with a limited shelf life. He knew the statistics, knew how long transplanted kidneys usually lasted.

Ten to fifteen years, with some lasting for twenty.

He was already thirty-three. It was looking like he would need the transplant at thirty-four or thirty-five.

Which meant he would need a new one by his mid-fifties at the latest, probably before then. And while he could probably still get one in his fifties, there was always the question of what happened after *that* kidney failed. While patients in their sixties still received transplants, most in their seventies didn't for a variety of reasons.

He wanted to be with Jo for forever, but what if his forever was only twenty more years? Forty years? And what if hers was sixty?

He couldn't abandon her like that.

She deserved someone who could be with her until they were old and gray, who would always be around to love her.

He might not be that guy.

Even if he got lucky and a new kidney lasted twenty years, and he was able to quickly get another one after that, there was also the increased risk of cancer from the anti-rejection meds. Sure, the majority of cancer cases among transplant recipients were skin cancer and fairly easy to take care of. But there were always those other cancers, the ones that weren't so easy to deal with.

The ones that could kill you.

And then there was the possibility of his body rejecting the new kidney completely, which would mean dialysis until he could get a new one. If he could get a new one. Hell, if he couldn't find a live donor to begin with (and how did he even ask someone to give him a part of them?), he would have to go on dialysis. He'd done his research, he'd even visited some dialysis centers.

They were kind of miserable places.

Places where people seemed to go to just prolong death.

He wanted to live.

He couldn't put Jo through that. He'd talked to enough people, read enough online to know that while dialysis and transplants were hard on the recipient, they were also very hard on the patient's loved ones.

He couldn't do that to her.

Knowing that this was coming sometime in the future had led to him being a bit of a lone wolf as it was. Obviously, he'd dated, been in relationships, and had sex. But he'd never allowed himself to get truly serious with anyone—until Jo—because he knew that this was a possibility and it wasn't fair.

Yes, he'd loved Jo as a teen, and had never completely gotten over her, but why now? Why had God put her back in his life *now*, when *now* was the thing he'd been protecting everyone in his life from?

Realizing he wasn't going to get any sleep with his brain such a mess, Chase got out of bed. Winchester lifted his head, sighed, and walked with him as Chase made his way from his bedroom to the living room with its big screen TV and satellite cable, hoping the distraction of mindless television would help him go to sleep, or at the very least help him figure out what to do.

CHAPTER NINETEEN

He knew what he needed to do.

With a feeling of inevitability, Chase texted Jo.

Chase: Dinner at my place tonight?

Jo: Our usual time?

Chase: That'll work.

It was currently just after ten in the morning. Friday.

He picked up his range bag after pocketing his phone.

He hadn't slept a damned bit last night. But hey, at least he now knew what he needed to do.

Yay.

Shaking his head to rid himself of maudlin thoughts— he really wasn't a fan of the pity party that had been going on inside his mind this week—he walked outside, where Owen was waiting on the patio, gun case in hand and range bag slung over his shoulder.

"You okay?" Owen asked as they began to walk towards the shooting range that was set up on the other side of the barn.

Chase shrugged. "Not really. But it is what it is."

They fell silent, caliche crunching under their feet and locusts rubbing their wings the only sounds for long moments.

"You know I'll gladly give you a kidney, right?"

Owen's statement caused Chase to stop in his tracks. "I couldn't ask you to do that."

Owen continued walking. "You didn't ask me—I offered."

"Still, though, I couldn't—"

Owen stopped, turned around and walked back to where Chase was still standing. "Yes, you could. Don't be a dick about it—you're going to need a kidney, I have two that work great and only need one of them. That's what friends do."

Chase swallowed past the lump in his throat. "You don't even know if we're the same blood type."

"Nope. Don't care. I'm just saying, I would gladly give you a kidney, and you would do the same for me if you could. Now let's go shoot some paper."

~~*~~

"Chase wants to have dinner tonight," Jo said as she sat down on the edge of Jenn's bed. Instead of going to Gran's last night they'd gone back to Jenn's and indulged in Mudslides made with ice cream.

Jenn yawned and stretched. "So? That's a good thing, considering y'all are together and all."

Jo couldn't fight the panic that somersaulted in her belly, though. "I've got a bad feeling about this."

Jenn sat and pushed her hair out of her eyes. "Okay. Why do you have a bad feeling?"

Jo shrugged and slid down on to the floor, her back against the mattress. She stared at the phone in her hands, the panic rolling through her. "I don't know. I can't quite explain it. But he's basically ignored me all week, and then when he texted me a few minutes ago he was pretty short about it."

Jenn slid off the bed and sat on the floor beside Jo. "I can see how that would make you nervous. But didn't he also say he was going to spend a couple of days up at the ranch? Sounds to me like he's coming home early because he wants to see you."

"Or maybe he's planning on breaking up with me and just wants to get it done and over with."

"Way to think positive there, counselor."

Jo sighed. "I know, I know. I just can't shake the bad feeling."

"Well, then, we need to make sure you change his mind *if* he's planning on making the dumbest move in the history of the universe."

"And how do we do that?" Jo turned her head and looked at Jenn, who waggled her eyebrows.

"We make sure he knows exactly what he would be missing."

~~*~~

In the end, Jo opted for the cotton sundress and cowboy boots she'd worn on the night before the Fourth, when they'd made love for the first time. She figured it had worked once, so it would probably work again. Maybe.

Besides, it was casual enough that she didn't come across as if she was trying too hard.

Even though she totally was.

Nervous, she wiped her palms on the skirt of the dress before letting herself into Chase's house. Cool air and Winchester greeted her.

She scratched his head before heading towards the kitchen.

Chase was bent at the waist, removing something from the oven. She sniffed and realized it was pizza.

"Hey there," she said once he'd set the hot pizza stone on top of the stove.

He turned around and smiled, but it didn't quite reach his eyes. Panic rolled once again, and she fought to keep it at bay.

"Hey. How was your week?" he asked.

She set her purse down. "Okay. Gran's doing really well. I missed you."

He nodded, but didn't say he'd missed her, too.

Oh, God, this really wasn't looking very good.

"So, ah, let me just get the salad out of the fridge and slice the pizza," he said before turning away from her.

He took salad and dressing from the fridge, set both items on the kitchen island where they'd made love to each other just a week ago one night while Matt was gone.

Had that seriously only been a week ago?

She watched as he sliced the pizza, and felt like her heart was being sliced right along with it. Tension tightened his jaw, and he was holding himself rigid.

Her eyes burned and she blinked away the tears that wanted to fall.

Winchester nosed her hand, and she absently buried it in his fur, finding at least a small amount of solace and comfort in the big dog's presence. She wanted to sit on the floor, hold him to her and cry her eyes out.

But she couldn't.

She wouldn't.

Instead, she watched, as if in a trance, as Chase took plates out of the cabinet, forks out of the silverware drawer.

The smell of the pizza joined the panic in her stomach, making her nauseous. There was no way she was going to be able to eat.

In thick silence, Chase plated their food.

"Outside?"

Jo swallowed. "Sure."

Out of habit she grabbed bottles of water for both of them, wishing she had something stronger.

They sat.

This is awful.

She wanted to cry, and she didn't even know what it

was she wanted to cry about.

They toyed with their food, neither of them even bothering to pretend to eat. Jo took a fortifying sip of water and finally said, "Okay, Chase, spill."

He sighed before turning those warm brown eyes on her, their depths filled with so much uncertainty and confusion and pain she wanted to gather his head to her bosom and simply hold him.

"How much do you know about why I was sick as a kid?"

She wracked her brain, trying to remember everything she'd been told or overheard. "Not much, honestly. You never seemed to want to talk about it, so I tried to respect that. All I know is that you had a lot of surgeries and that it was something involving your kidneys."

He nodded. "The very basic answer is that I had a type of reflux that caused urine to backup from my bladder into my ureters and kidneys. They didn't know what was wrong at first, thought maybe I had some cysts or some sort of growth, thus the first six procedures. The doctors finally figured out what was wrong, and did the first reconstructive surgery. That one didn't hold, so they had to do another one."

"That had to have been horrific."

"It was." He took a deep breath. Exhaled. "The issue is that because it took so long to get a proper diagnosis, and then with the first surgery not working, the reflux caused some kidney scarring. We knew then that the scarring could cause some long-term health problems, but since I was young, otherwise healthy and active the doctors were all hopeful that I either wouldn't have long-term issues, or that I could lead a normal life for a very long time before I did start having issues."

She didn't like the sound of where this was going.

Chase fiddled with his bottle of water, now unable to

meet her eyes. "Not long after I finished college, I found out I was in Stage 2 Chronic Kidney Disease. I managed it with diet and exercise, and didn't hit Stage 3 until about two years ago. For whatever reason, it's been a fairly rapid decline since then."

Jo swallowed, her thoughts pinging around her head. He'd been sick this entire time and she hadn't known. How had she not known?

"Six months ago I was in Stage 3. When I went in for another check up with my nephrologist on Monday, he told me I'm in Stage 4."

She blinked back tears. "So what does that mean?"

She knew nothing about Chronic Kidney Disease.

He couldn't meet her gaze. "It means I'm getting sicker. I could throw a bunch of technical medical terms at you, but I won't. Suffice it to say, my nephrologist thinks I'm probably a year away—at most—from needing a kidney transplant."

She wanted to reach out and touch him, comfort him, but the wall he'd put up around himself let her know that her sympathy either wasn't wanted or couldn't be handled right now. There were so many thoughts flying through her head she didn't even know where to begin.

Chase apparently took her silence as a signal to continue. "Obviously, I may not be able to get a kidney quickly—that would depend entirely on being able to find a live donor—which means I would have to go on dialysis while on the transplant list. Dialysis isn't pretty. It isn't easy. It's kind of like what I imagine a circle of hell to be."

"Circle of hell, huh?" Her attempt at levity fell pretty flat.

"You just sit there, hooked up to a machine for three or four or however many hours for three or four days a week. It wears you out, makes you tired. Yeah, there are other options like at-home dialysis or peritoneal dialysis, but neither of those are exactly a walk in the fucking park, either."

She couldn't not touch him anymore, so she placed a hand on his knee. He flinched.

"Let me help you, Chase. I don't know anything about kidney disease or transplants or dialysis, but I love you and you don't need to go through this alone."

He finally looked her in the eye, and the anguish she saw there made Jo felt like she'd been punched in the heart.

"I can't do that to you Jo."

"Can't do what to me?"

"Make you go through that. It's not fair to you. You didn't ask for this. You thought you were getting someone who was whole and healthy and who would grow old with you and give you babies. I'm not whole and healthy. I may not grow very old at all. And babies? There's no one else I would want to be the mother of my children, but what caused this is genetic and I can't take that chance. I can't do that to you, or any children we might have in the future."

Tears were slowly sliding down Chase's cheeks. Jo reached out and wiped them away, sniffling against her own. "We can work all that out. If you get a transplant, you'll live and I'll get to have you for a long time, right?"

He shook his head. "Not necessarily. Most kidney transplants last ten to fifteen years, some twenty. I could probably get another one in my fifties or sixties if I took care of the first one and did everything right, but after that…the boards that make those decisions tend to favor younger transplant recipients, and older patients don't handle the surgery as well."

"So I could still have you well into our seventies, maybe even eighties, right?" She couldn't imagine spending her later years without him, not when everything in her cried that *this* was the man she was supposed to spend the rest of her life with.

"That's not fair to you."

"What isn't fair to me, Chase? Because from where I'm sitting, this isn't exactly fair to you, either."

He shook his head. "This isn't about me. I've known this was probably my reality since I was a teenager. I've had time to prepare for this, to adjust and to plan. I've tried so hard to not let anyone get too close, because I didn't want to have to sit across from them one day and have this exact same conversation. Because it's not fair."

"No, it's not. But life often isn't fair."

"I can't put you through this."

"You shouldn't have to go through this alone. Let me help you."

He pushed her hands away. "I can't, Jo. You deserve…" he raked his hands through his hair, absently brushed the wetness off of his cheeks, "you deserve so much more than this, so much more than what I'll be able to give you."

She felt the tears falling from her eyes, the sting in her nose and the pressure in her chest as if from far away. She could feel her heart breaking, cracking in two at the clear anguish written all over Chase's face.

I didn't just find you again only to lose you again.

"I love you. So, so much. Words can't express just how much I love you, Jo. But I can't do this to you. So I'm asking you—no, I'm telling you—just walk away. Please, if you love me, just walk away, because as much as I don't want to say good bye to you right now, I know that saying good bye thirty years down the road would hurt even more. At least right now you could love again, find someone else who is healthy and whole and who will grow old and gray beside you and who can give you children if you want them, because you deserve that."

"I don't understand this, Chase. I love you, and the only person I want is you. I want to love you for as much time as we have together—whether that's one year or thirty years or God willing more than that. You're asking me to give up on us—on you—and I can't do that."

"Please don't make this harder than it already is. One day, you'll thank me for this."

"No, I won't."

You're being stupid.

She wanted to say it out loud, but knew that now was not the time. Somehow, despite the despair and the breaking heart and the tears and the panic, she knew that now was not the time to tell him how incredibly, utterly stupid he was being.

He stood, his fists clenched so tightly his knuckles were white. "Please, Jo. Just leave."

She stood, too, slowly cupped his face in her hands. He tried to avoid her gaze. She wouldn't let him, forcefully tilting his chin down and putting her nose tip to tip with his so that he had to look her in the eye. "I love you, Chase Ashley Roberts, and I'm not giving up."

She kissed him then. Soft, the barest of brushes of lips against lips, their tears mingling together for brief moments before she pushed away, walked back inside his house, gathered her purse and walked out, leaving her heart at his feet.

~~*~~

Jo didn't remember getting in her car.

She didn't remember starting the ignition, or driving to Jenn's.

She didn't really remember walking up Jenn's front walk and ringing the doorbell.

So when Jenn opened the door, Jo was a bit surprised to see her best friend standing there, a look of surprise on her face before Jo promptly burst into tears.

Jenn ushered her inside, closing the door behind her.

"Did you know?" Jo choked out.

A look of confusion passed over Jenn's face.

"Know what?"

"That he's sick?"

"Who's sick?"

Jo felt like she was breaking into a million tiny pieces, and those pieces were slowly being scattered by the wind until soon there would be nothing left.

"Chase," she choked out.

Jenn guided her to the couch, and Jo suddenly realized that they weren't alone, that Matt was also there, sitting on one end of the couch, watching her warily, like she was a rabid raccoon about to attack.

She turned to Matt, pointed her finger at him. "You. You knew, didn't you?"

Matt swallowed. Nodded.

Jo lunged for him, but before she could inflict any real damage he wrapped an arm around her, pinning her arms to her sides, and used his free hand to rub her back. In a soft, soothing voice she never would have expected from him, he said, "Just calm down, Jo. Breathe. That's it. Breathe."

All those millions of tiny pieces inside of her broke loose a little more, and Jo found herself burying her head on Matt's chest, sobs wracking her body.

I'm getting snot all over the highest paid pitcher in MLB history.

Slowly, as if waking from a nightmare, the sobs quieted. She felt tired. So, so tired.

Jenn sat down beside her, and Matt kept rubbing her back.

"You're kind of good at this whole comforting thing, y'know," she mumbled against his chest.

Matt snorted. "It's one of my secret talents."

"I'm afraid I got snot all over your shirt."

She felt him shrug. "That's okay. I have plenty."

She pulled back and looked. He was wearing a 2012

World Series t-shirt. The year the Wranglers won. "It's your World Series t-shirt!"

He smiled at her. "Jo, it's okay. I literally have a dozen of these. At least."

Embarrassed, she grabbed a tissue out of the box on the coffee table so she could blow her nose. "I'm sorry I attacked you."

"It's no biggie. I have to admit, I was kind of impressed—I don't think I've seen you that worked up since the time I stuck frogs in the back of y'all's bathing suits."

"Still, though, I shouldn't have done that."

"It's okay. So what got you so worked up to begin with?"

She looked from Matt to Jenn, for the first time realizing that she'd possibly walked in on something between the two of them. "Was I interrupting something?"

"Nope. We were just watching the game."

The TV wasn't on. Jo looked from it to Jenn, who at least had the decency to blush.

"We were about to watch the game. I just got here," Matt said. Covering for Jenn, Jo was sure.

Whatever, though. As much as she wanted to solve the mystery of Matt and Jenn, Jo was too heartbroken and too shattered to care beyond some good-natured teasing. Defeated, her shoulders fell and she slumped into the couch cushions.

"So what did you mean, Chase is sick?" Jenn asked, worry in her voice.

Jo rolled her head and looked at her best friend. "So I take it you don't know?"

"Know what?"

Jo sighed. Rolled her head to look at Matt. "What about you?"

He nodded. "The family's known since he was a teen,

and then he found out in his early twenties, I think, that he had Chronic Kidney Disease."

Jenn gasped. "He's been sick that long and never told me?"

"Don't get mad at him, Jenn. He probably kept it from you to protect you," Matt said.

"Kind of how he just broke up with me to protect me, you mean?" Jo asked. Bitterly.

"My brother's a fucking idiot."

"On this, I wholeheartedly agree with you."

Jo sniffled, and Matt handed her the box of tissues. "So I take it the CKD's gotten worse?"

She nodded her head. "From what he just explained to me, yes. His doctor thinks he'll probably need a transplant within a year."

Jenn asked, "Hold on. He's sick enough that he needs a fucking transplant? And he never told me? I'm his best friend!"

Jo closed her eyes, a tension headache forming at the base of her neck. "I'm his girlfriend. Was his girlfriend. Fuck if I even know what I am anymore. And he just now told me. So join the club."

The three of them fell silent, each lost in their own thoughts. Matt finally broke the silence by asking, "So what are you going to do?"

Jo sighed. "I don't know. I have to be back in Austin early next week for work, when what I want to do is stay here and show him I'm not that easy to push away."

In other words, it was a lose-lose situation.

CHAPTER TWENTY

"Are you out of your fucking mind?"

Chase looked up from the bottle of beer he'd been nursing for the past thirty minutes, noted the anger on Matt's face and looked away.

He shrugged, not even bothering to ask Matt what he was talking about. Jo. It all came back to Jo. "Probably."

Matt sat down in the patio chair across from him. "You're seriously just going to let her walk away? No, screw that. You're seriously just going to push Jo out of your life when now and the next few years are when you're going to need her most?"

Chase stared blankly at the swimming pool, numb. "You don't understand, Matt."

"No, I really don't. First, you don't tell anyone how bad it's gotten, and then when you do you break up with your girlfriend and shut everyone out. Then you throw a pity party—population one—and sulk like a sixteen-year-old who had his car keys taken away. And now you're sitting there looking like the poster child for a Prozac commercial. That's not like you, Chase, so no, I don't understand."

He wanted to be angry. Hell, he was kind of irritated at least. But Matt was right—his behavior since he'd gotten the latest diagnosis was completely not like him. Logically, he knew that. Illogically, though, he just wanted to shut down.

"What would you know, Matt? You've barely been around the past ten years," Chase goaded.

Instead of getting angry, Matt simply shook his head. "No, you don't get to use that card right now, because you and I both know it's bullshit. What's up with the poor pitiful me act anyway?"

Chase's shoulders sagged as if a giant weight had suddenly settled upon them. "Fuck if I know, Matt."

"I think you do." Matt paused before continuing. "So you're going to need a transplant?"

Chase nodded. "Not immediately, but sooner rather than later. The doctor thinks it's only a matter of a year or two."

"When are you going to tell Mom and Dad?"

"Soon. I don't know why I haven't yet. How'd you even find out?"

Matt waved his hand as if to indicate his answer didn't matter. "I was at Jenn's when Jo came in earlier bawling her eyes out. She hit me then got snot all over my shirt."

Chase finally took a good look at Matt at that, narrowed his eyes. "What were you doing at Jenn's?"

He shrugged. "I sometimes go over there and hang out to give you and Jo some privacy."

"At Jenn's?"

"Yeah. So?"

"So I thought you two hated each other for some reason." This was much better than thinking about his own mess of a life.

"I wouldn't say we've ever hated each other," Matt evaded.

Chase raised an eyebrow.

"There was just a bit of a misunderstanding years ago.

It's been cleared up now."

"I swear to God, Matt, if you hurt Jenn…" Chase let the implied threat hang in the air between them.

Matt raised his hands, palms out. "Not my intent. She's just nice to hang out with sometimes, that's all. We're friends."

"I've never known you to be friends with a woman."

"I'm friends with Jo. But I'm not the subject at hand here—you are. You and your idiocy."

"It's not idiocy." *Yes it is.*

Matt shot him a look that clearly said, "You're an even bigger idiot than I thought you were."

Chase swallowed past the idiot-sized lump in his throat.

"Since when are you in to heart to hearts? This is starting to feel like some Lifetime movie."

Matt snorted. "Hardly. As far as I know of neither of us has slept with a fifty-year-old woman who's twenty-year-old son slash lover wants to murder us."

"You know far too much about Lifetime movies."

"I had a lot of time to sit and watch cable TV in the hospital."

Chase felt a smile tug at his lips. He shook his head, wondering at the turn his and Matt's relationship had taken over the past month. "The truth is," he swallowed, picked at the label on his beer bottle, "I'm scared shitless, Matt. I've always been a bit of a loner, mostly because I've been in love with Jo since I was a kid, along with having the possibility of renal failure looming over my head. Finding out I was going to need a kidney transplant so soon…it's not fair to her. She's gone through so much, man. She's already lost both her parents. I can't do that to her."

"I don't think you're giving her enough credit."

"Probably not."

"That woman loves you, bro, and when you find

something like that you don't just throw it away like last night's leftovers. You hold on to that and don't let go."

Chase glanced up at his brother. "Where'd this philosophical side come from?"

Matt shrugged and looked slightly embarrassed. "It's always been there. Everyone's always seen what they wanted to see is all."

"So there's more to you than womanizing and a ninety-eight mile per hour fastball is what you're saying?"

Matt snorted. "To the public and my adoring fans? No."

Chase assessed his brother with new eyes, feeling kind of bad for assuming the worst about Matt just like everyone else always had. "How is it I've never seen this side of you until the past month?"

"I guess I never wanted you to. Facing your own mortality kind of gives you a new perspective on life, though."

Matt's comment hit home, and Chase rubbed his chest. "Point taken. Were you this scared when you came-to on the mound?"

Matt nodded, once. "Absolutely. I couldn't move for a few minutes. My ears were ringing and I could feel blood trickling down my face and neck. My head hurt like nothing I've ever felt before. Luckily I didn't know how bad it was at the time—just that the situation wasn't good. And when I woke up later, in the hospital," Matt shook his head, "I remember feeling lost and worried, mostly about Mom and Dad. It wasn't until a couple days later that the uncertainty of my baseball future really hit me, and that scared me, too."

"That's why you really came back home, isn't it? Because you were scared," Chase said with sudden clarity.

"Yeah." Matt sat back and sighed. "I was scared. I still am. Sure, my head seems to be healing fine, but baseball? I don't know if I'll ever be able to play again. I'm thirty-five and I'd already been thinking about retiring in another year or two, but I'd wanted to go out on my terms, y'know?"

"I had no idea you'd even thought about retirement. You've seemed so oblivious to the fact that you're kind of old for a pitcher."

Matt glanced at Chase and shook his head. "Again, everyone sees what they want to see. I'm not an idiot—I did graduate summa cum laude from Texas, y'know."

"Wait. What? But you were taken in the first round after your junior year. When did you go back and get your degree?" How had he not known this?

"In the off-season and through online courses. I finished it in 2008."

"Jesus, man. What other secrets do you have hiding out in there? I don't know if I can take much more."

Matt rubbed a hand over his jaw, looked at something over Chase's shoulder for long moments before turning his gaze back to him. "You know when you need a transplant I'll be the first one to offer a kidney, right?"

Chase sucked in a deep breath, blinked against the stinging in his eyes. He was not going to cry in front of his brother. "You don't have to do that."

"I know I don't, but you're my brother. We're the same blood type and siblings tend to be the best matches. My kidneys are in great shape, I'm healthy, and if I can do something to keep you alive as long as possible I'm going to."

He nodded, unable to speak past the lump in his throat.

"In the mean time, I suggest you figure out how you're going to apologize to Jo and grovel appropriately. You need her now, and you're going to need her in the future. Don't be a dick and make decisions for her—it's her choice to make, whether she wants to stick with you through this or not."

Chase sighed. "Do you know what the statistics are like for kidney transplant recipients? How long donor kidneys last? The complications, not to mention the cost involved?"

Matt crossed his arms over his chest. "Most donor kidneys will last on average fifteen years, with some lasting for twenty, possibly more if it's a really good match and the recipient takes their meds and takes care of themselves. That means you'd probably need another kidney in your fifties, and another in your sixties or seventies. Obviously, they're hard to come by the older you get, but it's not impossible. As for cost, the anti-rejection meds are incredibly expensive, but good insurance plans will usually cover at least a portion of the cost, and once you hit your out of pocket you pay nothing for the rest of your plan year. And yes, there's a risk involved with being on anti-rejection medications, including cancer, but most cases are skin cancer that's easily treated. You just have to be careful— wash your hands, use hand sanitizer, clean regularly, stay away from anyone who has the flu, that sort of thing. In other words, it's nothing insurmountable."

Chase was flabbergasted. All this time, he'd thought Matt was oblivious to everything outside of baseball and women, and yet he'd been getting a degree and apparently researching kidney transplants. "I feel like I owe you an apology."

Matt shrugged. "Nah. Like I said, people see what they want to see, and I don't do anything to dispel that image. It's more comfortable that way, honestly. But don't think for a minute I don't care, or that I haven't done research. You're my brother."

That damned burning feeling in his eyes was back. "I don't want to tell Mom and Dad."

Matt nodded. "I would imagine not. They can handle it, though. We've all known it was going to happen sooner or later." He grinned. "But wait until Mom finds out you broke up with Jo. You might wish you were dead then."

Chase rolled his eyes and flicked his bottle cap at Matt. "Shut it, asshole. I already know I screwed up big time in that regard."

"So what are you going to do to fix it?"

He cocked his head to the side. "You think you could help me with something?"

CHAPTER TWENTY-ONE

Jo sat back in her chair, rubbed her eyes and looked at the clock in the bottom right corner of her laptop screen.

2:47 a.m.

How had it gotten to be so late?

Yawning, she stood up and stretched, trying to remember how long she'd been sitting in front of the computer. It seemed like only a couple of hours, but felt like centuries.

Tired, she walked around her house, turning out lights, checking to make sure doors were locked and the alarm system was armed. She'd been back in Austin for a week, and hadn't heard from Chase since the night he'd broken up with her just over a week ago.

Of course that meant she'd thought about him every second of every day. And of course, she was up way too late, especially considering the school year officially began tomorrow. Once again, though, she'd gotten sucked in to the online world of CKD, ESRD, dialysis and transplants.

In an effort to better understand just what Chase was dealing with, she'd taken to Google every night since she'd been back home. The amount of information available was unbelievable, from research studies to online cookbooks to forums. She'd learned that while Chase's condition was incurable, it was treatable and he could have a pretty normal life even if he had to be on dialysis until he was able to get a transplant.

He just had to choose to have that normal life.

Apparently vesicoureteral reflux was rare, affecting only about one percent of children. Developing later problems in life was even less likely. In other words, Chase had won the childhood illness lottery.

She'd also found that transplanted kidneys were lasting longer and longer these days, thanks to modern medicine and better anti-rejection medications, but the chance of rejection or failure was always there. Most transplant recipients lived a completely normal life, going to work, having children and going on vacation.

Obviously, there were no guarantees, but from everything she'd read over the past week the road ahead for Chase wasn't necessarily easy, but it sure as hell wasn't hopeless, either.

Sighing, she climbed into bed, made sure her alarm was set and pulled the covers up.

The online forums had helped to shed some light on Chase's behavior and emotional withdrawal. Reading about the experiences of others who had gone through this before, or were currently living with End Stage Renal Failure and were on dialysis or waiting for a transplant, made it slightly easier for Jo to see things from Chase's point of view. Perusing the caretaker forums made it obvious that she wasn't the only one who'd been pushed away by the sick person.

Knowing those things, though, didn't make her heart ache any less. She closed her eyes, words and phrases dancing against the backs of her eyelids as she settled in to go to sleep, hoping that maybe tomorrow would be the day that Chase broke his silence.

~~*~~

A knock on Jo's office door the next morning pulled her attention away from the email she'd been reading to the unexpected interruption. When she looked up, she saw Rita, the school's receptionist standing at her door, flowers in her hand. Jo raised an eyebrow.

"Hey there. Come on in."

Rita walked in and set the flowers on Jo's desk. "These just came for you."

"For me?" Who the hell would send her flowers?

Chase, maybe?

But no, that wouldn't make any sense, considering he'd broken up with her.

Jo mentally shook herself and smiled, "Thanks, Rita."

"No problem," the older woman said before leaving her office.

Jo counted to ten before walking around her desk to get a better look—and to find the card.

The arrangement itself was beautiful; fat sunflowers and miniature orange roses in a squat, clear vase. It was simple and cheerful and pretty—exactly the kind of arrangement she would have been drawn to if she were buying them herself.

She searched and searched for a card, and couldn't find one, just a business card for the florist. Maybe she should call the florist, see if they'd accidentally not included one?

Jo rolled her eyes, situated the flowers just right on the corner of her desk and sat back down. The florist was a reputable one in the Austin area, so she was pretty sure the card hadn't been dropped or forgotten. She wanted to believe Chase had sent them, but if he had, why the anonymity?

~~*~~

The flowers were not the only anonymous delivery Jo received her first week back to school.

Tuesday she received a box of cookies from Tiff's

Treats, which she'd shared in the teacher's lounge after stealing a few for herself.

Wednesday she received a dozen red velvet cupcakes from Hey Cupcake!

Thursday was a bottle of what an internet research revealed to be a very expensive bottle of wine.

And Friday? Friday was a little box in a gift bag from a local jeweler, with a note. Finally, a freaking note. Except, no, her mystery gift giver didn't finally reveal himself (because, seriously, who else would send her gifts other than Chase?). Instead, he just gave instructions.

"Do not open until 5:00 p.m."

So now she was sitting at her desk, staring at the gift bag rather than answering emails and getting any work done. Granted, she was on her lunch break, but still, she hadn't been able to work all morning because of that silly gift bag.

"So who do you think it's from?"

Her closest friend in Austin and teacher of tenth-grade English, Heather, sat on the other side of Jo's desk and nodded towards the gift bag. Jo swallowed the bite of the sandwich she'd just taken and sighed.

"I think it's from Chase. I think everything this week has been from Chase."

Jo had told Heather about her summer romance the first day of teacher in-service. Heather, being a hopeless romantic, had been both jealous and sympathetic, and had even cried when Jo had told her about the break up. No doubt the perky teacher was even now getting romantic notions in her head about happily ever afters.

Heather popped the lid on to the now empty plastic container that had held homemade spaghetti. Her brown eyes twinkled as she asked, "What do you think it is?"

"Well, it's obviously jewelry."

Heather balled up her napkin and threw it at Jo. "No

shit, Sherlock. But what kind of jewelry?"

Jo shrugged, but her heart was in her throat and her stomach was a nervous mess. She put down what remained of her sandwich, suddenly unable to eat any more. "I have no idea. I can't imagine it being what you're thinking it is, though, considering we haven't even spoken in three weeks. It's probably just a bracelet, or earrings or something."

Heather peeked into the bag. "Considering the size of the box, it's not a bracelet. That, my friend, is either a ring or earrings."

"Or a necklace, maybe a charm for a necklace or bracelet."

"Except you don't have anything you would need a charm for."

"That's beside the point."

Heather snorted and tucked a lock of outrageously curly black hair behind her ear. "Well, I hope it's a ring and that he's come to his senses and realized how lucky he is to have you."

Jo felt the sting of tears and blinked rapidly.

"Oh, hell. I didn't mean to make you cry."

She practiced deep breathing for long moments until she got her emotions somewhat under control. "It's okay. I'm pretty much an emotional mess these days. Thank God it's been a pretty light week so far."

"Knock on wood, my friend. It's Friday afternoon and the first week of school—shit could still hit the fan."

"You don't teach with that mouth, do you?" Jo teased.

Heather snorted. "Only in my dreams."

~~*~~

Luckily shit did not hit the fan that afternoon, and Jo found herself breathing a sigh of relief as the last voices of students faded down the halls. Her gaze once again fell on the gift bag on her desk. It was just after 4:30, and she still had some paperwork to wrap up and emails to respond to before she could leave for the weekend.

Not to mention almost thirty minutes until she could open that damned box.

She looked around, and then back at the bag. Wait a second. Why was she even waiting to open the stupid thing? It wasn't like he would know if she'd opened it before 5:00, considering he was in Del Rio.

Ugh.

She reached for the bag, withdrew the box. Hands only slightly shaking she made quick work of the gift wrap.

It was definitely a jewelry box.

Not that she'd expected anything else considering the name written in elegant script on the gift bag.

She took a deep breath, wrapped her hands around the velvet container, and cracked it open.

"I thought my note said not to open that until five?"

The box snapped shut, pinching Jo's finger. She yelped and turned towards her office door and the voice she'd missed more than air itself for the past few weeks.

She sucked on her pinched finger before glaring at Chase. "So it was you."

His smile was unsure, and she wanted to leap over the desk and wrap herself around him, but she wasn't going to make things that easy for him.

Oh, no, it was his turn to apologize and grovel for making a stupid decision.

Not that he'd ever really made her grovel, but still.

Payback was a bitch.

Or something like that.

"Can you leave yet?"

His hands were in his pockets, and for the first time Jo really took note of how he was dressed. Charcoal gray trousers, blue button down shirt and a black jacket. This was Chase all grown up, looking every bit like a confident, self-assured businessman.

It was kind of hot.

She nodded and said, "Let me just shut everything down and we can go somewhere private to talk."

A part of her wanted to make him wait and squirm, but she just didn't have it in her.

He nodded, and she went through the motions of shutting down her computer, turning off her desk lamp and the Scentsy warmer she had on the bookshelf behind her. She straightened up her desk, made a couple of notes to herself for when she came back in Monday morning, grabbed her purse out of her desk and was ready to go.

She took a deep breath to calm her nerves. "Okay. We can get out of here."

She walked towards him, and he smiled and asked, "You forgetting something?"

She was close enough now to smell him, that unique combination of sunshine and warm skin that was Chase, and her senses were just enough on overload that she had to stop and think about what he was saying. "Forget what?"

He reached around her, grabbed the jewelry box off her desk, and said, "This."

"Oh, yeah."

He shoved it into a pocket and gave her half of a grin. "Let's get out of here."

~~*~~

Chase followed Jo towards the back of the school, barely noticing his surroundings he was so engrossed in the woman in front of him.

He was having a hard time reading her mood, but he was man enough to admit that that was all on his shoulders. He'd been the one to shut her out then push her away, and considering how bad he'd felt when she'd done that to him back in high school, he could only imagine what she was feeling now.

Her palm hit the release on the door, and they stepped out into bright sunshine and sweltering humidity. Just being back in Austin for a day had made him appreciate the relatively lower humidity in Del Rio.

She stopped short just in front of him before pointing at the black Cadillac sedan idling in the parking lot and asking, "That yours?"

"Ours, if you're willing."

She slid him an unfathomable look before shrugging. "Well, I'd hate for you to have gone to all this trouble for nothing."

Chase bit back a grin as they headed towards the vehicle. The driver stepped out and opened the back door, Jo slid in and Chase followed. The door closed behind them and they were ensconced in cool air and leather.

As the driver pulled out of the high school's parking lot and headed towards Highway 71, Chase searched for something to say to fill the space between them.

Jo finally broke the silence by asking, "So where are we headed?"

"It's a surprise."

She raised an eyebrow. "A surprise? You think you can just waltz into my office after not speaking to me for three weeks and whisk me away for some 'surprise' I may or may not enjoy?"

"I'm sorry, Jo." He sighed. He wasn't about to force her to go somewhere with him if she didn't want to. "We can turn back around and you can get in your car and go home."

Okay, so that sounded a bit more defensive than he'd intended.

She snorted. "I'll play along with this surprise thing for now, cowboy."

Chase smiled, for the first time in weeks feeling like everything was going to be okay. "Fair enough. I think you'll enjoy what I have in mind, though."

She glanced towards the driver and back at him, a blush staining her cheeks.

He leaned forward and whispered in her ear, "Get your head out of the gutter."

She laughed but didn't respond, instead turning towards the window to look out of it. "So, seriously, where are we going? It looks like traffic's a nightmare."

"Austin traffic's always a nightmare."

"You have a point." She paused. "So you're really not going to tell me where we're going?"

He sat back and grinned. "Nope. Just enjoy the ride."

~~*~~

An hour and a half later they passed a huge stone sign that read "The Reserve at Lake Travis," and Jo turned to Chase, confused. "What are we doing out here?" As far as she knew, The Reserve was a luxury home community with real estate prices beginning at three times what she'd paid for her little house in south Austin.

"Just a couple more minutes, counselor. We're almost there."

She rolled her eyes and turned back towards the window, watching as sprawling homes that could only be called mansions flew past them. Tennis courts on the right. More homes with lushly manicured lawns. They rounded a bend in the road, turned left and came to a stop. She peered out of Chase's window and saw a scattering of small, high-end cabins. Behind them, she could just make out the waters of Lake Travis.

Chase's door opened from the outside, and he stepped out. Jo followed, grabbing on to his hand for stability. He pulled his wallet out, handed a few bills that Jo couldn't see to the driver and said, "Thanks, Mark. I'll see you again on Sunday."

The driver—um, Mark—tipped his hat and smiled

before closing the back door behind them. Chase led her down a path as she heard the car drive away.

Too busy taking in her surroundings—these cabins were absolutely gorgeous—she paid no attention to where they were going. Chase drew to a stop in front of one of the smaller cabins, withdrew a key from his pocket and placed it in the lock. He opened the door and stepped back, gesturing for her to enter first, which she did.

The first thing she noticed was the smell of something absolutely delicious that made her mouth water. The second was the modern, yet somehow natural feeling décor. The ceilings were surprisingly high, the walls painted a neutral stone color.

"This place is beautiful."

"You like it?"

She nodded. "And what is that smell? I'm suddenly starving."

She set her purse down on a chair and wandered around the small space. The source of the wonderful food smell came from warming dishes that had been set on the counter top, along with plates, silverware, two wine glasses and a bottle of wine chilling in a bucket of ice. She touched the dome of one of the warming plates, found it to still be warm, and turned to Chase. "I'm guessing this hasn't just been sitting here for a couple of hours."

He stuck his hands in his pockets and rocked back on his heels, a nervous gesture that was so unlike him that she barely managed to resist the urge to walk to him and wrap her arms around him. Sure, she was going along with things for now, but she wasn't foolish enough with her heart to risk it all again without knowing what the lay of the land was.

"I texted the lodge about fifteen minutes before we got here to let them know to bring it on over and leave it. I figured a private dinner and conversation would be better than a public one."

Fair enough. "It feels kind of weird, getting here and immediately eating."

"The food will keep warm for a little longer."

She shook her head. "No, I'm actually starving."

God, this was so freaking awkward.

"Okay," he said before walking over to the sliding glass doors, sliding back the curtain and revealing a private patio area with a table for two. Well, that answered one question she'd had.

Curiosity getting the better of her, she began to pull off the warming covers and discovered what looked to be herb-crusted prime rib, fluffy mashed potatoes, and roasted green beans, already plated. Another dish revealed little wells of what looked to be au jus and horseradish butter. There was also a basket of crusty, still warm bread that smelled heavenly, with individual pats of butter tucked in here and there.

By silent agreement, Chase took their dinner, and Jo managed to grab the condiments, butter and bread. They carried their fare out to the little patio, arranged it to their liking and then went back inside for silverware, bread plates, the wine glasses, and wine, which Chase opened before going back outside.

Once settled, they looked across the table at each other, and Jo almost smiled.

Chase poured them each some wine, giving her more than he did himself. From all the research she'd been doing, she guessed he was cutting back on alcohol due to his kidneys—not that he'd really drank all that much to begin with.

They each took an appreciate sip of the red wine, set their glasses aside and then simply stared at each other across the table.

After long, silent moments, Chase cleared his throat.

"So this is kind of uncomfortable and awkward."

Jo shrugged, somehow managing not to smile again, and then picked up her steak knife and fork. "It's been better, that's for sure."

He sighed and picked up his utensils, too, but didn't seem as interested in the meal as she was.

She relented, just a little. "Eat. This conversation will go much better if we're not both hangry."

"Hangry?"

"Yup. Being hungry makes people angry. You combine hungry and angry and you get hangry."

He shook his head, but he at least seemed to relax enough to enjoy his meal (which really was superb).

They ate pretty much in silence, broken only by small talk about work how the Wranglers were doing. Safe, fairly neutral subjects. Nothing like the conversations they used to have over countless shared meals.

It was awful and awkward and there had to be a way to get past it.

Jo just wasn't sure how.

~~*~~

Once the dishes had been cleared from the table and placed in the sink for the lodge's staff to retrieve, Chase led Jo to the sofa inside the cabin, unwilling to have this conversation outside where anyone and everyone could hear them. Yes, the cabins had wood privacy fences that were impossible to see over unless you were maybe a professional basketball player, and with it being the beginning of the school year most of the other cabins were empty, but what he had to say to Jo was between the two of them and nobody else.

He refilled her wine glass before taking a sip out of the bottle of water he'd grabbed for himself after dinner. The jewelry box in his pocket felt like a lead weight, and the one in the bedroom taunted him.

He hoped like hell what he had to say was enough to make Jo forgive him.

Although to be fair, he was still struggling with forgiving himself.

She waited patiently, and he knew her silence was her way of getting him to talk. God, he'd been stupid to push her away.

He took a deep breath, studied the water bottle in his hands for long moments, and then slowly began to speak.

"That day I broke up with you, I was out of my mind. I was scared. So I pushed you away because I was trying to protect myself and you. At the time, I knew it was stupid. I knew it felt all wrong. But all I could think about was how unfair this was to you, and how you deserve someone better, healthier, who'll live to grow really old with you. I felt like if I stayed with you, I would be condemning you to a life of doctor's appointments and medical scares and uncertainty. You've had enough instability in your life, I didn't want to pile on."

He looked up at her then, met her gaze head on and saw the tears swimming there, felt his own eyes burning and continued. "The thing is, Jolene Dolly Sommers Westwood, I'm an idiot. I was scared of having a short life to spend with you, so I ended it now instead of getting to spend the rest of my life with you, no matter how short that life might be."

A tear spilled over and onto Jo's cheek. He reached out and brushed it away with his thumb, feeling his own threatening to fall. "But then I got to thinking about that, and realized that there are no guarantees in life. For all we know we could die tomorrow, a year from now, ten years from now, or live until we're eighty-five. We just don't know. And the longer I thought about it, the more I realized that a life without you—no matter how long or short that life may be—isn't living at all. What I have, yeah, it's a bit of a death sentence, but that doesn't mean I should stop living between now and when my name is called.

"I'm sorry for being an idiot. I'm sorry for hurting you—that's the last thing I want to do, and yet I did it. I'm sorry I made you cry. Most of all, I'm sorry that I was so willing to throw our love away out of fear of the unknown. Life is short, but what good is life if you're not actually living?"

Jo sniffled, set her wine glass down on the coffee table and grabbed a tissue out of the box on the end table beside the sofa. She swiped at her eyes, blew her nose and then said, "So all the gifts this week, those were from you?"

He grinned. "I wasn't sure how much I needed to butter you up. Sorry if I went a little over board."

Her smile was wobbly, but at least she was smiling now, which was better than the past few hours had been. "It was kind of sweet, if not a bit exasperating. I'm not sure what was worse—knowing they were from you but not knowing why you were sending things anonymously, or the questions I kept getting from all of my coworkers. Why did you send everything anonymously? It's not like I couldn't figure out it was you."

He shrugged. "Honestly, I'm not really sure. I think I was a little scared that if you knew they were from me that you would refuse to accept them, which meant it really was over."

She scooted closer to him, leaned into his body and wrapped her fingers around his. "Chase, honey, things will never be over between us. Even after the good Lord decides it's your time to go I'll still love you. You'll always have my heart, no matter what happens."

He kissed the top of her head. "I love you so, so much. I don't think I can apologize enough for being so stupid."

"This is a pretty good start. And I love you, too."

They sat in companionable silence for long moments,

until Jo finally spoke again. "I hope you don't mind, but I've been doing some research about End Stage Renal Failure, dialysis and kidney transplants."

He raised an eyebrow. "How much research?"

"Maybe just a few…dozen…hours' worth?"

He laughed. "I don't mind at all. What have you found?"

She told him about everything she'd found, from online support groups to news articles about the kidney transplant black market to research institutions developing artificial kidneys that would work in lieu of biological ones.

"You really have been busy, haven't you?"

"Just a little. I couldn't help it, though. I wanted to better understand what's wrong with you and what you were dealing with. From what I've read, you're not the only person to kind of freak out when given a less than stellar diagnosis. I've also read so many stories about people living pretty normal lives while on dialysis or after receiving a transplant. It's not a death knell, you just have to adjust to a new normal."

He tightened his hand around hers. "Are you sure you're willing to go down that road with me?"

She nodded and looked up at him. "Absolutely."

His heart swelling with an emotion that went far beyond love, he leaned in and kissed her, just a light brushing of lips over lips. "God, I love you."

She smiled and kissed him more fully, nibbling on his lower lip until he opened his mouth and met her tongue with his. They caressed each other with lips and tongue and hands, saying "hello" and "welcome home" with touch rather than words.

After long moments he broke the kiss, remembering the box in his pocket. "Oh, yeah, you never got to open your gift."

He pulled the box out of his pocket and held it out to

her. She gently took it from him and just as slowly opened
the lid before peering down and gasping.

"Chase! This is beautiful."

He'd contacted a jeweler friend of Matt's and found
something he thought fit Jo perfectly—a thin silver chain
with a horizontal infinity pendant. One of the curves of the
infinity symbol held the word "love" in cursive, accented
by both of their birth stones.

He didn't give a shit how corny Matt had said it was—
the look on Jo's face let him know he'd chosen well.

She removed the necklace from the box, unclasped it
and turned so that the back of her neck was presented to
him. "Help me put it on?"

He took the necklace from her and clasped it around
her neck. When she turned back around, he was relieved to
find he'd chosen the correct chain length. She smiled up at
him and kissed his cheek.

"Y'know, I was pretty determined to make you squirm,
but it ends up I don't have it in me."

"I'm glad."

"Hell, me too."

Chase rested his forehead against hers and simply
breathed her in. Jo closed her eyes and wrapped her arms
around his waist. They sat there, silent, for long moments
until Chase spoke. "So I was going to wait until tomorrow,
but there's something I need to show you."

Jo pulled away and glanced up at him. "Well that
sounds vague."

"Sorry." He got up from the sofa and then pulled her
up, too, before leading her around the fireplace wall and
into the bedroom. "Wait here."

"Okay…"

He turned and walked over to his suitcase, unzipped
it and pulled the box he was looking for out of it. He then
walked back over to Jo, his hand curled around the box so

she couldn't see it, and said, "Close your eyes."

She knitted her brows but did it anyway.

He took a deep breath, and the sound vibrated through the room. "The thing is, when I said earlier that I want to spend the rest of my life with you, no matter how short it may be, I meant it."

He closed his eyes, opened them back up and cupped Jo's cheek with his free hand. "I've loved you since we were kids, and I've been in love with you since I was fourteen years old. You're the only woman I've ever loved, and the only one I want to spend the rest of my life with. I know there are no guarantees, and I feel like a selfish bastard even asking you this considering the road I have ahead of me, but I can't not ask you to marry me."

He placed the box in one of Jo's hands and wrapped her fingers around it. "We've already wasted so much time, and I don't want to waste any more. I love you, Jolene, and would love nothing more than to be able to spend the rest of our lives together—no matter how long or short those lives might be."

Jo opened her eyes and looked at him and then down at the box in her hand. He swallowed past the lump in his throat, his heart pounding in his chest. This felt like every last out he'd ever thrown rolled into one, multiplied by about a hundred.

Or maybe a thousand.

After long moments of Chase feeling like he could throw up at any time, Jo finally spoke. "First, I love you, too. Second, I want to spend the rest of my life with you, too. Third, yes, I will marry you."

He stepped closer, joy bouncing through him, but Jo pressed a finger to his lips and held him in his place. "Fourth, you're not a selfish bastard. And fifth, if I ever hear you say again that I don't deserve this, that I don't deserve the stress and worry and fear that goes along with loving someone who one day will be very, very sick, I will kick you in the balls and leave."

He couldn't hold back the chuckle that escaped.

"Oh, you think I'm not serious? Believe me, Chase Ashley Roberts, I am very, very serious about that last one. And I may not literally kick you in the balls, but I will not tolerate you talking down on yourself for something that isn't your fault to begin with, and I definitely won't tolerate you thinking you know everything that's best for me." Her brow was knitted in frustration, and the finger she'd had at his lips was now poking him in the chest. "No one deserves to go through what you're going through and what you will go through. But no one deserves to go through that alone, either. So if we do this, it's not just a marriage, Chase, it's a partnership. We're a team. And you know how in wedding vows there's that whole part about 'in sickness and health'? That's there for a reason, and believe me when I say that when I speak those vows I will mean them with every fiber of my being. For better or for worse, in sickness and in health, 'til death do us part, for as long as we both shall live. You better believe that as much as I do, or else the ring I suspect is in this box won't be going on my finger."

Chase fought the smile that wanted to spread across his face, and instead pulled her to him until she was flush with his body, the hand holding the box trapped between them. "For better or for worse, in sickness and in health, 'til death do us part, for as long as we both shall live."

Jo sniffled. "Now that we've got that settled, can I open this box?"

He stepped back, and Jo slowly opened the box, revealing the engagement ring he'd had Matt's jeweler friend find. The ring with a vintage vibe had screamed "Jo" as soon as he'd seen it; the ring was white gold, with a thin infinity band of diamonds, topped by a traditional round-cut diamond surrounded by smaller diamonds set in rose gold.

"Oh, wow." She looked up at him, tears swimming in her eyes. "Chase, this is…holy…have you been looking at my Pinterest account?"

"I didn't even know you had a Pinterest account."

"Please. I'm a woman in my early thirties who up until a couple of months ago was woefully single yet dreaming of her wedding day. Of course I have a Pinterest account."

He smiled and took the box from her, removed the ring and took hold of her left hand. "So I guess that means you like it?"

She smiled. "Like it? I love it! Put that thing on my finger already!"

He chuckled and slid it onto her ring finger, smiling as he did so. She laughed, looked down at her hand in the way that all females do, and then wrapped her arms around his neck and met his mouth with hers.

After long moments, she pulled away just enough to say, "I love you."

"I love you, too." And then he kissed her again and there was no more room for words or worries about the future. In that moment, it was just him and the woman he wanted to spend the rest of his life with—no matter how long that life may be.

~~*~~

Dear Reader,

Thank you so much for taking a chance on this book—and me—and purchasing it. I hoped you enjoyed reading it as much as I enjoyed writing it.

Like it often does, art certainly imitated life while I was writing this book—or maybe it was the other way around and life ended up imitating art. The idea for this book first came to me while listening to a local sports reporter talk about a childhood illness of a particular quarterback, and how he'd overcome that illness. This quarterback happened to be the younger brother of another quarterback who went to the same university. The older brother was successful and is to this day beloved by university fans; the younger brother, not quite as much. But it got me to thinking—what must it be like to have that kind of pressure on you, to be the younger brother of someone who's beloved by a pretty rabid fan base? And what must it be like when you throw in an illness no one knows about on top of that?

As I began writing the book, I changed Chase's illness to something vaguely involving his kidneys, just needing a jumping off point for research. I was about halfway through writing Between the Seams when my husband got sick. For months my writing went almost completely on hold as we tried to figure out what was wrong with him. Six months later we had an answer—he was in renal failure, and we'd had no clue. What followed was a crash course on End Stage Renal Failure (sometimes also called End Stage Renal Disease), dialysis (which they put him on while in the hospital, just days after finding out his kidneys were functioning at around 10%) and transplants.

The scenes in which Chase are talking to his doctor, and then his interactions with people immediately afterwards are admittedly all drawn—at least partially—

from my life and from the reality of facing dialysis and/or a transplant. The cause of Chase's kidney disease is different from what caused my husband's, but the emotions that Chase and Jo feel while dealing with this disease are very, very real.

The reality of kidney transplants is sobering: according to the National Kidney Foundation there are currently over 101,000 people on the kidney transplant waiting list. The average wait for a kidney from a deceased donor is 5 years, but in some states it's closer to 10. There are fewer than 17,000 transplants performed each year, but nearly 3,000 people are added to the wait list each month. In 2013, 4.453 people died while waiting for a kidney transplant. I'm not one to use fiction as a platform, but in this case I do hope that my writing about such an awful (and widespread) disease causes at least one person to register to be an organ donor (www.donatelife.net).

So where do Chase and Jo go from here? Never fear—their story will continue over the course of the next three books in the series as their relationship and Chase's looming need for a transplant will play a role in upcoming books.

Next up, though, is Jenn and Matt's story, which has been incredibly fun to write. Keep reading for an excerpt of Baseball and Other Lessons, and feel free to follow me on social media and sign up for my newsletter to be the first to know when Book 2 of the Devils Ranch Series will be released.

Cheers!

Aubrey

BETWEEN THE SEAMS PLAYLIST

Honeybrowne – "Texas Angel"
Josh Abbott Band – "Touch"
Reckless Kelly – "Nobody's Girl"
Miranda Lambert – "Mama's Broken Heart"
Aaron Watson – "3rd Gear and 17"
Imagine Dragons – "Demons"
Randy Rogers Band – "Kiss Me In the Dark"
Casey Donahew Band – "Give You a Ring"
Gary Allan – "Watching Airplanes"
Josh Abbott Band – "Oh, Tonight"
Jon Wolfe – "I Don't Dance"
Kelly Willis and Bruce Robison – "Border Radio"
Radney Foster – "Nobody Wins"
Eli Young Band – "Guinevere"
Eminem f. Rhianna – "The Monster"
William Clark Green – "Rose Queen"
Alex Clare – "Too Close"
Matchbox twenty – "Busted"
Wade Bowen and Brandy Clark – "Love In the First
Degree"
Jack Ingram – "Barefoot and Crazy"
Pat Green – "Take Me Out to a Dancehall"
Sugar Cult – "Pretty Girl (The Way)"

PREVIEW: BASEBALL AND OTHER LESSONS

The hardest lessons are a lot like a line drive to the heart.

Texas Wranglers' ace Matt Roberts had it all: fame, fortune, his dream job. Until one line drive to the head ended it. Well, at least that was the case according to Twitter. Needing time to let his fractured skull heal—along with his psyche—Matt heads home to Del Rio, Texas, with one goal in mind—getting back to baseball. Unfortunately a certain redhead keeps driving him to distraction.

Seventh grade English teacher Jenn McDonnell is not happy that Matt's come home and is staying with his brother—aka her best friend—while his thick skull heals. And she certainly could do without all the questions their group of friends suddenly has, like, "Why do you hate Matt so much?" Yeah, she totally has no desire to answer that one.

Unfortunately for Jenn the questions aren't letting up, and unfortunately for Matt he can't get Jenn off of his mind. Can Jenn put past hurt aside and teach Matt that there's more to life than baseball? Furthermore, can Matt convince Jenn that this relationship isn't doomed to strike out?

CHAPTER ONE

Matt Roberts' career ended with a tweet.

@ESPN: Sources confirm @MattRobertsTX career likely over. 35yo pitcher suffered cracked skull, brain bleed. Surgery successful.

Next came the Deadspin article.

ESPN Reporting Matt Roberts, Texas' Ace, Out Forever

Followed by the piece from Bleacher Report.

Texas' Matt Roberts' Career Over, Next Steps for Texas to Fill Gap

Sports Illustrated jumped on it next, followed by the *Sporting News*, Yahoo! Sports, *The Dallas Morning News* and SB Nation. From there, the barrage was endless as social media took one stupid—and highly inaccurate to his knowledge—tweet as gospel.

Matt's head pounded. He wasn't sure if it was because of his stitched up skull or if his blood pressure was getting too high. When he noticed his hands were shaking, he figured it was probably his blood pressure.

He sat back on his brother, Chase's couch, closed his eyes and took a few deep breaths, tried to find some internal peace. Instead, all he could find was that damned tweet. Sighing, he opened his eyes and looked back at his open laptop, giving the offending tweet the evil eye, before picking up his cell phone and dialing his agent.

The man answered on the first ring. "Hey, Matt. Don't worry, man, we're on it. I don't know who ESPN's sources are, but they're wrong. We haven't heard anything from the front office other than they want you to have a full recovery and that your health comes first."

Matt sighed and pinched the bridge of his nose. "Dammit, Darrin, where the fuck did this shit come from? I've barely been out of the hospital for a week. Nobody knows the future of my career right now, especially not some lowlife who'll give crap information to ESPN."

"I know. Like I said, we're trying to track down the source. I also have a call in to Reed. Hopefully I'll hear something soon and can get this mess cleared up."

Reed Thornhill was the team's president and general manager, and the person who would ultimately decide Matt's professional fate. He and Reed had a pretty good relationship, and Matt couldn't see him making such a definite statement without having all the facts. And the facts were, Matt couldn't even begin rehab until the fucking stitches were out, and that wouldn't be for a couple more weeks probably.

"Thanks, Darrin."

"No problem, man. So how are you doing?"

Matt blew out a breath and looked around his brother's living room. How was he doing? He was going fucking stir crazy. That's how he was doing. "Effing crazy, D. I'm bored out of my mind."

"You know you could have stayed in Dallas, in the comfort of your own condo and all the take out you desire at your fingertips."

Matt snorted. "I know. Mom was worried sick, and I knew she'd be calling me multiple times a day. I also didn't feel like having the media breathing down my neck."

"How's the ranch doing?"

Matt, along with Chase, Chase's friend Owen, and Darrin were all owners of a managed game ranch just north of Del Rio, on the Devils River. "You know about as much as I do. Chase and Owen do a great job keeping up with it, and Daniel runs the place flawlessly. I'm hoping to get up there some time soon, just have to have clearance to drive."

"Any word on when that'll be?"

"I have an appointment in San Antonio next Monday. Hopefully he'll give me the go-ahead then."

"Keep me up to date. In the meantime, I've gotta go— lunch with Mercer to discuss the contract extension the Cowboys offered him."

Clint Mercer was the Dallas Cowboys' all-pro tight end, Darrin's client, Matt's friend, and all-around good guy. "Getting ready to milk the Cowboys dry?"

"As dry as I can." Darrin chuckled. "Anyway. Stay off of Twitter and message boards for a while, and I'll call you as soon as I know something."

"Thanks, D." Matt ended the call and tossed the phone back onto the couch beside him. He rested his head against the plush back and looked up at the ceiling. God, he was bored.

~~*~~

Jenn McDonnell surreptitiously watched Matt as she and Owen played a game of pool.

She didn't like Matt. Didn't trust him. Sure as hell didn't want to be around him.

It hadn't always been that way. Once upon a time they'd kind of been friends. Not great friends like she and Chase, but kind of friends, the type that are just above acquaintance but not someone you would exactly tell secrets to. They'd once gotten along okay, kind of like siblings but not quite.

Somewhere along the way, though, her feelings

towards Matt had changed. People sometimes asked her what had happened to make her dislike Matt so much. She would just shrug her shoulders and say something flippant, or that maybe it was the fact that since he'd made it to the Bigs eleven years ago he'd rarely come back home to see his family (and Jenn knew for a fact that Mrs. Roberts missed her "baby boy"). Or maybe she'd tell people that it was because he came across as an arrogant dick, like being blessed with a 98 mile per hour fastball and a nasty slider somehow made him better than the mere mortals who wore his jersey and cheered his name.

Somehow, along the way, she'd gotten pretty good at evading the truth.

So she would put up with him—when she had to—because Chase was his brother and one of her best friends. Like a brother, really. And tonight she was putting up with Matt more than she wanted to because she was trying to give Chase and Jo—her other best friend since childhood—some time alone together to try and figure out whatever was going on between the two of them (they were obviously meant for each other, but still hadn't come to terms with that fact).

Speaking of…

From the corner of her eye, she saw Chase lead Jo out onto the dance floor, saw the way they looked at each other and smiled. It may have been the night before the Fourth of July, but Jenn was willing to bet money that there would be fireworks tonight.

She missed her shot, turning the table over to Owen Daniels. As her other best friend—she really was lucky, wasn't she, to have three best friends?—lined up to take his shot, Jenn sipped from her margarita and watched Matt from the corner of her eye.

Even with his current crazy haircut, the man was hot. Her gaze kept wanting to skitter up to the stitches on the shaved side of his head—stitches that had happened after he'd been hit by a line drive and suffered a cracked skull and brain bleeding just a few weeks ago.

Looking at the stitches, though, did funny things to her stomach. She'd never been good with blood or injuries; they always made her feel squeamish and jittery inside. Seeing Matt's head—and remembering the moment the injury had happened since she, Chase, Jo and Owen had been watching the game together—made her uncomfortable.

It made her want to care.

Jenn sipped her margarita and focused her gaze on the row of cue sticks on the opposite wall.

"You can look at them, y'know."

Matt's voice, deep and low, a whisper against her ear, startled her. She jolted. Slushy liquid sloshed in the glass in her hand.

She took a half step to the side, away from him. "Look at what?" she asked, not looking at him.

"The stitches. My head."

She shrugged.

"Unless you're one of those women who gets turned on by pain. That shit's too kinky, even for me."

Jenn closed her eyes. Gritted her teeth. "They make me feel squeamish."

She could feel him beside her, hot and big and the epitome of Alpha Male. If he'd been a character in the Regency romances she loved to read, he most definitely would have been a rake.

And she? She would have been a wallflower. Or a governess.

A woman who most definitely did not garner attention from outrageously attractive males with hazel eyes, a lean body sculpted with muscle and lips that would make most women think about hot kisses and raunchy sex.

Jenn, though? She really just wanted to wipe the smirk from those sinful lips and not be aware of that muscled body.

"Stitches make you squeamish?"

Matt's voice was deep and seductive, like the promise of silk sheets, dark chocolate and a bottle of wine. She steeled herself against it, knowing that he was all too aware of his...potency.

"Yes."

He sighed. "You're a strange woman, Jenn McDonnell."

She snorted, watched Owen as he lined up to pocket the eight ball. "I'm strange? You're the one walking around with half of your head shaved."

"It's different. I like it."

"Or you just haven't gotten to a stylist yet." She somehow doubted he was a Super Cuts sort of guy.

Owen sank the eight ball and asked, "You up for another game?"

"Nah. I'm gonna go grab another drink, make sure Jo and Chase haven't mauled each other by now."

Jenn made her way through the bar, set her empty glass on a table holding other discarded drinks, and headed for the ladies' room. She sang along as the DJ switched from Josh Abbott Band's "Oh, Tonight" to "Fuzzy" by The Randy Rogers Band. The song's tale of drunken escapades always made her think of *The Hangover*, which never failed to make her smile.

She finished up in the bathroom and walked out to the main bar area, didn't see Jo and Chase and figured they'd stepped out to the back patio to get some air. She stepped up to the bar, ordered another margarita and walked back to the pool tables.

There were three women surrounding Matt, the same three that had fluttered around him when Jenn and Jo had first arrived. They'd scattered, but apparently had decided that Jenn and Jo weren't competition.

Jenn stayed back, sipped her margarita as the fake redhead with fake boobs leaned into Matt and trailed her fingers down his chest and towards the waist band of his jeans. Owen caught her eye, shook his head as he lined up a shot. Jenn stifled a giggle.

The redhead's fingers trailed lower, dipped inside Matt's jeans. Jenn saw him roll his eyes before removing the redhead's hand. She couldn't hear what he said, but apparently Ms. Wandering Fingers wasn't too happy about it, if the mulish expression on her face was any indication.

She was stifling laughter when she felt a tap on her shoulder, turned around and saw Jo, her cheeks flushed, eyes bright and hair slightly mussed. Jenn raised her eyebrows.

"I, uh, feel a migraine coming on. Chase is going to take me home. I'll see you later."

"Migraine, huh?" Jenn teased.

Jo's blush deepened, but Jenn could tell she was trying not to smile. "Yeah. A migraine."

Jenn laughed and hugged her best friend. "Well, I hope you find a way to get rid of it."

Jo did laugh then, before turning and walking away. Jenn looked down at her margarita, contemplating the sugar crystals on the rim of the glass as a smile tugged at her lips.

Looked like she'd been right about those fireworks tonight.

~~*~~

Matt watched the exchange between Jo and Jenn, vaguely aware of the three women surrounding him. He'd never been a huge fan of jersey chasers to begin with, but having them surround him in his hometown seemed like a little too much even for him to take right now. Jo shook her head at something Jenn said, and Matt noted the tousled hair, swollen lips and beard burn on her neck.

Looked like little brother was finally going to score.

At least someone was.

Disgusted with his self-pitying thoughts, because, really, he was one of the best pitchers in the league with a healthy bank account, wise investments and women at his beck and call if he wanted them, Matt breathed deeply and tuned back in to the jersey chasers currently trying to score with him.

Yeah, that wasn't happening.

Even if he'd been interested, the doctor had specifically told him no sex. Apparently repetitive motions and strenuous activities could still cause complications with the damned head wound.

Fan-fucking-tastic.

"So, Mattie, how 'bout we go back to my place?" The brunette—Kara or Katie or Karma—asked with a pout as she trailed an index finger over his left bicep. "We could play pitcher and catcher, if you know what I mean."

Jesus. Talk about a bad pickup line. "Thanks but, uh, no thanks."

"Oh, come on, Mattie. It'll be fun. Jeanine could join us if you like." The brunette batted her eyelashes at him. Matt couldn't remember which one Jeanine was, nor did he really care.

"Sorry. But I can't. Doctor's orders." He shrugged, adopted an innocent expression and hoped like hell it worked. Despite not liking jersey chasers, he only got tough on them when he had to.

Kara/Katie/Karma lifted up onto her toes and whispered in his ear, "I'll let you do me any way you want, Mattie. My pussy's dripping wet and aching for that cock of yours."

She nipped his ear lobe before lowering herself to her normal height, bit her lower lip and looked up at him with big green eyes. Matt sighed. Time to play hardball, apparently.

Normally, he would have someone with him he could pawn the girls off on—whether it be Darrin, a teammate, or a friend who was more than willing to take one for the team. Tonight, though, he had Owen—a guy he knew would be more likely to crack a joke than show any interest in any of the three women—and Jenn, who he was pretty sure would outright refuse to help him, especially after what had happened the last time she'd assisted in a Jersey Chaser Extraction.

Feeling somewhat hopeful, despite the feeling in his gut, he looked up and caught Jenn's gaze, mouthed, "Help me" and hoped like hell she'd put that last Extraction behind her.

~~*~~

ABOUT THE AUTHOR

Aubrey has been reading and writing since she was about two and a half and has been an avid romance reader since she read her first romance novel in the 6th grade. She wrote her first novel in high school. It was an ~~awful~~ imaginative historical romance that involved a cross-country trip via covered wagon, and maybe some Indians. She thinks it's still on a floppy disk somewhere (DOS computer, y'all), but can't be too sure. These days, she writes contemporary romance with a lot of humor and sass and characters that have issues.

She graduated from Seton Hill University's Writing Popular Fiction program with a Master of Arts in 2008. When she's not writing, she can be found with her husband and their two dogs at home in Austin, on their ranch in west Texas, watching a football or baseball game, or with her nose stuck in a (usually virtual) book.

Connect with Aubrey at
http://aubreygross.com

Publisher's note: This is a work of fiction. Names, characters, places, and incidents are a product of the author's imagination. Locales and public names are sometimes used for atmospheric purposes. Any resemblance to actual people, living or dead, or to businesses, companies, events, institutions, or locales is completely coincidental.

Book layout © 2015 Indie Book Design
Book cover © 2015 by Indie Book Design

Between the Seams/Aubrey Gross -- 2nd ed.

Epub Edition April 2015 ISBN: 978-0-9962821-0-9

Print Edition ISBN: 978-0-9962821-1-6